ACEDIA

SHADES OF SIN

ACEDIA

COLETTE RHODES

ILLUSTRATED PAPERBACK ISBN: 978-1-7386106-0-0
HARDCOVER ISBN: 978-1-7386106-1-7
DISCREET PAPERBACK ISBN: 978-1-7386106-2-4

COVER ART BY COLETTE

ACEDIA IS A MONSTER ROMANCE BETWEEN A HUMAN AND HER NOT-QUITE-HUMAN PARTNER, SUITABLE FOR READERS OVER 18.

CW: SEXUAL CONTENT; PERIOD SEX (NO BLOOD PLAY); CHILDHOOD NEGLECT.

"IN THE DEPTH OF WINTER, I FINALLY LEARNED THAT WITHIN ME THERE LAY AN INVINCIBLE SUMMER."

- ALBERT CAMUS

IRIS

CHAPTER 1

The heating was playing up again.

That happened sometimes, though it seemed especially unlucky that it was happening on Christmas.

"Chin up, Iris," Nana said sternly. "Are you not grateful for this delicious dinner?"

"I'm very grateful, Nana," I replied immediately, straightening up and silently instructing myself to stop shivering.

The dinner was a little chilly too, but it always took a little while to make its way up from the dining table downstairs where my parents and twin brothers ate to the attic where Nana and I lived.

"Have you tried the turkey? It's very good, Iris. Even better than last year's."

My fingers twitched, wanting to touch the food on the plate so I could build a picture in my mind of what I had and where it was, but Nana hated when I did that. Blindness was not an excuse for poor etiquette, as she always reminded me. Instead, I gingerly moved my knife and fork around the plate, softly prodding and poking until I found something that felt like meat.

I couldn't reply for a long moment as I made my way through the small bite I had taken. It had a much chalkier texture than I expected, but perhaps that was normal.

"How is it?" Nana asked, a sharp edge to her voice that dared me to complain.

"Delicious," I rasped, immediately grabbing my glass of water to wash it down as I struggled to swallow it.

"Yes, it is," she said firmly. "Eat the rest of your food, Iris. Then straight to bed."

"Yes, Nana."

"We have much to be grateful for this year," she mumbled. Her utensils chittered faintly against the ceramic plate—they always did, her hands were increasingly shaky with age. But it was worse than usual tonight. She was shivering more than I was.

"Perhaps I could ask Clara to bring up that little space heater we used last time?" I suggested tentatively, not wanting to anger Nana by complaining but also not wanting her joints to ache from the cold.

"What on earth for?" she snapped. "Clara doesn't want to spend her Christmas hauling appliances around the house."

"Of course," I replied quickly. "I'm sorry, Nana. I shouldn't have said anything."

She tutted. "No, you shouldn't have. You were thinking of yourself, Iris. Thinking of what might make *you* happy and not at all thinking about poor Clara and the inconvenience it would cause her."

I'd been thinking of Nana, but it would only upset her more if I pointed that out, so I forced another cold potato into my mouth instead. Clara had worked with our family for years—she was a Hunter who'd sustained an injury bad enough that she wasn't able to hunt any longer, and had been assigned to domestic duties here instead. There had been a helper like that before her too—Margaret—who'd worked for our family until she died, and she'd been much friendlier.

I shook off the disrespectful thought. Clara hadn't wanted to be here, and from what I understood, knowing about my existence put severe limitations on her life. I should be more grateful.

Be grateful, be grateful, be grateful.

"I worry, you know," Nana sighed heavily. "You're getting more difficult each year. More opinionated. Sometimes, I think you don't even care about being kind anymore. You used to be so good at remembering that it was the most important thing you could be."

I nodded, immediately contrite. Kindness was free. Kindness was unlimited. Kindness required nothing but my own effort.

"I won't be around forever," Nana continued. "You're going to have to prove to your mother that you're not a burden. That you shouldn't be sent away to one of those awful places—you don't want to go there, Iris. They'll do awful things to you there. And there's no one else who can watch you once I'm gone. Certainly, no one would expect your brothers to undertake such an onerous task."

I bowed my head over my plate, letting my hair fall around my face like a curtain as I blinked back tears. I didn't like thinking about my future. Nana was the only person who'd ever cared for me. I'd be all alone in the world once she was gone, and I had no idea how Moriah and Giles would respond.

I didn't want to go to one of the group homes where the other broken Hunters went. I was so fortunate that I hadn't been sent there already. Moriah had been very generous in letting me stay.

Tilly whined at my feet, leaning heavily against my legs. It was probably only her body warmth that was stopping me from shivering more. She was my guide dog in more ways than one. Tilly was my eyes, my heart, and my best friend. Nana had gotten her for me three years ago, and the fight between her and my mother had been so bad that I couldn't even think of it without my hands trembling.

"Oh, don't cry now, my Iris," Nana grumbled, hating displays of emotion. "There's no need to cry. You just have to do the right thing. Put your best foot forward. Don't make life difficult for your mother; I'm sure she'll let you stay in the attic alone. You're more than capable, so long as Clara helps out now and again. You'd like that, wouldn't you?"

"Yes. Of course," I agreed in a raspy voice. It would be the height of ingratitude not to, even if the idea of spending the rest of my days in these few rooms was...

Well, a little disheartening.

What was the world outside this house like? What were people outside my family and Clara like? Nana liked having the TV on most of the day, and I had list upon list in my head of all the things I'd heard about from her films and shows that I'd like to try for myself.

Cheesecake. Champagne. Sand between my toes. Swimming. I wanted to go on an airplane and sit on the back of a motorbike. Failing all of that, I'd settle for going for a walk on a concrete sidewalk instead of the dirt paths that wound through the forest around our house. I wanted to experience *something*. Anything.

She grunted a sound of assent. "Finish your dinner, and as a treat, we'll stay up and watch a Christmas movie. How about that?"

"That would be lovely. Thank you, Nana."

"And then you can play me *Silent Night* before we go to bed."

I perked up immediately at the thought of playing my harp. It was always such a centering activity for me. I had a lot to be grateful for. Life in the attic was all I'd ever known, and while the idea of doing it without Nana was a scary one, it wasn't one I needed to think about now. The future was a distant, nebulous thing. We had the present—Christmas dinner and a cozy movie and some music before bed, and Tilly on my feet to keep me warm until the heating kicked on again.

Grateful. There was a lot to be grateful for.

I huddled down in my blankets, trying to ward off the chill in the air. The heating must have gone out again—it was freezing today. Usually, Tilly woke me up each morning with her demands to be let outside, but today it was the noise from below that had me stirring. The hustle and bustle downstairs was loud, and the sound drifted up through the vents into my room so that I heard almost every word with perfect clarity.

"We need to be on the road already," Moriah was saying. "Isn't Lucas Thompson a cousin of yours? A relative somehow? He's the one who found her—this could be a real advantage for us, Giles. I don't want to squander it."

Giles grumbled in response. "Fourth cousin or something, I don't know. How certain are we that the woman is even who he says she is? What did you say her name was?"

"Verity de Jager. The pictures we have of her are years out of date and she's looking a little worse for wear having appeared unconscious in a canyon, but I think he's right. This is our chance to make an example of one of the traitors. To really restore the family reputation."

Giles groaned as Tilly wriggled and huffed by my feet. Apparently, it was early enough that even she wasn't in a rush to get up yet.

"The entire Council is going. Why do we have to?" Giles complained. He'd never been particularly fond of leaving the house. Or of change. Or people. Nana said that was why her daughter had married him. Moriah had needed the balance of being public enough to maintain her career in the Council, while being private enough to hide me. Giles had given her both.

He and Nana had never particularly gotten along, but someone had to take care of me, so Nana lived here in his grand house too. Well, in the attic with me. It was harder for Nana here than it was for me—once upon a time, she'd lived her own life. She'd been a valued member of the Hunters, and her husband had served on the Council like Moriah did now. But as Nana liked to remind me, age came for us all.

"Imagine how it would look if we didn't?" Moriah objected. "My reputation is already in tatters—"

"Whose fault is that?"

She let out a sound of frustration. "Perhaps if you were a more supportive husband—"

"I've done nothing *but* support you," Giles interjected, raising his voice. I pulled the covers up a little higher, wrapping myself tightly in the familiar, threadbare fabric. "Every decision made under this roof revolves around you—*your* career, *your* dreams, *your* reputation. And for what? It's all gone so fucking disastrously lately, I'm questioning what the point of it all was."

"Giles," she gasped while I winced under the blankets. From what I'd overheard, things hadn't been going well for Moriah at the Council recently, but Giles had never been anything other than supportive. "Yes, things have been difficult lately, and perhaps we were too ambitious in some of our plans, but *here* is the opportunity to fix that! Half dead in a canyon, ready for us to take control of the narrative. Don't look a gift horse in the mouth, Giles."

I kicked off the blankets and crept out of bed, not wanting to hear anymore. I hated when Moriah and Giles fought—neither of them ever remembered to be kind. Nana said that they didn't have to because they were busy and important, but it seemed as though life would have been a lot more enjoyable for them both if they did.

Or perhaps their lives would be more enjoyable if they weren't quite so involved in the Council? From the conversations I overheard, it sounded very stressful. And everything they talked about was so negative and frightening—it was enough to put anyone in a bad mood.

Once I was up, Tilly leaped off the bed with a loud yawn and followed me into the shared living space, making for the outside door with the stairs that led down to the yard. I let her out, leaving the door open before heading for Nana's room. It was unlike her not to be up already—she wasn't a very good sleeper—and sometimes, she needed a cup of tea to help her get up and moving, especially if her joints were bothering her.

"Nana?" I called, making my way through the living room that I knew like the back of my hand to knock gently on her bedroom door. "Nana, do you want a cup of tea?"

There was silence on the other side of the door, which was very unusual. I knocked again and waited, a strange foreboding feeling settling somewhere between my shoulder blades.

I hadn't ventured into Nana's room in years—not since I'd outgrown the nightmares I'd gotten as a child—but that heavy feeling of dread nudged me forward, insisting that I go inside—that I verify what I was pretty sure I already knew.

I wasn't sure how or why I knew it was true. Only that I was deeply, deeply certain of it.

I fumbled around, knocking something over as I searched for the cast iron bed frame.

"Sorry," I whispered into the silence, acutely aware that Nana would have told me off immediately for my carelessness if she could.

My fingers traced the intricate stitching of her quilt as I made my way up the side of the bed, feeling around until I touched her arm above the blanket.

"Nana?" I asked again, startling at how cold her hands were. "Wake up, Nana. It's morning time. You need to wake up now," I rasped, suddenly feeling very small again. Like the little girl she'd carried around the house for so long to stop me from bumping into things that I hadn't learned to walk until I was nearly three.

No. No, this wasn't happening.

Except that it was. It was happening right in front of me, and yet I felt incredibly far away from it all like I was in someone else's body.

"Mommy is yelling," I whispered, kneeling down next to the bed, still holding her hand. "Mommy and Giles are fighting. Wake up, Nana. I don't know what to do. What am I meant to do?"

At some point, Tilly was at my side, which was strange because she knew she absolutely was not allowed in Nana's room. I had no idea how long I stayed there, the attic growing increasingly chilly from the outside door that was still open, occasionally banging in the wind.

Perhaps it was the sound that caught Clara's attention, eventually. Her footsteps thundered up the stairs—the easiest way to tell when she was in a bad mood. I felt as though I was taking it all in while floating above my own body somehow.

"What is going on up here?" she demanded from the living area, pulling the outside door closed with a bang. My voice wasn't working anymore. I opened my mouth to formulate a response, but nothing came out. Maybe because my soul still felt disconnected from my body. "Where are you both? What's going on?"

The light switch clicked, and Clara screamed. I stayed still and quiet because there was no point making noise. There was no point in anything.

"Get back, Iris!" she shouted, grabbing me beneath my armpits and hauling me backward. I landed on the ground with a thud, pain radiating up my tailbone. "Get out of here. Get out of this room."

"I need to stay with Nana—"

"OUT!" Clara yelled, her shrill command penetrating the haze in my brain. I crawled along the floor to the door, too disoriented to get to my feet, while Tilly whimpered next to me, pressing her body against mine. I kept going until I found the sofa in the living area, clambering onto it and curling up in a ball with Tilly half on top of me.

I wrapped my shaking arms around her middle, burying my face in her fur. She felt like the last tether that was stopping me from floating away entirely. Tilly needed me. We needed each other. Through every family argument and freezing cold night and moment of frustration where I longed for my life to be more than what it was, she'd been by my side.

For Tilly, I had to be strong.

Why did I go into Nana's room this morning? I never went into her room. I should have stayed in bed. Gone back to sleep. Started today over.

Maybe it wasn't too late. Maybe I could reset it all.

"What's going on?" Moriah yelled, several sets of footsteps coming up the stairs. "What is all the screaming about?"

The words were muffled; I didn't hear anything else. No one paid me any mind as I shrunk further and further down into the sofa cushions, wishing that I could be anywhere but here.

"She's a curse!" Clara was arguing, and I forced my brain to focus. "First Margaret, now your mother! I'll be next!"

"They were both old!" Moriah shouted back, the frustration clear in her voice. "You *will* stay here and watch Iris because *that* is in your job description!"

Clara let out a noise of frustration. "If you put me in such a high-stress situation, who knows what I might accidentally say when I'm talking to my friends and family."

Silence.

No one could argue with that.

Nana said that Clara had signed paperwork that said she couldn't tell anyone about me, but ultimately, it didn't matter. If word got out, the damage couldn't be undone. The knowledge Clara held meant that she always had the upper hand.

Giles was arguing back, but it didn't sound like he was having much success. I squeezed Tilly tighter, wishing we could fly away somewhere, just the two of us. Somewhere peaceful. Quiet. Welcoming. What would that be like?

"What are we going to do with you?" Moriah asked coolly, making me startle. I hadn't heard her approach, and now she must have been standing right over me. "We're all going to Utah. We have Council business to attend to."

"Oh," I said, understanding dawning. I didn't want to be a burden. I didn't have to be. I didn't want to be sent away. "I'll be okay here on my own. I can look after myself."

"No you can't," Moriah snapped. "You can't *see*. You'll probably fall down the stairs the moment we're gone. We've got enough on our hands to deal with right now."

"She'll have to come with us," Giles grumbled. "Call your brother to come and deal with... your mom. The body. God knows he didn't take care of her when she was alive. Seems like the least he can do now she's dead."

Dead. It was such a harsh, permanent word. Did he have to say that? I couldn't think of Nana that way. I *couldn't*.

"Come with us?!" Moriah shrieked, ignoring the latter half of what he'd said. "Do you have any idea how many high-ranking officials will be there? What do you mean, *come with us*? Someone will find out about her!"

A fresh lump rose in my throat at the reminder of how very unwanted I was, and I swallowed it down painfully. There was no point getting upset about that—it wasn't anything I hadn't heard my entire life. It just felt a lot more frightening without Nana's presence to soften the blow. I'd been a burden to her too, but at least we'd been in it together since Moriah and Giles had struggled to accommodate her needs too.

Still. The idea that my very existence would cause problems for my family never ceased to pain me. If only I could be who they wanted me to be. Who I was *supposed* to be, if I'd been born with eyes that drained the way they were meant to.

"Obviously, Iris will have to stay in a separate hotel. I don't want her in the house alone, Moriah. What if she burns the place down? It's been in my family for generations. You've just gone and pissed Clara off—"

"Don't blame *me* for Clara's attitude—"

"We don't have time for this. If we're driving, then we need to get on the road now if you don't want to be too far behind all the other Councilors who are flying in."

"Why don't we just fly?" Justin asked in a whiny voice, entering the attic.

"Your mother doesn't like flying," Giles snapped. "Make a decision, Mor. Iris will be fine in a hotel room alone during the day. The boys can drop off food in the evenings. We'll figure out a long-term plan for what to do with her when we get back."

I bit my lip, wondering if saying anything in support of Giles's idea would ruin it. Would I really get to leave the attic? Even if it was just for a little while and I was only going to be trapped inside another room, it would still be somewhere different from here. At any given moment, I wanted to explore the world outside the attic, but now more than ever. The memories of Nana were everywhere in these rooms, and I needed a reprieve from them before they overwhelmed me.

Maybe I could prove to Moriah and Giles that I was able to look after myself just fine in the hotel room, and they'd realize they didn't need to worry about me so much.

Maybe if I was *really* good, they'd let me live by myself somewhere. I knew from their conversations that they owned lots of properties around Denver. They could put me in one on my own and I'd be as quiet as a mouse and never let anyone know that I was related to them. And they wouldn't have to worry about me making any noise in the attic when they had guests over and giving my presence away. It would be to everyone's benefit.

Giles and Moriah moved away, and I couldn't make out the quiet words he was giving her but I could tell from the tone that they were ones of comfort. Giles was such a soothing presence for Moriah. Nana had always been proud that her daughter had found such a wonderful, perfect husband.

The second time around.

"No one wants you there," Travis hissed, startling me. He was so very good at sneaking up on me.

"I won't get in the way," I whispered, trying to make myself smaller.

I bit my lip to stay silent as he gripped the skin of my arm between his thumb and forefinger, pinching until tears sprang to the corners of my eyes. *Boys will be boys,* I reminded myself, breathing through the pain. That's what Nana would always say. She'd shoo them away at the same time, though. She was the only one who noticed how rough they could be.

My last line of defense was gone.

"Please stop," I whispered, not wanting to enrage Moriah anymore by crying out.

"No," Travis replied, tightening his grip while I clapped a hand over my mouth to stop myself from screaming. "No one is going to save you now, Iris."

"We can have all the fun we like," Justin added, popping up on my other side until the twins were boxing me in. They were seven years younger than me, and it felt like just yesterday that they'd been smaller than me. They certainly weren't now. "Look how upset Mom and Dad are because of you. You always get in the way."

"It doesn't seem fair that we have to stay in the RV at some random Councilor's house with Mom and Dad while Iris gets to stay in a hotel by herself," Travis pointed out, finally releasing me. I sucked in a breath as the blood rushed painfully back in.

"Yeah, that's bullshit. Mom! Why can't we stay in a hotel?"

"We'll sort it out on the drive," Moriah snapped. "And Samuel Winston is not some *random Councilor*. If you were more respectful, perhaps the two of you would be in more impressive positions *within* the Hunters by now. Do you know how humiliating it is that my own sons have such mediocre records?"

That definitely silenced the twins. I wasn't quite sure what made them mediocre—that didn't usually come up as a topic of conversation through the vents. Perhaps Giles and Moriah didn't like to reflect on it too often.

"You and your mutt will have to travel in the RV, Iris," Moriah added. "There's no room in the truck for you. Let's go."

"Don't fuck up," Travis taunted in my ear, his voice too low for anyone to hear. "You're not supposed to exist, remember? If you make a mistake, they'll *kill* you."

"No, they won't," I whispered tentatively.

"If they don't, we might," Justin laughed quietly. My brothers were always saying things like that—Nana had told me they were just rambunctious. They just had overactive imaginations and a silly sense of humor.

I hope you're right, Nana. I wish you were here to reassure me.

But she was gone, and I was alone except for Tilly. It was terrifying, but I was also *leaving*. Venturing out of the attic, if only for a little while, and experiencing some of the world around me.

Nana, I'm going to make you so proud.

IRIS

CHAPTER 2

I was jolted awake as the vehicle came to a stop after hours of travel. Tilly whined piteously, and I felt awful at how long it had been since she'd had a bathroom break. Hopefully, wherever we were, this was our final stop.

The door opened with a bang, and I could tell it was Giles based on the heavy breathing. He grunted in annoyance as Tilly shot out, her paws clicking and scrambling on the RV floor.

"Hope your mutt doesn't run away, I'm not chasing her," he grumbled. "This is your stop, Iris. A hotel was too risky with so many Hunters coming into town. Your mother—I mean, Moriah, has rented a house for you to use for the time we're here. It's got two bedrooms so the twins can come and stay if they need a break."

I nodded uneasily, dread trickling down my spine. I didn't want to be left alone with my brothers.

With shaky hands, I felt around the RV for the bench that would take me to the steps, hoping I didn't fall out now. To my surprise, Giles grabbed my wrist, half supporting, half yanking me down until I was on solid ground before rapidly letting me go.

Tilly licked my hand, sticking close to my side as I followed my brothers' voices up the path, walking slowly and cautiously so I didn't fall. If Nana were here, she would have linked arms like we did when we walked through the forest paths, but that would never happen again. My throat grew tight at the thought, but I couldn't cry now. This was not a time to show weakness.

It was so *loud* here. Giles's house was surrounded by trees, and when the television wasn't on, I mostly heard the swaying, rustling sounds of them outside as well as the creaks and whistles of the wind blowing through the attic.

Here, all I could hear was the traffic from the road nearby. I tripped on the threshold, catching myself before I fell on my face, though no one seemed to notice at least. The central air was on, and it made a buzzing sound that seemed to needle into the very back of my brain. Tilly whimpered slightly, pushing her nose into my hand, and I stroked the top of her head, unsettled and unsure.

All I'd ever wanted was to leave the attic. Now, I wondered if perhaps I'd been too ambitious with those goals.

"Clara packed you a bag of clothes and snacks," Moriah said dismissively as something landed with a thud on the floor. "The yard is fenced—you can let your beast out there. If you're lucky, we'll be back for you when it's time to return to Denver. Boys, come on."

"Can't we just stay here?" Justin whined.

"No. We need to greet the rest of the Council and talk about the next steps. I expect my children to put their best foot forward and make a good impression."

If there was anything she could have said to get them moving, it was that. Not because they wanted to make a good impression, but because it gave them an opportunity to be smug that she claimed them as her children, and not me.

"Of course, Mom," Justin said sweetly, bumping the sore spot on my arm as he headed out the door.

Moriah left with them, but the door didn't click shut. I hesitated, wondering if I was alone or not.

"I'll send a food delivery to the door," Giles muttered, making me jump. "Don't make us regret the trust we're placing in you, Iris. Your grandmother isn't here to fight your battles anymore. Lock the door behind me."

With that chilling pronouncement, he was gone.

My limbs shook with each step as I felt my way to the door, banging my hip on something and then my elbow. Eventually, I found the door and fumbled until I felt like the lock had clicked into place.

If only they'd told me a little about the layout, that would have been so helpful. The last time I'd moved was when Moriah had married Giles and we'd moved out of Nana's house and I'd gone into the attic. I couldn't even remember that time, and Nana would have helped me get accustomed to the unfamiliar space.

Now, it was just me.

I'd never had a cane before—the one time I'd quietly suggested one having heard about it in a movie, Nana had gotten me Tilly instead. She'd said she'd found Tilly easier to stomach as an aid. That she could pretend she was just a pet, and that there was nothing wrong with me. In the small space that I knew as well as I knew myself, that had been fine.

I really wished I had a cane now.

Fortunately, I stumbled into the bathroom first since Tilly hadn't been the only one holding on for the long drive. I opted to take the bedroom right next to it, since it would be easier to get to in the middle of the night if I had to.

There was one other bedroom on the other side of the small house, behind the kitchen area. The yard was a small square with seemingly no plants—I could run my hand along the wooden fence the entire way around, so at least Tilly would be safe outside.

It must have been late by the time I got my bearings. I tripped over the bag that Moriah had left on the ground, crashing onto the carpet on my knees, but at least I was able to find the small bag of snacks that Clara had packed for me and have some popcorn for dinner before getting ready for bed.

For all my dreams of leaving the attic and getting to explore the world outside those walls, thus far it was proving a little less exciting than the movies had made it seem. So far, it was worse in nearly every way, in fact. But every inch of the attic contained memories of Nana, and I wasn't sure how I was going to cope when I was forced to confront those again.

The sheets were starchy and uncomfortable compared to the well-worn ones of my bed at home, and trucks seemed to pass by all night long, making the windows rattle each time. Tilly was practically curled up on my neck, as uncomfortable as I was, and even if I'd been at home, I doubted I would have gotten much sleep. I couldn't turn my brain off.

Would there be a funeral for Nana? I wouldn't be allowed to go, even if there was. Would Moriah let me live in the attic by myself? Did I even want that? If I wasn't blind, maybe this would be my opportunity to run away and start a new life like they always did in the movies. But if I wasn't blind, I wouldn't need to. I wouldn't be a faulty Hunter, and my mother wouldn't have rejected me as her child. There would be no reason for me to want to leave.

Fortunately, I found the TV remote on the second day and was at least able to replicate the comforting background noise of home. Unfortunately, Giles seemed to have forgotten his words about having food delivered, and I rationed the snacks as much as I could, wondering how long I could make them last. Days dragged on that way, and I slept as much as I could, hating the harsh reality of being awake.

Hating *myself*. For the first time in my life, I was unsupervised. I could leave, and no one would ever find me again. Except, I couldn't. I'd probably walk directly into traffic and that would be that.

"Open up, Iris," Justin called through the door, banging on it loudly and making me startle. Tilly grumbled in irritation at the disruption. "We forgot the key."

I quickly twisted my damp hair off my neck, having just gotten out of the shower, and pulled on a comfy long dress with t-shirt sleeves. If I had time, I'd go back to my room and grab a baggy sweater—an extra layer of protection for my skin in case my brothers got pinchy again—but it took me so long to get around this place still and I didn't want to risk angering them.

I knocked my shin on the corner of the coffee table on my way to the door, sucking in a quiet breath at the sudden sharp pain. Hopefully, they'd brought food.

"Finally," Travis grunted, knocking me with his shoulder as he barged his way in. "We're going to hook up the console in here to play games for a bit. It's so fucking boring over there, we need a break. Don't get in the way."

"Oh. Right."

"Um, hi," an unfamiliar voice said, startling me as I closed the door. "I'm Lucas."

I stood with my hand on the door handle, frozen like a statue, while Tilly trotted over to position herself at my feet. They'd brought someone back here? Why would they have done that? No one knowing about me was the number one rule in our family.

It had never really been put to the test before. It was easy to hide me away at home, where only the attic was off-limits. It hadn't taken Justin and Travis long to crumble at the very first hurdle, though.

Nana would have been so disappointed in them.

"Hello," I replied eventually, shrinking back against the door. Tilly grumbled a quiet, unhappy sound, almost sitting on my feet.

"Ignore her," Travis instructed Lucas. "Come, sit here. What do you want to play? Iris, don't be weird. Lucas is family. Not *your* family, obviously."

Lucas laughed uncomfortably, moving away so I could close the door. The three of them got comfortable on the couch, and I hovered awkwardly, wondering what I should do. Maybe I should just go and hide in the bedroom? That felt weird—and I'd have to walk past them all, and that idea was mortifying.

Eventually, I felt my way over to the small two-person dining table and took one of the seats. I was behind the couch where they were sitting all facing the TV, and maybe if I stayed still and quiet enough, they'd forget I existed. Tilly plonked down on my feet with a sigh, seemingly as unsure of what to make of a stranger in our presence as I was.

The boys decided on a game that sounded horribly violent, and I made myself as small as possible while they played—for hours it felt like, though I had no way of checking unless I asked. What was I meant to do? They'd come into my space, and yet I felt like the one who was intruding. My face burned with humiliation as my stomach grumbled so loudly that they all must have heard it. I suspected that Travis and Justin wouldn't react well if I got up to get some jerky and reminded them of my presence.

"Should we order pizza?" Lucas suggested casually. "I'm starving."

"Sure," Justin replied distractedly, before uttering a string of curse words so foul that I was glad Nana wasn't around to hear them.

"What does everyone want?"

"BBQ chicken for us," Travis said. "Don't worry about her."

"I'm ordering for everyone," Lucas said firmly. "I'm sorry, I've forgotten your name."

Was he speaking to me? Probably.

"I'm Iris," I mumbled. He was quiet for a moment, and I wondered if he was considering the irony of my name. It certainly wasn't lost on me that my irises were one of the worst things about me.

"Iris, what kind of pizza would you like?" Lucas asked kindly.

I'd never eaten pizza before. Clara—Margaret before her—or Nana had always prepared my meals at home, and Nana had been strongly averse to any kind of fast food. But I knew from movies that pepperoni was a popular choice.

"Pepperoni?" I suggested tentatively.

"How do you know what pepperoni is?" Justin scoffed. "She can have a slice of ours—you don't need to order anything special for her."

"I like pepperoni too," Lucas said easily.

There was a brief awkward silence before they resumed playing their game, and I shuffled a little in my seat to get comfortable as my butt started to go numb. Tilly adjusted her position with me, and I wished we were sitting on the sofa so I could haul her onto my lap and cuddle her like a lifeline.

She perked up right before someone knocked on the door, and there was some movement and murmurs of conversation in the background before the room was filled with the smell of cheese.

It smelled *really* good. My stomach rumbled loudly again, desperate for any kind of food but especially anything that wasn't jerky and chips.

"I'll get hers," Justin said begrudgingly, pulling plates down in the kitchen before slamming one down in front of me.

"Here. Don't say we don't ever do anything nice for you."

"Justin, you weren't meant to bring anyone here," I whispered, walking my fingers along the tabletop until I found the edge of the plate.

"Lucas is family. He'd already heard rumors about you anyway," Justin replied dismissively. "You know how annoying all the bullshit Council politics are, right Lucas? Just pretend you never saw her."

"Right," Lucas agreed uncomfortably, though I wasn't sure my brothers picked up his tone.

"Wear long sleeves next time," Justin added, flicking the bruise on my arm and making me wince. "You're so clumsy—we don't want to see this ugly eyesore."

I gritted my teeth, refusing to give him any more of a reaction than I already had.

"Lucas is the one who *found* one of the Hunters who defected to the shadow realm—he recognized her and reported her right away," Travis said in a relaxed tone that sent a chill down my spine. Nothing good ever came from that tone. "We haven't been allowed to see her, but I hope we get to soon. I'd *love* to know what the shadow realm is like for her. Wouldn't you, Iris?"

"I've never really thought about it," I replied eventually as the silence extended. I didn't know much about the shadow realm—only what I've overheard from downstairs in recent months about them waging some kind of war on us.

The correct assumption based on the family I'd been born into was that the shadow realm had to be bad because Shades lived there, and they were the monsters that all Hunters were trained to kill.

But I'd always struggled with making that assumption stick in my head.

As far as humans went, the Hunters that I'd encountered were pretty monstrous.

"So cool that you identified her and called it in right away, bro," Travis added. There was a slapping noise, like he'd clapped Lucas on the back.

"It really wasn't a big deal," Lucas replied, sounding almost embarrassed, which was strange. Nana was always telling me stories about the heroic Hunters and the evil Shades—surely Lucas would be proud of himself for making such a discovery?

"Fuck yeah, it was a big deal," Travis admonished. "We've got to make an example out of Hunters like that one who defected. Burn those harlots at the fucking stake like they used to back in the days when the Hunters used to have some goddamn integrity. I told Mom that's what they should do but apparently they want to, like, sweet talk her for a bit first or whatever. Try get some information out of her. She can't even remember anything."

I felt suddenly queasy, but I felt tentatively around on the plate in my hand, sinking my fingers into melted cheese. After a little more fumbling, I came to what I thought was the crust, though it was still incredibly difficult to get a hold of the piece of pizza, which seemed to flop around in every direction no matter how I tried to move it.

"May I?" Lucas asked, alarmingly close.

"Sure," I squeaked, flinching instinctively.

After a long pause, he gently gripped my hand, helping me bend the pizza so it cooperated between my fingers.

"Easier?"

"Yes, thank you," I replied awkwardly.

Justin groaned—a distinctive sound he'd made since he was a toddler that had always made him easy to distinguish from Travis. "Don't be annoying,

Iris."

"Okay. Sorry."

Only once the sounds of their game started up again did I bring the pizza up to my mouth to cautiously nibble on the end of it.

And, *oh*. It was glorious. Like a combination of Nana's grilled cheese and Clara's spaghetti, but somehow better. And those were my two *favorite* meals.

"Do you like it, Iris?" Lucas called from the other side of the room.

"Yes, thank you." I nodded enthusiastically, wanting him to know that I was appreciative.

Tilly rested her head on my lap, sniffing loudly, but I shifted the plate away, not knowing if it would make her sick or not. Better to be safe than sorry.

"Oh, I have some beers in the back of the truck," Justin said, walking past me on his way out of the front door. "Pause it. I'll go grab them."

How had he even gotten hold of that? The twins were only nineteen.

"I'm sure Iris wants her room back—" Lucas began. What time was it anyway? It felt like it was getting late, but it seemed as though they had a lot of game left to play.

"Nah, she's probably grateful for the company. She just sits here alone all day," Travis said bluntly.

"Right," Lucas replied slowly. "Iris, do you want me to let your dog outside?"

Why was he being so kind to me? I didn't know what to make of it.

"I can do it—" I began, moving to stand.

"I didn't think you couldn't, I was just wondering if you'd like me to. I'm over here by the sliding door anyway."

"Oh okay. Then, yes, please. Tilly, outside."

She immediately trotted away as the door slid opened, which meant she'd probably been waiting to go out since she didn't move very promptly otherwise. I finished my food, huddling in a little closer on myself as the cool breeze blew in from outside.

"Shit, Mom's calling. I better take this," Travis said, his footsteps heading toward the yard.

Lucas cleared his throat, and I realized that I was alone in a room with a man I'd never met.

"So, you're their sister. Right?" he asked quietly.

"Did they tell you that?"

"No."

"Oh." How could he know then?

"You guys look like triplets," Lucas added. "You're like the girl version of them."

"Oh. I didn't know that." Nana had occasionally mentioned how strong her genes were, but she'd never explicitly stated that the three of us looked alike. I wondered if it was because she knew it would make me sad.

That appeared to be how I was feeling, though I didn't entirely understand why. Sure, they were my brothers. But they'd hated me since the moment they were old enough to understand what hatred was. They'd been explicitly taught that skill by their parents.

"When Giles married your mother, there were some rumors in the family about how she'd had a baby from her first marriage, you know. I remember them. But I guess when no kid materialized, everyone sort of forgot about that. It's crazy that she's managed to keep you a secret—Moriah is pretty infamous after winning the bid for the treaty negotiations and the Shade-

Hunter marriage and then, you know, botching the whole thing."

"I don't really know anything about that. I'm sure Moriah has a lot of pressure on her," I offered weakly.

"You don't call her Mom?"

"She prefers that I don't. It's best for everyone. I'm sure you've noticed that I'm blind. What use is a Hunter who can't hunt?" I asked, repeating back the words Moriah and Giles had said to me so many times over the years. That even Nana had said a time or two, though she always seemed to feel bad about it right after.

"Don't say that," Lucas murmured uneasily, falling silent as my brothers came back into the room and Tilly noisily lapped at the water in her bowl.

Justin returned with beer, and the already painful evening got markedly worse as the drinks flowed. Fortunately, they were all content to leave me alone and I had the taste of pizza to savor, so it wasn't entirely bad.

But the *fear*... this brand new fear that the past few hours had brought me was crippling. Someone knew that I existed, and who my mother was. That information was out there in the world now, and my entire life felt as though it was at the mercy of this strange man.

It was terrifying. And yet, in an odd way, thrilling. If nothing else, my life would never be entirely the same again, even if I ended up locked in the attic alone for the rest of my days.

Someone knew I existed.

DAMEN
CHAPTER 3

Ruvyn!" I called, striding up the corridor to clap him on the shoulder. "Where have you been? It's been years!"

"Months, at most. You exaggerate, Your Highness," he replied with a slightly sarcastic tilt of his head.

"Surely, it's been longer than that." I searched my brain, trying to think of the last time we'd laid around, drinking wine and debating the meaning of life.

"I haven't visited since the new arrivals moved in. Things have been busy recently in the field of academia. I don't have the luxury of frequent visits to court these days."

"Nonsense, you could always just come for the night. Is there a special reason for this trip?"

"I've been doing a lot of theoretical research on the history between Shades and Hunters. I suppose it occurred to me recently that I should spend some time at the palace and see them for myself rather than keeping my nose buried in my books."

"A fine idea—I'll introduce you to my sister-in-law. Come sit in my drawing room with me after dinner and I'll call for some wine."

"Here was me thinking I might be able to leave without a sore head this time."

"And I can always send for tea if you're so worried about your head?"

He laughed. "No, no, I want the good wine you keep here at the palace."

"Then that's what you shall have," I assured him. For a noble, Ruvyn was a little rough around the edges and didn't take himself too seriously. It was a refreshing change from the courtiers. We'd both been sent to finish our education at The Itrodaris as many nobles were, but while I'd gotten out of there as soon as I was allowed, Ruvyn had stayed on and pursued a life as a scholar.

I watched him closely, noting that he didn't look quite as at ease as he usually did. "Are you well?"

"Fine, fine," he said dismissively, always loathe to talk about himself. "I'll see you after dinner. We can talk properly then."

"Abandon me to the high table with my brother, will you? Though, you can always join us—you'd be my esteemed guest."

"Oh, how you suffer," Ruvyn replied wryly, already walking away. I'd already known that he'd want no part of that offer. Sitting at the high table would be far too much attention for Ruvyn's liking.

I did actually suffer a little, I grumbled internally, traipsing up to the high table—late, as Allerick and Ophelia had already made their grand entrance and taken their seats. It was a miserable experience having to sit next to such a sickeningly happy couple every evening while I was all on my lonesome. I'd prefer to go and sit at one of the long tables and chat to a friend, but Allerick said it wasn't a good look.

The chances of me ever sitting on the throne were negligible now that Allerick was mated, married, and intending to procreate, but they weren't zero yet. I still had to maintain the illusion of the kind of bland, inoffensive dignity that royals were expected to have.

"Look who's finally joining us," my brother grumbled.

Ophelia smiled at me, always open and friendly and seemingly immune to her cantankerous husband's moods. "Hi, Damen. How was your day?"

"The same it usually is," I replied, pouring myself a glass of wine. I was nothing if not consistent with my daily habits. "How was yours?"

Ophelia exhaled slightly, her smile tight. "Fine."

I met Allerick's gaze over the top of her head, understanding that meant her day was not, in fact, fine. Verity was still stuck in the human realm, despite Soren and Astrid's best efforts to get her back. The court had to run as normal, but the strain of Verity's absence was definitely being felt, even though she'd already moved away.

Allerick would never admit to it, but sometimes I wondered if he was in a little over his head between helping the ex-Hunters get settled here as well as maintaining the delicate pause in hostilities between the Shades and Hunters in the human realm. There were also Shades here who disapproved of the way he was running things, and would happily see him overthrown. The power stores were slowly but steadily draining from the realm's exclusive reliance on them rather than feeding from fear in the human realm as we'd done for centuries.

It was all a "shit show," as Verity would describe it, if she were here.

And she'd be back. I knew she'd be back. If any ex-Hunter would find a way back from the human realm to give her mate hell for his idiotic choices, it would be Verity.

Allerick was a good ruler, but he was in unchartered territory. And he was proud—it took a lot for him to admit that perhaps he didn't know as much as he thought he did. I'd offer to help out more but nobody wanted my opinions anyway. I didn't know anything.

As always, Ophelia kept up a steady stream of conversation throughout dinner—mostly gossip, which I appreciated. No court could run without gossip to fuel it, it was the way of the world. She was distracting herself too, from her worry for Verity, and I was more than happy to be of assistance in that regard.

"May I introduce you to my friend, Ruvyn?" I asked Ophelia as we finished our meals. "He's visiting from The Itrodaris—I believe he's studying the historical relations between Shades and Hunters."

"Ooh, yes, please. I would love to meet him." Ophelia beamed—though not quite as brightly as usual—while Allerick scowled, inconvenienced by any sort of social interaction. I imagined it was a real liability to enjoy conversing with others so little as ruler of the realm.

I waved Ruvyn over once we'd descended the few steps of the dais, and he immediately inclined his head at my sister-in-law.

"It's a pleasure to meet you, Your Majesty."

"We don't have to bother with all that. You can just call me Ophelia."

"Though I'd recommend you didn't," Allerick muttered under his breath. He was so dramatic. When I eventually found a wife to put up with me, I wouldn't be half as overbearing as he was.

Ophelia rolled her eyes affectionately at her jealous beast of a husband before returning her attention to Ruvyn. "Damen mentioned your studies—it sounds very interesting. Do you have a lot of evidence to go on? I thought there wasn't much available."

"More than we thought. We weren't looking in the right places before, but we've narrowed down the area and found some new and promising records. Unfortunately, much of what we've collected is in languages that haven't been in use for centuries, so translation is proving difficult. Not impossible, though," he added hastily, as though worried he was going to get fired from his post. "I'm confident we'll figure it out soon."

"How exciting!" Ophelia replied, looking so genuinely interested that it was impossible for Ruvyn not to look gratified. She was exceptionally good at being encouraging.

"Anyway, we're going to go have a drink now," I interrupted because Allerick looked on the verge of complaining. "You're welcome to join us, of course."

"Next time," my brother said dismissively, already reaching for his wife. "Enjoy your evening."

"I'd love to talk to you again sometime!" Ophelia called over her shoulder, laughing as Allerick banded one arm around her waist and lifted her clear off the ground, carrying her away.

"She's not what I expected," Ruvyn admitted, falling into step beside me as we headed for my set of rooms.

"No? What were you expecting?" I tried to remember what I expected the Hunter queen to be when she showed up here for the first time to marry my brother. Scared, I thought. She'd never been that.

"Quieter, I suppose. More subdued. The impression I have of them from my research is that they're quite shy and retiring."

Meera, perhaps. I wouldn't describe any of the others that way. Austin might actually perish without attention.

"I wouldn't say that's a fair assessment. The ex-Hunters are as varying in temperament as any group of Shades would be."

"Yes," Ruvyn replied absently, briefly looking troubled before shaking it off.

A tray of wine and cakes had already been set up in my drawing room, the fire burning low and steady in the grate.

"Come, come. Sit," I insisted, heading over to the fire to throw some more wood on. It was cool enough tonight to warrant the use of it.

"So," Ruvyn began, pouring the wine. "Tell me, Crown Prince of the realm, where is *your* ex-Hunter, hm?"

I laughed. "It appears I've failed to find one."

It stung a little, I could admit. With both Shade females and Hunter women, no one ever seemed to know what to do with me, which was absurd because my expectations of a partner were very few. I would like someone who took me seriously at least some of the time despite my cheerful personality, who wasn't either intimidated by my title or disappointed that I'd never challenge Allerick for the top spot, and who would let me lick their pussy for several hours of the day. Was that really too much to ask?

"How can that be? If rumors are to be believed, the *Duke of Lindow* secured a Hunter bride. Mate. Whatever you're calling them. How dire are your conversational abilities if he was able to successfully court one and you weren't?"

"You wound me—Theon is far more brooding and mysterious than I am. I never stood a chance." Brooding and mysterious, yet also somehow being the most dramatic Shade I'd ever encountered. Perhaps I'd be the same if the lifestyle and fame I'd been accorded due to my role were suddenly snatched away from me. "Besides, Theon and Verity seem almost made for each other— if you saw them together, you'd know that there couldn't be one for them but each other."

He probably didn't know that Verity was missing yet, and I wasn't sure I wanted to be the one to divulge it. Undoubtedly, news of Theon's arrest would spread soon enough.

"And all the other ex-Hunters who have moved here?"

I shrugged, accepting the goblet he handed me. "I spoke to all of them when they arrived here to see whether any sort of romantic connection would come of it, but it wasn't meant to be."

It was a little frustrating, of course. Unfortunately, something about me seemed to make it hard for anyone to take me seriously, and I suspected some of the ex-Hunters had been intimidated by my title on top of that. Perhaps I should be more solemn and difficult like Soren and my brothers, that seemed to work well in attracting a mate.

Though, the kind of dynamic they shared with their mates would never work for me. They were all content to stand back and let their mate shine, and I'd never excelled at that. I liked attention too. I might like attention *most*.

Plus, there wasn't much I could do about the title part. Not until Allerick and Ophelia produced an heir of their own.

The jealousy I would feel when that happened would be unbearable. Not because of the loss of my spot in the line of succession, but because I wanted children of my own more than anything. I'd be a far more fun and involved father than mine had ever been to me.

"Does it bother you?" Ruvyn asked, his voice deceptively light. "That you haven't found someone?"

"Why do you ask?" I sat down and leaned back on the chaise. "Are you feeling the weight of singleness too?"

He grunted, taking a sip of his wine. "Perhaps a little. If I want someone in my bed... Well, that's never been a problem. But it's companionship I'm seeking now. At the same time, The Itrodaris is a demanding mistress—more a lifestyle than a job. I'm constantly busy, and I'm unsure that I'd be able to offer a wife the time that she might need."

"Maybe you just need to find a wife who's also busy and content to do her own thing. Though, when you would have the opportunity to meet, I have no idea."

Ruvyn laughed roughly, draping his arm over the back of the sofa, the goblet dangling loosely between his fingers. "You have the opposite problem, no? You have an abundance of time. Perhaps something to occupy your days with would do you some good, especially if you're surrounded by happy couples at all times."

I snorted. "Why would I add stress to my life when I could simply *not*?"

Life should be easy and enjoyable at all times. It shouldn't be challenging. It shouldn't be complicated. It should be *leisurely*. I was a Shade of conviction, and that was the one I held dearest.

"Don't you ever get bored?" Ruvyn asked curiously. "I've always wondered this about you—even in our youthful days at The Itrodaris. Your ability to do absolutely nothing is truly unmatched."

"I get bored sometimes," I replied, only a little defensively. "But I find ways to entertain myself when I do."

Admittedly, that was now harder than it used to be since everyone else was constantly preoccupied these days, falling in love and whatnot.

It was very rude of them.

"I'm sure you do," he laughed. "I can't fathom what your life is like, Damen. Few Shades in the realm could imagine having so much leisure time."

"That's probably true, but not at court," I pointed out. "There are lazy Shades in abundance here—I am but one of many. Tell me, how have the new developments in the realm been received at The Itrodaris? Do they have any opinions on having an ex-Hunter queen? Or an influx of ex-Hunter residents?"

Allerick and Ophelia had toured the realm a little, and I'd accompanied them when I felt like it, but they were hosted by noble houses wherever they went, as was the tradition. Ophelia had gotten a few wary looks in that crowd, so I imagined that opinions among the wider populace were just as mixed.

Ruvyn gave me a look that made me feel very out of touch for a brief moment. It was an odd feeling. "They just want to be able to feed once more, Damen. I'm sure there are some very interesting conversations happening here at the palace in order to facilitate that. I'm sure there are philosophical questions being asked about what it means to be a Shade and to be a Hunter and what the future of both will look like. But in the everyday world of the shadow realm, Shades just want to feed safely and stop drawing from the precious reserves of the energy stores—for many, it's a blow to their pride to use the stores at all. Most Shades don't much care who the queen is."

I nodded, taking a long sip of my wine, appreciating the much-needed reminder that what mattered at court often didn't matter at all in the rest of the realm.

"Why don't you visit?" Ruvyn suggested, taking a swig from his own goblet. "See it for yourself. You can't convince me that you're too busy—you've already admitted that you have an abundance of time."

I laughed. "True, I've given myself away. You know The Itrodaris holds nothing but unhappy memories for me."

"Liar," Ruvyn scoffed. "You were always a very capable student, Damen. You impressed all of the scholars with your extensive knowledge and memory. You're just lazy."

"Don't you start," I groaned, slumping down in my seat. "All I ever hear about is how lazy I am. It's exceedingly bad for my ego."

"Your ego seems to be holding up just fine."

"No thanks to you or my brothers," I laughed. "I am a simple, unimpressive Shade, who longs for attention despite doing nothing to earn it. Is that such a difficult concept for everyone to grasp?"

Ruvyn shook his head, exasperated. "You're an intelligent, lazy princeling. It will probably come back to haunt you one day."

I yawned loudly, stretching out in my bed and wondering if anyone would truly care if I opted to sleep through breakfast. Then again, Allerick might barge in and drag me out of here by my horns just to prove a point. He was always so relentlessly annoying about me attending these sorts of gatherings even though I didn't have to be there and had nothing of value to add to the conversation.

Ugh. Better to just get it over and done with. At least the tea would be hot and the meat freshly roasted.

"There he is," Soren said dryly as I emerged from my room, finding him walking along the corridor with Astrid toward the breakfast room. "Did you have a late night?"

"I may have enjoyed a few goblets of wine with Ruvyn last night. He so rarely visits the palace, it would be rude not to."

How had we parted ways? My memory was a little hazy, but if I recalled correctly, I had promised to pay him a visit at The Itrodaris. Perhaps I would someday, though it sounded like a lot of effort. As a member of the royal family, I'd be expected to meet with the administration and so forth. It would all be very tedious.

Soren looked unimpressed, though the effect was somewhat dulled due to the fact that he always looked unimpressed. "Yes, well, The Itrodaris demands a lot from its scholars. I'm sure it's difficult for Ruvyn to take a break."

That felt like a pointed comment, but I might have been reading into things.

"What's new with you two?" I asked. "Gone on any rescue missions recently?"

"Did you forget that Verity is still in the human realm?" Soren asked impatiently.

"No, of course not," I replied guiltily. I hadn't forgotten that at all—I was worried for her, but also confident that she would be back. Theon wasn't going to let her get away, he loved her too much.

Failing that, Astrid would murder her way through any captors that stood between her and Verity, and drag Verity back herself. I was confident that all would be well.

"It's not an easy time for us, Damen," Soren huffed.

"I could be the hero. Point me in the direction of the damsels who need saving, and I'll take the job off your plate." I gave Soren my most charming smile and he gave me a flat stare in return.

"Finding them *is* most of the job," Astrid shot back. Sometimes, I got the impression that she didn't like me very much, which was patently absurd because I was delightful company and everyone in the realm knew it.

"I'll help," I said, more seriously this time. "I've *been* helping. With Theon. Remember?"

Soren grimaced, but declined to respond. He wasn't particularly fond of Theon at this moment, or ever. I dragged my feet slightly as I followed them into the breakfast room and took my seat, wishing I could return to the cheerful oblivion of last night instead of the cold reality of today.

CHAPTER 4

The living room smelled awful.

The boys had all come back here again last night—this time with more beer—and they seemed to be sweating it out in their sleep in the most repulsive way. They also all snored like nothing I'd ever heard in my life, and I didn't think that Tilly and I had gotten even a second of sleep, despite the fact that we'd been in the bedroom.

The twins were meant to sleep in the other room, but it seemed they all passed out in the middle of their awful game. The TV had been making irritating sounds all night.

Lucas had brought over tacos this time, though. I couldn't decide if I liked tacos or pizza more, everything was so delicious. I would miss the food from this trip when I was back in the attic.

I moved around the kitchen as quietly as I was able to, feeling my way across the bench to get myself a glass of water. When were they going to leave? Surely, Moriah would send for them at some point.

Was that the sliding door? I paused. Maybe someone was already awake? I heard Tilly's claws tapping on the floor, so at least she was getting to go outside. Before I could grab the glass, a hand clapped over my mouth, muffling my scream.

"Shh, I just want to talk. It's okay," Lucas whispered urgently. "I just want to talk. Don't scream."

He lifted me around the waist with one arm like it was nothing despite my struggling, keeping his hand pressed firmly over my mouth. A door shut behind us, and I guessed that we were in the spare bedroom.

"I just want to talk. Please don't scream," Lucas pleaded, setting me down gently and slowly removing his hand from my face. "You know it won't help anyway—your brothers wouldn't come to your aid."

"Is that supposed to make me feel better?" I rasped, fumbling around for some semblance of my bearings. I was confident that Lucas was standing in front of the door, but I edged my way beside a dresser, keeping the piece of furniture between us.

"I know you won't believe me, and this is going to sound insane, but I'm genuinely trying to help you. One of the options the Council is considering is opening up a portal and sending through a negotiating party to discuss sending Verity back. I'm not sure if those discussions are in good faith or not, but they clearly see an opportunity for bargaining here, and they're going to take it."

"What does that have to do with me?"

Lucas hesitated. "I'm sure you know your brothers aren't overly fond of you."

"I'm well aware," I replied, surprised at the bitterness in my voice. It seemed silly to be bitter about it at all at this point, it had always been this way.

"They see the portal opening as an opportunity to..." he trailed off with a noise of frustration, like the words were too awful to get out. But I didn't feel that way. A sense of perfect calm and understanding washed over me as I saw the future laid out in front of me that I should have always predicted.

"They see a chance to get rid of me. They want to push me through the portal. Into the shadow realm."

Lucas cleared his throat. "Yes. Or into the in-between, at least. It's a dark nothing space between the two realms, and it can be difficult for Hunters to navigate. Your brothers seem to think that because I reported Verity's existence to the Council that this would be something I'm interested in helping them with."

I didn't care to question that. Lucas was clearly offended at the slight against his honor, but I had more pressing concerns.

Moriah and Giles wouldn't help me if I asked them to protect me from the twins. They'd probably throw me through the portal themselves on principle. But also...

Would that be the worst thing?

If there was one thing I knew from the conversations I'd heard through the vents, it was that the Hunters who went to the shadow realm were disgusting harlots who got by there by using their bodies. Something about the Shades being able to feed off of our lust, rather than human fear like they did in the human realm.

I experienced lust. Oh, did I experience lust. That part of me worked just fine.

If there was one job I could absolutely do, it was contribute lust.

Maybe being a disgusting harlot there would be better than being my brothers' punching bag here? Or maybe I was being naive, and I'd be walking into a situation much, *much* worse.

Lucas let out a sigh of frustration. "I kind of feel like... like I fucked up.

Sorry. I mean, that I *messed* up."

"You can use curse words," I assured him. I wasn't a little girl, despite the sheltered life I'd led. I was twenty-six years old. And with Justin and Travis for brothers, I'd heard plenty of curse words.

"Right. Okay. I fucked up. In hindsight, reporting the Hunter who defected to the shadow realm might not have been a good call."

"Was it not the right thing to do? Isn't that the rules?"

"What if... what if the rules aren't right, though?" Lucas muttered. "What if I should have used my own best judgment instead of doing what I was told? The way everyone reacted... I don't know. I feel like I set this huge thing in motion. I thought they'd just send out a couple of people and, you know, deprogram her or whatever. But it was a whole production, and I felt like I'd... like I'd falsely reported a crime that was going to send someone to the gallows."

I was ill-prepared for this sort of conversation. What would Nana say? Probably something about him needing to stand by his choices and stop complaining. I didn't want to say that, though. Not when Lucas sounded so upset.

Besides, I'd never really understood why Nana was so virulently against having regrets when she also believed that every experience in life was a lesson.

Were regrets not lessons too? Even if they left a bitter aftertaste?

"I want to set this right. I want to... I don't know. I could lie. Your brothers aren't that smart—no offense. If I told them that I knew of another secret portal and I was sneaking you through that, they'd probably believe me. And then I could help you find somewhere to live. To hide out. Away from your family."

He didn't sound very certain of that, and I wasn't about to place my safety in the hands of someone who wasn't convinced they could secure it. I'd rather make my own decisions—right or wrong—and live with the consequences of them, knowing the choice had been mine.

I'd never gotten to make my own choices before.

"How hard is the in-between to navigate? It's not like I'm afraid of the dark," I pointed out gently.

"What do you mean?" Lucas asked sharply. "If you navigate it correctly, you end up in the shadow realm."

"Yes," I agreed. "How hard is that to do?"

"Why would you want to?"

I was quiet for a long moment, trying to come up with an answer that incorporated everything I wanted to say without bursting into tears and making Lucas uncomfortable.

But in the end, I couldn't.

"Why would I not?" I settled on.

"Because," he spluttered. "They're... bad."

"My brothers are bad."

"Well, yes. But I can help you get away—"

"No, you can't," I interjected softly. "Not here in the human world. Moriah has a lot of resources at her disposal—she's in a powerful position on the Council. And she won't be happy if I disappear because it'll mean the possibility of someone finding out I'm related to her is always there. She'd never stop looking for me. If I'm going anywhere, I want to go somewhere that's out of her reach. With Tilly, of course. I'm not leaving without her."

"You know Tilly isn't a proper guide dog, right?" Lucas asked dubiously.

"What do you mean?"

"I mean, she's a good dog. But I'm almost positive that she wasn't trained as a guide dog. Does she actually help you navigate? Avoid obstacles? Can she locate objects for you?"

"She brings me my slippers," I replied slowly. "And her lead?"

"I don't think those are guide dog-specific skills."

"She hasn't really been put to the test," I said a little defensively. "This is the first time I've had to navigate an unfamiliar place. I'm sure she'll help me a lot in the shadow realm."

Besides, she was great company and my bestest friend. I wasn't going anywhere without her.

"Look, we don't have to make any decisions right now. Verity is still in the hospital. They're not going to do anything about a portal until she's been discharged. You've got time to think this over. And I'll come up with an alternative—somewhere here in the nice, safe, Shade-free human realm that you can live peacefully."

I made a noncommittal sound, not believing for a second that there was anywhere on this earth that the reach of the Hunters Council wouldn't be able to find me.

"Do you know what they *do* to Hunters in the shadow realm, Iris?" Lucas asked in a low voice.

"Have sex with them?"

He coughed loudly, choking on his own saliva, and I listened out to see if the ruckus would wake my brothers. "Yes. I thought it was just a rumor, but I've overheard some stuff while being in close proximity to the Council over the past few days. Stuff that isn't exactly widely available knowledge to the rest of the Hunters. That they feed off our *lust*. I... Do you know much about lust?"

"Of course I know what lust is," I replied, keeping my voice gentle but not entirely able to hide the impatience in it. I experienced desire just like anybody else. I had wants and needs.

I got lonely.

I got lonely a lot.

"You can't possibly want that. They'd... *touch* you."

I didn't know *how* they'd touch me. Maybe it'd be cruel. Maybe it would be worse than the bruising pinches my brothers gave me.

Or maybe it wouldn't. Maybe it'd be gentle.

Maybe it would feel good.

If they were feeding off lust, if they *needed* lust... Surely, it would be more efficient to use pleasure than pain? It was an alluring motivator. With each year that passed, I craved physical touch more and more—I *ached* with it some days. And if I could provide something they needed, then I might not be a burden. I might actually be valuable.

I wanted so badly to be valued by the people around me.

Of course, it would mean overlooking my other flaws and the Shades might be just as repulsed by me as everyone told me the Hunters were. But on the off chance that they weren't...

What were Shades even like? Nana had always described them as mindless and evil, but I'd struggled to reconcile that description with a group who we were negotiating a treaty arrangement with, sealed by a marriage between our kinds. From what I'd overheard, there was nothing mindless about them at all. What my parents had attributed to evil seemed more like the Shades fighting for their interests—the exact same way we were.

Had Nana ever said anything else about how they looked? I knew they had a solid form in their own realm and a ghost-like one here.

"In their realm, their den of iniquity, they look like demons that have crawled up from some ancient underworld. Your grandfather saw drawings in

the archives once—he said they were the most repulsive creatures you could ever imagine in their true forms."

That didn't bode particularly well as far as lust was concerned. Then again, I couldn't see them. Their touch would matter the most to me, and maybe that felt good? Maybe they smelled nice. That would be a bonus.

"I guess you wouldn't be the first," Lucas muttered. "Other Hunters have defected. Maybe their families were raging psychopaths too."

"That seems a little excessive." I wasn't very sure of the words, but it felt disloyal to not try and defend their honor at least a little.

"It's actually an understatement. You do appreciate that it's not normal to hide your child in an attic their entire life, right?"

"The twins told you about that?"

"They boasted about that."

That was an uncomfortable thought. "I know it's strange. But it would have been disastrous for Moriah's career in the Hunters if anyone had found out about me. It was really for the best."

"No," Lucas said firmly. "I'm sorry. I get that you have Stockholm Syndrome or whatever, but there's no world in which that was an appropriate solution. There are homes where Hunters who can't hunt for whatever reason are sent to live. Where they can still contribute to the cause and have a community, and live normal lives."

I'd heard all about those places in hushed tones from Nana. From what she'd described, they weren't the idyllic dreamy villages of rejected Hunters that Lucas seemed to think they were.

What would he know about them, really? He didn't have to learn about those places. He was strong and healthy and an asset to the Hunters. He didn't have to worry about people or places like that.

There was a noise from the other room and Lucas cursed under his breath. "Hold on, let me see if the coast is clear for you to sneak out of here."

I'd never really snuck anywhere before, I realized with some amusement. When guests were at the house, I had to be quiet but the TV was always on because Moriah told everyone that Nana had an apartment in the attic. No one had ever trusted me to *sneak* before.

Lucas did whatever he was doing before coming back into the room, whispering at me to stay quiet as he gently grabbed my wrist and led me out of the room, depositing me back at the kitchen counter where he'd found me.

"I'll go let Tilly in," he murmured, pushing the glass into my hand that I'd been patting the counter, searching for.

If he was a bad person, he was doing a very good job of hiding it. So far, I felt much more comfortable in Lucas's presence than my brothers'. But I also knew not to trust my own judgment because Nana had regularly told me how naive I was to the ways of the world.

I startled as a phone rang, sloshing water all over my hand. One of the twins groaned, answering it groggily. "What's up, Mom?"

Whatever Moriah was saying, she didn't sound happy about it. I wondered if it was because she could tell through the phone that Travis had been drinking last night—his muttered grunts and replies sounded extremely rough.

"Yeah, alright. Yes! Okay. We'll be right there. Sorry. No, we really are sorry—"

There was a dull thud, then Justin groaned.

"Come on," Travis snapped. "She's been discharged—she's going back to that big house they're all staying at. We're supposed to be there already. Lucas—sorry, man—you have to come too. Mom's orders."

"Of course," Lucas agreed quietly. There was a lot of shuffling around and muttered complaints from the twins, and I huddled quietly in a corner of the kitchen, hoping they'd just leave without acknowledging me. The second they were gone, I was opening the sliding door. I didn't care how cold it was. They seemed to have been sweating out the beer they drank last night through their skin, and it was the most rancid smell.

"Bye, Iris," Lucas said gently as the three of them filed out, the door shutting with a deafening click.

I shook my head slightly, trying to clear that odd conversation we'd had this morning from my mind. Realistically, that was probably the last time I'd ever meet Lucas. If he was smart, he'd take this opportunity to get away from my brothers and pretend he'd never met me.

An urgent pounding on the door woke me up from the nap I didn't realize I'd been taking on the couch.

"Iris!" Lucas whisper-shouted. "Let me in—if you're going to go, it has to be now. Verity escaped, everything is in chaos."

Tilly barked—which was very unlike her—and it felt like she was hurrying me along, encouraging me to pounce on this unexpected opportunity.

Or plunge headfirst into this very real risk.

The moment I unlocked the door, Lucas was inside, hurriedly shutting it behind him. "Can I pack your stuff? If we're going, we need to go now."

"Is the portal open?"

I heard his pause of hesitation. "No. I'm not letting you be thrown through some random portal and hoping for the best—"

"That's *my* choice, Lucas."

"—when safer options are available. I know where Astrid Bishop has been hiding out, watching the hospital. I left her a note, asking if she could guide you through safely."

Oh.

"That sounds less intimidating," I admitted. "If that's something she'd want to do."

"Astrid was the leader of the last exodus into the shadow realm. She'll welcome you with open arms," Lucas said, sounding slightly resigned by the fact. "I still don't feel good about this. My human friend in Tucson has a trailer you could hide out in if we could get you there. We could drive through the night and be there by morning. I just want you to know it's an option."

I shook my head. No, that wasn't what I wanted. A trailer in Tucson had the potential to turn into another attic in Colorado. Another four-wall limit that I couldn't go beyond, because if the wrong person found out about me, it was all over.

Wherever I went next, I didn't want to be in hiding.

Although I'd never given him an answer, I heard Lucas rushing around, packing my things. Tilly gave a half-hearted growl like she wasn't sure whether this was acceptable or not before flopping down next to me with an exhausted huff.

"Alright—let's go. Come on, Tilly. I imagine someone will be here soon to collect you two since Verity disappeared. Half the visiting Councilors had cleared out already by the time I left."

He ushered me out the door, keeping a hold of my wrist as he guided me to a vehicle and opened the door. "It's high, there's a step to get in."

My stomach dipped in alarm as I scrambled to get in, having no concept of what I was clambering into. I eventually settled awkwardly on my seat as Tilly clambered into the small space at my feet, ignoring Lucas's instructions for her to get in the backseat.

"How do you think Verity got away?" I asked as Lucas climbed in next to me and started the vehicle. I startled, not expecting the rumbling engine to be quite so loud. "It must have been hard with so many Councilors in one spot."

"I wasn't high-level enough to be let in the room, but they were saying something about a temporary portal—I've never heard of anything like it. Are you going to put your seat belt on?"

"Oh. Um. I don't know how. On the way here, I just sat in the RV. I can't remember the last time I was in a vehicle before that—it must have been when I was a toddler."

The silence felt very loud.

"Right. I'm going to lean over you, okay? A seat belt is a strap that goes across your body to secure you in place. I'm going to reach over and grab it."

I nodded. I had heard of them, of course. From movies. I just didn't know where they went and how they were shaped.

Lucas got right into my personal space to tug the strap from somewhere above my shoulder, and I sat perfectly still, weirded out by the sensation of his breath on my skin.

It had me second-guessing my ability to provide lust in the shadow realm just a little. I was great at being lustful all by myself, but I didn't enjoy the physical proximity to Lucas at all.

"Are we going to your house?" I asked awkwardly after the seat belt clicked into place and Lucas moved back, immediately getting the vehicle moving.

"We're going to Denver," he answered, voice strained. "Astrid wants the meeting to happen on her home turf. She set the location."

"Oh." My hands shook a little. It seemed very risky to return back to my hometown. Then again, perhaps it was a bold enough choice that my mother would never think to look for me there?

"Oh no, Lucas," I gasped, immediately wracked with guilt for not thinking of it earlier. "This could be really bad for you if Moriah founds out you helped me—what are we going to do? Will you come to the shadow realm with me?"

He let out a surprised laugh. "I definitely wouldn't be welcome there, Iris. Not after what I did to Verity. I'm covering my tracks here. Worst case scenario, I think I have enough dirt on your brothers to get them to at least help me out—they wanted you gone anyway, right? I'm doing them a favor."

I don't think he meant the words to sound as callous as they did. He was just pointing out the honest truth of the situation. It was a painful truth, though.

The farther we got, the more relaxed Lucas seemed to become. "How are you feeling, Iris? I know it was a pretty spontaneous decision, but you're... Well, you're free."

I let out a shaky breath, burying my hands in the fur on Tilly's neck. "Yes."

I didn't know how long for, or what the consequences would be.

But for now, I was free.

CHAPTER 5

Come," Allerick grunted. "Sit with me awhile."

I silently joined him on the sofa in front of the fire in the drawing room, dragging over the small cart with goblets and a decanter of wine as I went. We both needed it.

"Ophelia went with Verity?"

Allerick nodded in confirmation, staring at the empty grate. "Soren will accompany her back later."

I poured us each a goblet of wine, and for a long moment we sipped our drinks in silence.

"Do you think Theon will forgive me?" Allerick asked, taking me by surprise. It was unlike him to even want forgiveness from anyone who wasn't his wife.

"Probably. Will it bother you if it doesn't?"

"I think so." He cut me an odd look. "You've grown closer to him. You have a real knack for building relationships."

That sounded like a vast exaggeration. "And yet here I am—single and unwanted," I joked, trying to lighten the mood.

"It is strange that you're single," Allerick agreed. "When everyone agrees you have the vastly superior personality. Are you very off-putting to your romantic partners?"

"No," I replied, offended. I didn't *have* many romantic partners to begin with, and I certainly hadn't been off-putting to any of them.

"Are you courting anyone right now?" Allerick persisted.

"Since when is this a topic that we discuss?"

"I'm concerned that you're sad and alone now that so many of your closest confidants are coupled up."

"You're the off-putting one," I muttered. "No, I'm not courting anyone. I don't know why this is so hard for everyone to grasp, but just because I'm *friendly* doesn't mean I always *like* everyone I meet. When I meet someone who I like enough to want to court, I'll know. There won't be any doubt in my mind. You don't have to worry about me being sad and alone," I added, just in case he was actually feeling bad and not just antagonizing me.

He nodded absently, swirling the wine in his goblet. For a brief moment, I felt oddly hopeless. I suspected that Allerick needed assistance, but I wouldn't have the first clue about how to provide that. It wasn't really my role. I was the fun one, not the problem-solving one.

"Since Theon's not going to prison anymore, you could always resign and let him deal with ruling the realm," I joked, trying to lighten the mood.

Allerick sighed heavily. Maybe I'd missed the mark on that one. "You're next in line, Damen. Not Theon."

"He's better qualified than me."

"Doesn't matter. You challenged him, and you won." He was quiet for a long moment. "I know you've been coasting by even more than usual recently, banking on the fact that Ophelia and I will have a child who will inherit the throne. But a baby hasn't... well, it hasn't happened yet. Don't get complacent."

"I didn't realize you were trying," I said awkwardly. "I thought the plan was to wait a little while."

Allerick grimaced. "I do my best to ignore the pressure of the court and the Elders for the most part, but the issue of an heir... Well, in this regard, they seem to be unwilling to leave it alone. I was content to ignore it but it has particularly gotten to Ophelia."

I nodded silently, wishing I knew what to say to offer him some comfort. Then again, that wasn't really the kind of relationship we had.

"I'm sure it will happen for you eventually," I volunteered. "If Ophelia were a Shade, you would be assuming that it would take years for conception to happen."

"Yes. But she isn't, and she's worried." His shoulders slumped slightly, and I wondered if I'd ever seen him so defeated. "Ophelia is the light of my life, Damen. Her unhappiness is excruciating to me."

She was my sister, and I adored her, but selfishly, the pang in my chest in that moment wasn't for her sadness but mine. My envy. What I wouldn't give to have the kind of love that those two had.

But if it meant experiencing the kind of vulnerability that Allerick was experiencing, I wasn't entirely sure that I was capable of it.

"Anyway, enough of my moroseness. I should probably go and smooth things over with the Council of Shades—they've been very unhappy with me recently."

"Would you like me to come with you?"

Allerick shook his head, setting his goblet down and pushing to his feet. "I know I'm always encouraging you to get more involved, but I would still shield you from this unpleasantness, Damen. Slighted Elders are a nightmare to deal with. Enjoy your evening."

"What's the plan today?" I asked Soren around a yawn as we made our way to the breakfast room. "To visit with Theon and Verity again?"

"I hope you will do that," Soren replied crisply. "Astrid has been asked to collect a Hunter from the human realm."

"How? By who?"

"Someone knew where Astrid was stationed while we were watching for Verity. They left a note."

"That sounds... like a trap?" I hedged. Granted, I wasn't the authority on these things, but it certainly sounded like it had the potential to be a trap to secure Astrid's capture.

That would be a massive accomplishment for the Hunters if they got her back. From what I gathered, Astrid had been their greatest loss, and she was now their biggest threat.

"Believe me, I have concerns," Soren said wryly. "So does Ophelia— she's relaying them to Astrid right now. My mate has many talents, but listening to other's very valid reservations is not one of them."

I laughed, able to imagine perfectly the look of haughty disdain on Astrid's face whenever someone so much as hinted that she might not be able to do something.

"Do you want me to come with you?" I offered.

"No. I'd only worry about you as well if you did." He paused for a moment, thoughtful. "It might be useful if you could be there to greet the new arrival when she shows up, though. Allerick is dealing with the fallout with the Elders, you're the next highest ranking royal."

"Right. You need me to do some kind of formal greeting?"

Soren grimaced, looking as thrilled with the idea as I felt. "It's probably the right thing to do, isn't it? Respectful and such."

"I've yet to meet a single ex-Hunter who cares about that, but sure. I'll perform as required." It was deeply refreshing to me that the ex-Hunters didn't seem interested in the pomp and ceremony of court. They seemed amused by it if anything.

Everyone scattered after breakfast, and I opted to go to Orabelle's room until I was required for greeting duty. I knew in my bones that she was happy to see me—I was practically her second son—but she always made a great show of scowling in annoyance whenever she had to interact with anyone. I suspected it was just habit at this point.

"At least one of you comes to visit me," she sighed dramatically, ringing a bell for tea. "Where is Allerick? Has he forgotten that his mother still lives?"

"He's busy running the realm, Ora. You shouldn't have birthed such a strong child if you didn't want him to inherit the throne."

"You know very well I had no control over that, you little rascal. Come here, let me look at you."

I winced as she grabbed my horn the moment I leaned down, turning my head this way then that.

"You've not been feeding enough, Damen. You look peaky."

"You're one to talk." Even before the human realm ban and the reliance on the energy stores for all Shades to feed, Orabelle had been loathe to use them. Like many older Shades, she found it an indignity to feed that way when she'd once been young and strong and able to fend for herself.

Allerick was frustrated by her stubbornness, but I understood. Without meaning to, sometimes the way help was offered was insulting rather than empowering.

"I'm not long for this world. I can do what I like," Orabelle sighed dramatically, even though she'd probably outlive all of us. "When are you going to settle down and give me grandchildren?"

"Settle down? I was thinking I'd leave a string of assorted infants in my wake the way my father did. Surprise myself whenever a new one pops up—like a gift to my future self. Oh look, a new progeny! That sort of thing."

Orabelle cackled quietly to herself. "You're too sweet for that, Damen. You don't have your father's philandering streak."

"More's the pity," I sighed, though we both knew I wasn't serious. My father had left a trail of chaos wherever he walked. I had no desire to emulate any of his behaviors.

I took a seat opposite her, pouring us both tea in silence. I felt a little out of sorts, though I couldn't think why. Perhaps it was just because everyone else was off doing important things today while I sat and had a cup of tea with my mother figure, ignoring all of the very real problems that seemed to be unfolding around me.

But what could I do? I wasn't qualified to be of use anyway.

"Are you happy, Damen?" Orabelle asked shrewdly.

If I could be honest with anyone, it was Orabelle. Or rather, if there was anyone I couldn't lie to, it was Orabelle.

"Allerick said I shouldn't get complacent as he has no heir yet and I may still inherit the throne someday," I said, opting to share just one of the things that was bothering me.

"And you don't want it?" Orabelle guessed.

"No one wants that," I laughed. "The realm would fall to pieces if I was in charge."

She sighed heavily, leaning back in her seat. "We both know that's not true. You just diminish your skills and talents before anyone else has the chance to. Everyone knows how capable you are, Damen. Even you."

I valued my life so I didn't argue with Orabelle, but I didn't agree. If I was in charge of the realm, every day would be a celebration and no one would have to work. Maybe I *should* be in charge, everyone would be far less stressed.

"Spend the day with me," Orabelle demanded gently. "I wish to walk in the gardens—you may accompany me."

"Gladly. Though I'll have to leave at some point—Soren has gone to collect a new Hunter. I'm to greet her on arrival."

"Another one?" she grumbled.

I laughed. "Don't try that with me. I've seen for myself how fond you are of all of the ex-Hunters who've come here. Ophelia may have even replaced *me* in your affections—I'll try my best not to hold it against her."

"I would be *very* cross if you held it against her," Orabelle sniffed, not contradicting my claim. Lucky that I couldn't begrudge my sister anything. "Perhaps this Hunter will be the one to win your affections," she added, perking up considerably.

"Perhaps," I agreed without much enthusiasm. If history was anything to go by, she'd be intimidated by the title, then not take me seriously as a romantic prospect when I tried my best to move past it. However, it was nothing to get upset about.

Maybe I could even introduce her to Ruvyn if I thought the two of them would be compatible? That was a very good notion. I wasn't entirely useless—I had good ideas.

Mind made up, I helped Orabelle to her feet and we made our way slowly downstairs to take a turn around the gardens.

At least if today's meeting was horribly awkward, it would be over quickly. I would divest myself of my duties immediately, nudge the new ex-Hunter in Ruvyn's direction if she was suitable, and resume my life of leisure.

IRIS

CHAPTER 6

We don't have long," Lucas muttered. I winced as he tugged my head a little harder under the faucet in the motel bathroom to rinse the dye out. "I don't even know if this is going to help. You won't have blinding blonde hair anymore, but the dog is still kind of a giveaway. Are you sure you won't leave her behind?"

"Absolutely not," I replied, my voice muffled by the basin.

Lucas huffed but didn't object, and I tried to say as little as possible, not wanting to annoy him. Even though he'd been nothing but kind in the time we'd been hiding out here, I still half expected him to pinch me the way my brothers did if I said the wrong thing.

I couldn't have slept more than two hours last night—my nerves had been relentless. What if I was making the wrong decision? Was I putting too much faith in Lucas? He seemed kind, but maybe his intentions weren't pure and I was just too ignorant about the world to realize it.

Lucas pushed a towel into my hands the moment he was done, and I roughly dried my hair as best I could over the basin. Despite the circumstances, there was a small frisson of excitement penetrating the cloud of nerves.

This was the most interesting thing I'd ever done.

I'd spent my entire life listening to movies and stories and songs about going on adventures and chasing dreams, assuming that I'd never go anywhere beyond the confines of my attic.

And while this experience wasn't quite as romantic as the ones I'd heard described in stories, it was still the start of a new chapter for me.

The start of a moment in time that would either make my future or break it.

"Alright," Lucas exhaled. "Let's do this. You're due to meet Astrid soon—she'll take you through to the shadow realm. I don't really know how, I assume a Shade helps with that part."

"Are you sure you won't come with me?" I asked, nervous both about going to a new world by myself and for Lucas. The silence from Moriah had been eerie. Lucas seemed to think she'd assumed I'd run away and had simply chosen not to look for me, but I knew I couldn't be that lucky.

"I'm definitely not welcome there," Lucas said firmly. "Though it's horrible to think that I'll never see you again."

Was it? I had assumed that Lucas would be glad to see the back of me.

Maybe once I was in the shadow realm, I could convince them to come back for him. He seemed very remorseful for calling in the higher-ups when he found Verity—surely that had to count for something.

"Have you heard from my brothers?" I asked.

Lucas made a quiet noise of discontent. "They asked if I'd taken you and I said I didn't know anything about that, and they had no further follow-up questions. I believe they've returned to Denver now, though your parents—sorry, Moriah and Giles—are still in town."

"Looking for me?"

"I'm not ruling that out, but I haven't heard anything specific through the grapevine, if it helps. If they're looking, they're being *very* discreet about it."

They didn't have a choice if they wanted to keep my existence a secret.

I shouldered the small backpack of things I was taking with me, and held onto the elaborate contraption Lucas had attached to Tilly—it was some kind of handle and harness contraption that she was very begrudgingly wearing.

If I said anything at that moment, I might have burst into tears. Lucas was a stranger to me, and yet he'd repeatedly shown me more kindness than my family ever did.

That's not kind, I scolded silently. *It's* because *Lucas is a stranger that he can be so patient with you. You haven't become a burden to him yet.*

"It's a short walk to the meeting point," Lucas murmured, gently gripping my elbow as we headed outside, the wind immediately chilling my face.

"Is there anything I need to know before I get there?" I asked, wishing I had a coat on to ward off the chill.

"Almost certainly," Lucas replied. "I don't know where to begin. The Shade king's name is Allerick—he is married to Ophelia Bishop, the exiled Hunter that your mother sent over to the shadow realm to secure the treaty. Or to lure them into a false sense of security. I'm not really sure—the reports we received were pretty mixed. Astrid defected to help her sister, and took some other exiled Hunters with her." He was quiet for a long moment. "That wasn't the story that we were told at the time, but that's the information I've gathered after spending several days with the Councilors."

He sounded so quietly betrayed by that, and I had no idea how to respond. Was it such a surprise for him to find out they'd been lied to? Perhaps

I had an advantage in that respect. Through the vents, I'd heard Moriah tell someone one thing in their presence while saying something entirely different the moment they left my life.

"You'll probably fit in just fine with the ones who have already gone over there, Iris. They all didn't fit in the Hunters' mold for one reason or another."

That bolstered my confidence slightly. How lovely to start off with something in common.

Lucas's steps slowed, pulling me to a stop with him. "Can you walk the rest of the way alone?"

"I don't know," I replied honestly, taking a steadying breath. "I'm not used to doing things on my own. Tell me what to do."

Lucas grabbed my wrist and pressed my palm against a rough brick wall. "Follow the curve of the building. Astrid should be waiting for you in an alleyway down the side of it. I'll wait here for a little while too—to guard the entry and make sure she actually shows up to collect you."

"You won't come with me?"

Lucas gave my wrist a brief squeeze before releasing it. "In theory, you're safe with Astrid. I'm not."

Oh. That made sense.

"If you've changed your mind—" Lucas began.

"I haven't. I know this must seem crazy to you but in my bones, it feels like the right decision. Nana always said that my gut would tell me what my eyes couldn't." I found myself smiling at the memory, a sense of peace washing over me. "It seems insufficient to say this after everything you've done for me, but thank you for your help."

Lucas blew out a shaky breath. "I hope this is the right call. Helping you means helping the *Shades*, and I feel pretty fucking weird about that, but

I guess this is the side of the coin we've landed on. Let's hope it was the right one. Now, go."

I didn't hesitate, pressing my palm hard enough against the wall that it stung as I picked up my pace with Tilly right in front. My breathing was so loud that I was certain they would hear me coming from a mile away. If that didn't give me away, then my thudding heartbeat surely would.

Running away had been the bravest, most reckless thing I'd ever done, and I was already replacing it with a new bravest and most reckless thing.

Perhaps Nana had been right to worry about how I would behave once she was gone.

Tilly slowed, alerting me to the fact that there was someone ahead of me. I picked up the faintest shuffle of someone's feet, though they were very quiet.

Should I say something first? Maybe. I was the intruder here, after all. I was the one in need of a favor.

"Hello. My name is Iris."

There was a long pause. "Um, hello."

I suddenly recalled that most Hunters knew each other—or at least *of* each other. It was quite a tight community that I had no part in.

"Iris *Nash*. We've never met," I added needlessly. I was confident that she would have never met a blind Hunter.

To be completely honest, "Nash" wasn't even my surname, but no one had ever told me what mine was so I'd decided to copy my brothers.

"Nash? As in Moriah Nash?"

"My mother." How strange to admit that out loud.

"Moriah Nash doesn't have a daughter," Astrid said, quiet and uncertain.

"Not one that she wants people to know about. No Hunter wants a *blind* daughter. Especially not a Councilor." Should I tell her about the attic? I had the oddest feeling that the revelation wouldn't be well received. "It's a big house, though. Plenty of places to hide a spare child."

I'd been trying to keep my tone light and relaxed, but I suspected, based on the heavy silence, the words hadn't landed the way I wanted them to.

"Do you... Do you want to come to the shadow realm?" Astrid asked eventually. "I can't imagine you've heard many good things about it, living in the Nash home."

"Not a single one, but I know my mother. She wouldn't be so furious if there was no cause for concern. There must be something there to entice Hunters such as yourself and Austin—successful, *popular* Hunters—to leave this world behind." I jiggled the backpack I was carrying. "I'm all packed. Though it's mostly kibble for Tilly."

"Right. Then let's go, I guess." Astrid sounded a little baffled by the entire interaction. Maybe other ex-Hunters had approached the move differently. "No pressure, okay? If you don't like it, let me know and I'll bring you back."

"I'm not coming back. I've been imprisoned my entire life. The shadows are going to set me free."

"Alright," Astrid replied, sounding much more certain this time. "Then let's go."

While I couldn't see the in-between, I didn't need to know the exact moment we stepped into it. The background noise of the world disappeared. The air cooled—it felt like the mist of the morning fog that sometimes hung in the air when I'd walk the forest paths outside the house. And the odd, faint sensation that had been tickling one shoulder became a solid, heavy hand all of a sudden.

"This is Soren," Astrid said offhandedly. "Captain of the Guard, et cetera, et cetera. He's my mate. That's like... a husband or whatever."

Soren snorted, perhaps at her rather unromantic description of their relationship.

"Nice to meet you, Soren."

"Nice to meet you too, Iris," he replied in a low, even voice. Despite the fact that I *knew* Shades had two forms and they were more human-like in their own realm, it was still a little jarring to hear him speak.

Tilly whimpered a little and I pulled her back to my side so I could scratch her ears, letting us both be led by Soren rather than having her walk up front.

"It's okay, Tilly. You're such a brave girl," I murmured.

"She is brave," Astrid agreed. "This must be weird for her. And for you," she added after a moment's pause.

"A little. It's quite exciting to go on an adventure, though."

"I guess," Astrid replied, though she didn't sound *that* enthused. Based on what Lucas told me, Astrid probably went on multiple adventures each day—undoubtedly, this seemed very boring to her. "We've set up a temporary entry to the shadow realm for you—we're nearly there. Usually, we'd emerge right outside the palace, but Lucas's note made it seem like you might prefer a quiet introduction to life here."

"That was kind of you to go to the extra effort." Though I wished they hadn't. I was already making more work for people. "What was it about Lucas's note that made you come back for me? He seemed to think you weren't very fond of him."

"Oh, I'm definitely not," Astrid agreed. "And I absolutely wondered if I was walking into a trap. But there was something about the letter that was compelling, I guess."

"Did he tell you I was blind?" I asked, wondering if pity had been the compelling factor.

"No. That must have slipped his mind," Astrid said dryly. "Here we are. Keep hold of Tilly, this might feel a little odd for her."

I tightened my grip on the handle, but she didn't try and bolt or anything as we stepped out into a whole new world. There was a gentle breeze and warmth on my skin, and I could hear rustling trees and running water, as well as the faint buzz of what I assumed were insects, though they weren't ones that I recognized.

"Tallulah, Meera, this is Iris Nash," Astrid announced. "And Tilly."

"It's a pleasure to meet you," someone said. They sounded worried, and I did my best to be as calm and self-assured as possible when I replied to put their mind at ease.

"It's so nice to meet you too."

There was an agonizingly long silence after that, and I tightened my grip a little on Tilly's harness as I waited. Sometimes, when there were long stretches of no conversation in films, Nana had explained that the characters were communicating with their body language instead. I wondered if that was what was happening now, and wished I didn't feel so left out.

"What is this?"

Based on the sharp intakes of breath, I wasn't the only one taken by surprise by whoever this new arrival was. It was a masculine voice—noticeably different from Soren's. A little brighter. A little *happier.*

It immediately made me feel happier too.

"What a magnificent creature," the nice voice said.

Me? I supposed that I had come here knowing that I would need to be providing my lust in exchange, so I shouldn't really be shocked. Perhaps it was just the word "creature" that had thrown me off? It just sounded so unsexy.

"He means Tilly. They don't have dogs in the shadow realm," the woman who'd spoken earlier said, hurrying out an explanation. "Prince Damen, this is Iris Nash and her dog, Tilly."

A prince? My only frame of reference for them was the kind they had in fairy tales. Was he like that?

"My service dog," I added, needing them to know how crucial Tilly was to me. "I'm blind. Tilly is my eyes."

"Well, you and Tilly are both most welcome here," the prince said. He really did have such a lovely voice. It was strong and steady without a trace of anger, and it was something that I didn't know I liked—I'd never heard anyone speak like that before.

I doubted that I would get to exercise my abundance of lust on him, since he was a prince and all. They probably had important Hunters who fulfilled that role. Perhaps they could send me someone like him, though? Would I get to choose? It took all of my self-control not to reach over and touch him, just to get some idea of what he was shaped like.

No one had brought up the lust thing yet, or mentioned that I would need to contribute in order to stay here. It was all very polite.

"I hope you will find the shadow realm a happy home for both of you," he continued. "Tallulah and Meera stay in the accommodation that has been set aside for ex-Hunters, but perhaps you would be more comfortable in the palace, Iris? I believe it would better suit you and Tilly."

The palace? I was hardly palace material. I almost objected on principle—somewhere like the attic would be perfectly suitable for me. Then again, this was an adventure, and I didn't want to keep living the life of seclusion I'd always had.

If I was going to do this, I needed to be brave and say yes to opportunities as they arose. "Well, I've never been inside a palace before, just heard about them in fairytales. It certainly sounds like the kind of place where anyone could be comfortable."

"We'll accompany you over there," a different feminine voice said.

"Um, we'll just start walking straight ahead. It's about two hundred feet away. The path curves a little on the way, but it's flat."

I smiled in the direction of the first woman, grateful for her thoughtful description as we set off on the path. So far, everyone was being very kind and welcoming. I wished I could go back and tell Lucas that there was nothing to worry about—that maybe he could even come too—though I recalled Astrid's affirmation that she wasn't fond of him, and wondered if this was for the best. Maybe in time I could convince her that he was really quite kind.

"What made you decide to come to the shadow realm?" someone asked.

"Well, my parents kept me hidden away because they were ashamed of me. And my nana who raised me, recently passed away, so the options of what they were going to do with me were looking quite bleak. Bleak enough that one of the Hunters decided that this would be a better option for me."

"One of the Hunters decided that?"

"I suspect what my parents had planned for me was very grim indeed for him to make that decision. But it was very kind of him to help me. I owe him a great debt."

Perhaps if I planted the seeds now about Lucas's good nature, it would be easier to convince them later on to let him come here. Despite his confidence, I was terrified that Moriah would realize what he'd done and punish him for it.

I'd have to find a way to speak to Verity first—she was the one who'd been harmed by Lucas's decision to call the Council. She didn't seem to be one of the ex-Hunters who'd greeted me here today, but hopefully I'd have a chance to meet her soon.

One of the women offered me their arm as we went up some stairs, and the room we stepped into was echoey in a way I'd never experienced before. The ground beneath my feet was hard and smooth, but also uneven, and I barely resisted the urge to bend down and run my fingers over it to find out what it was. Everything felt different to the attic and the little house in Utah I'd been staying in.

There was a lot of noise and I listened with interest at the hushed whispers of everyone trying to decide where I would be most comfortable. I was used to hushed whispers about me, but never because anyone was worried about my comfort.

The woman behind me seemed to be heatedly telling the prince that he needed to help make some decisions, which I was struggling to reconcile with what I knew of royalty and how they were usually spoken to.

Maybe things were different in real life than they were in movies? And, of course, human royalty and Shade royalty wouldn't be exactly the same. I decided to treat him like he was any other person or Shade I was meeting for the first time, to be safe.

"Damen, you handled things really well out there. It isn't realistic for King Allerick to personally address every logistical issue that the ex-Hunters face in moving here. You could really help us in this area," she whispered, a clear thread of impatience in her voice.

"You're right. Okay. Yes. There's a ground-floor guest apartment with a small garden area out front, near where Captain Soren and Astrid stay. Please ready that room."

Oh, that sounded *lovely*. I wondered if the garden would be safe for Tilly to explore—that would be so nice.

"Have you eaten, Iris?" the woman asked me.

"No, but I'll be fine."

"I'll send for food," the prince said decisively.

So far, this was all proving to be a very pleasant experience. Everyone had been very kind and welcoming. They were possibly a little intimidated by me—or at the very least, didn't quite know what to do with me—but they'd definitely been friendly.

"And some water for Tilly. Perhaps we could eat in the dining hall?" Tallulah-or-Meera said—I really needed to figure out who was who—before lightly touching my arm. "We'll give you a tour of the place now while it's empty."

"I would appreciate that. Thank you."

"Great, let's go. We're going to make you feel so welcome here, Iris. Anything you need, just let us know."

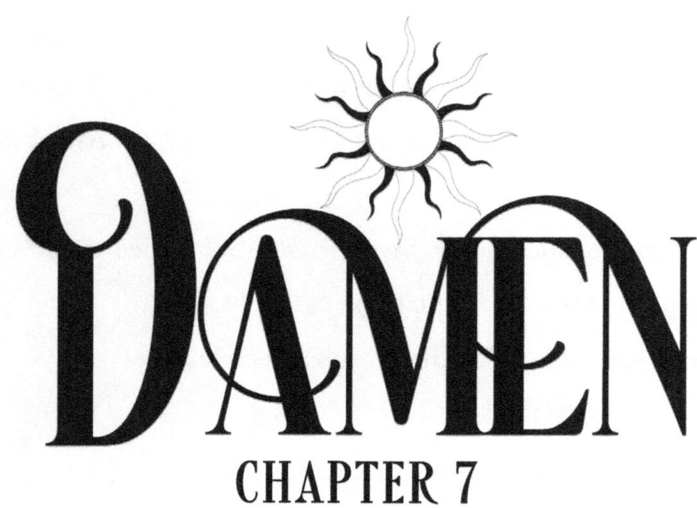

DAMEN
CHAPTER 7

I just show up, and the food is already prepared?" Iris asked dubiously after Tallulah finished telling her about the dining hall and explaining the meal schedule. "What do I need to help with?"

"Nothing," Tallulah assured her. "It's all part of how the palace runs."

"Oh, how *lovely*," Iris murmured, amazed. "Though, I really would like to help with something. Somewhere. Whatever I can do."

"Just find your feet first," Tallulah recommended. "Get used to the shadow realm, to the palace, meet everyone. There's no rush."

"I'm so grateful I came here," Iris said wistfully, a soft smile on her face.

Fuck Ruvyn, I definitely wasn't going to be introducing Iris to him.

Not that I'd had much of a chance to speak to her or anything, but something about her had me feeling... out of sorts.

I always knew what to say. Perhaps not what to *do*, but at least how to charm anyone enough that it didn't really matter if I didn't have the answers they were looking for. But Iris was waiting so expectantly, so *trustingly*, for us to come up with a solution—and Tallulah was basically demanding that I step up and find one—and now I was too stressed to make anyone smile.

Worse still, Iris seemed like she'd be content with whatever half-cooked idea I came up with, and that didn't sit well with me. She had a soft optimism to her that should be preserved at all costs. Like she'd come to the shadow realm with an entirely pure and unshakeable belief that life here was going to be better for her.

I was going to make sure that was the case.

"The room is ready. If you'll follow me," I said, having gotten the go-ahead from the staff that they'd finished preparing it.

It was as close as Iris could be to the dining hall whilst also having a private courtyard for her delightful little beast companion. Unfortunately, all of the ground-floor rooms were small because most of the communal spaces were down here.

What if Iris didn't like it? I got the distinct impression that she wouldn't tell anyone, and I was oddly displeased by it. Usually, I liked easy-going personalities.

"I think this room will work best for you," I told her, pushing open the door. "It has a small courtyard directly outside and its own washroom."

"That sounds perfect, thank you," Iris said with a smile that could have melted the coldest of hearts.

"That's... okay."

Huh. It was strange to be thanked for something. I supposed I didn't usually do things that required gratitude.

I liked the way that Iris spoke to me the same way she spoke to Tallulah and Meera, even though she knew I was a prince. And she was very lovely, I had to admit. Her hair was an odd color compared to what I'd seen of the other ex-Hunters—a dismal sort of pale brown with odd patches of a lighter color—but it didn't detract from the elegance of her face. Interestingly, she had the kind of beauty that was particularly prized in Shades. Sharp, angular features, high cheekbones, a pointed jaw, and a long, graceful neck.

But there was nothing Shade about that soft, welcoming smile and those blunt, harmless teeth.

Or her complex, interesting scent. Iris seemed to be processing a range of emotions, though seemingly none of them were negative. She must have a very joyful disposition to walk into this situation alone—*blind*—and feel anything close to contentment.

It made me want to stay close to her. To absorb some of that brightness for myself, as well as shelter her, so nothing could dim her light. It wasn't a sensation I'd ever experienced before, so I surmised that I must be in love with her. What else could it possibly be?

Based on scent, she didn't appear to love me back yet, but we hadn't spent much time together. I'm sure we'd get there eventually.

"Weren't you going to arrange food?" Tallulah reminded me. She was always confident, but she seemed more assertive than usual today. Or annoyed. I wasn't entirely confident which.

I lingered in the doorway, but even the usually mild Meera turned to give me a *get out* look. Perhaps they wanted time alone for "girl talk," as Ophelia always referred to it? I supposed I could come back later and get a feel for whether Iris was in love with me or not yet.

Leaving them to it, I headed down the corridor, sending an instruction down to the kitchen with a staff member to have a tray brought up.

Would it be possible to keep every other Shade away from Iris until she'd chosen me for her mate? That didn't seem like too much to ask.

Conveniently, Soren was pacing in the corridor as I emerged like he wasn't quite sure what to do with himself.

"Is Iris okay?" he asked.

"Yes. She's magnificent actually, she's adapting very well. Soren, the doors in the palace only lock via shadows. I didn't bring it up with Iris yet as I didn't have a solution, but we can't expect her to stay in an unlocked room."

Elverston House could be secured with a drawbar from the inside, but there was no such thing on the individual rooms within the palace.

"I hadn't thought of that." Soren briefly glanced at me in surprise, like he was shocked that I had. "She's in the end room. I'll see to it that the others are left unoccupied—they're for temporary visitors anyway—then station a guard rotation for the entire corridor. It's not ideal, I admit. Iris is new here and she has no reason to entrust her safety to Shades in general, let alone the Guard."

"I don't think that will bother her," I admitted. "She seems to have a very trusting disposition. Only put your very best on duty here," I added in a warning voice. I didn't like to think that any member of the Guard was dishonorable, but I didn't want Soren taking any chances.

"Of course," he agreed, narrowing his eyes slightly. "I'm glad to see you're taking more of an interest in goings-on around the palace, Damen."

"I always take an interest in things," I replied, waving him off. "Shall I go update my brother on this new development while you arrange a guard rotation for this corridor? Did he know she was coming?"

Somehow, that seemed to make him more suspicious, though I had no idea why.

"That would be unusually helpful of you, thanks. He knew Astrid and I were collecting someone, but the details of the note were vague."

"I'm always helpful," I assured him, clapping him on the shoulder before making for the throne room where Allerick would probably be meeting with... I don't know. Subjects, I supposed. He never used to use that room, but since he and Ophelia had thoroughly desecrated it, he was rather fond of the place.

It must be nice to have someone to desecrate important state rooms with.

Perhaps that would be me someday soon.

"Damen," Allerick said in surprise as I walked in, finding him speaking to a couple of the most boring elders on the Council of Shades. I was doing him a favor by rescuing him from this conversation.

"May I have a word?"

"Of course."

The two elders inclined their heads deeply to Allerick, then with less enthusiasm at me before excusing themselves.

"Where's my favorite sister?" I asked, climbing the stairs up the dais and sitting on the top one. I leaned back on my forearms so I could peer up at Allerick while he spoke from his ugly throne. If I were king, I'd have redecorated.

"Napping," he replied, almost bashfully for my cocky brother.

"Are you running your poor wife ragged again?"

He narrowed his eyes. "Watch it, Damen."

Right, right. I felt a twinge of guilt at my thoughtless joke after what he'd confided in me the other night.

"You will be able to retaliate in kind shortly," I assured him. "I've met my wife."

"You've... what? Who?"

"The new ex-Hunter who just moved to the realm. The one Soren and

Astrid collected. Her name is Iris. I think I'll marry her someday. Ideally sooner rather than later."

"You're going to... Are you feeling okay?"

"Of course, I am." I sighed, exasperated with Allerick's limited emotional range. "What part of 'I met her today and I'm going to marry her' are you finding difficult to comprehend?"

"All of it. You've never expressed that kind of interest in anyone before. It's unusual for you."

"I was just waiting for the right one, clearly."

"Yes," he agreed slowly. "Clearly. Why don't you tell me about her?"

"Well, she's very kind. The kindest of all the ex-Hunters who have moved here, I'm sure of it—though I don't mean that as a slight against your wife." Allerick made a grumbling sound but didn't say anything. "She is pleased by the simple things and talks to me like I'm the same as anyone else. Iris is also beautiful, which is a pleasant bonus. She's sweet and curious. She has a very agreeable nature which is something that I would like in a wife as I don't have much desire to be challenged on anything—"

"Words that every wife desires to hear from her spouse."

"—and I believe that we could live a very content life together. She inspires a feeling of protectiveness in me. What else is there?"

He looked at me for a long moment. "Have you asked Iris what she wants?"

"That seems a little forward, Allerick. I just met her."

He groaned, slumping down in his throne and resting his forehead on his palm. "And yet you are content to project whatever ideas you wish about her onto a future marriage you've made up in your mind?"

"It's very romantic of me," I agreed. "Planning out our future this way.

Someday—once we're engaged, ideally with my mating mark on her neck—I'll tell her that I knew from the very moment I saw her that she was the one and I even informed my brother as such immediately after the fact. I assume you'll be supportive and reaffirm how smitten I was when she asks."

"Everything you're saying is *I, I, I*. What will Iris say about the moment she first saw you?"

"She didn't see me, I suppose," I mused. "Perhaps she'll reflect back on the first moment that she heard me? I should have touched her—just on the arm or something, relax—something to make the moment magical so it would exist as clearly in her mind as it does in mine."

"What are you talking about?"

"Oh, right. Iris can't see. Her eyes don't... function. I don't know how it works," I admitted. Shades didn't get injured like that—our power healed us. Though Evrin, a member of the Guard, had been born without horns entirely. Maybe it worked the same way? Perhaps Iris didn't have eyeballs?

It didn't make her any less desirable to me. Should I tell Allerick I was in love with her? He'd probably be as negative about that as he was being about everything else I was saying.

Allerick straightened, looking worried. "You didn't think that was pertinent information to lead with? Damen, that makes her very vulnerable. She's in a brand-new world, and she can't see her surroundings."

"We put her in a room here in the palace rather than Elverston House for her comfort. And she has a pet beast who helps her navigate things. And I'll take care of her."

"You're not to propose to her."

"What?! Why not?" I narrowed my eyes, contemplating challenging Allerick for his throne. Once upon a time we'd have been equals, but now that he was feeding from Ophelia, I suspected I wouldn't stand a chance.

"Stop looking at me like that—you don't want my job. You can't propose to her right away, at least. Give Iris time to settle in and get familiar with the place. She might not even like it here. She might not even like *you*."

"Everyone likes me." Granted, I hadn't had any luck romantically with any of the other ex-Hunters, but that had been entirely mutual—I hadn't felt anything for them, and they hadn't felt anything for me.

"A month," Allerick stated firmly. "Wait a month. Give her time to settle in. Get to know her—make sure that the connection you think is there is real—"

"It *is* real. And a month is barbaric."

"—and in the meantime, I'm going to wake up Ophelia. I think she'd like to be involved in this to make sure the right arrangements are in place to accommodate Iris. I'll see you at dinner—don't do anything ridiculous before then."

"Apparently, I have to wait a month first," I snarked, annoyed at Allerick's high-handedness, but he was already gone.

Fine. I could wait a month. Iris needed time to get to know me anyway, so her scent would sweeten into that delightful lovey-dovey smell that ex-Hunters got when they were smitten. There was a faint niggle of doubt in the back of my mind that she might not reciprocate the immediate love I'd developed for her, but I squashed it instantly.

I would woo her and charm her. Gently suggest that it would be fun to be a princess. Iris would be my wife in no time.

CHAPTER 8

The bed in the palace was the most comfortable bed I'd ever slept in. If I hadn't been hovering on the edge of overwhelm all night long, I was confident I'd have had the best sleep of my life. As it was, it had been a fitful, rather restless night, and I felt as though I could have stayed in bed for several hours longer.

Tilly disagreed.

She bumped my arm with her nose, snuffling slightly in a clear request to be let out. Tallulah had assured me that the small courtyard outside was completely secure and private, and it felt like such a blessing to be able to just walk a few steps and open the door to let Tilly out somewhere safe.

Unfortunately, I hadn't gotten my bearings yet at all in this room. There were heavy drapes around the bed, and in disentangling myself from those, I almost immediately knocked my hip against the heavy nightstand as I was climbing out.

"Just a sec, Tilly girl," I wheezed, clutching my hipbone as pain radiated out. Once it had subsided, I felt for the edges of the nightstand, wincing at how sharp the corners were. Luckily I'd bumped into the side instead, which was slightly less treacherous.

I gingerly took a few steps, nudging the ground with my toe to avoid tripping. There were low stools and cushions on the ground, as well as a coffee table in the center of the room. Off to one side was a small dining table and chairs, and there were other larger bits of furniture against the walls which I presumed were storage.

In truth, it wasn't the easiest room for me to navigate, but I didn't want to be rude and ask if I could shuffle things around a little.

Tilly appeared at my side, and I softly held her collar as she guided me around the obstacles and directly to the door.

Clearly, I'd been taking too long for her liking.

"There you go," I murmured, pushing it open so she could get out. The familiar sound of birdsong from home didn't greet me, but the air was fresh and cool, and there were definitely sounds of nature even though they weren't familiar to me.

I wondered what Nana would say if she knew I was here. If she'd be able to forgive me for the choices I'd made, or if she'd treat me with the same shame and revulsion that Moriah had always treated me with.

That was a depressing thought.

I startled as someone knocked on the door, letting themselves in before I had the chance to stumble my way over to it.

"Breakfast," a feminine voice called. "I have a tray here for you fresh from the kitchens."

"For me?" I asked, surprised.

"Yes. Prince Damen thought you might find it easiest to have your breakfast delivered here for the time being. Until you learn the layout of the palace."

"Well, that's very kind of him. I'll be sure to thank him. Or perhaps it would be best to send along a message? I doubt I'll meet him again soon—princes must be very busy."

Perhaps it was my imagination, but I could have sworn the Shade woman scoffed. To my horror, I realized that I had no idea who I was speaking to. Nana would be appalled at my manners—she'd always drilled into me how I should act if I met someone new even though I'd never gone anywhere.

"What is your name? It was very rude of me not to ask earlier, I'm sorry."

There was a slight pause. "Hela."

"Hela," I repeated firmly to lodge the information in my brain. "Thank you for bringing me breakfast. I'm Iris."

"I know."

Right. I supposed there weren't *that* many ex-Hunters living in the shadow realm. How odd to go from completely hidden away to relatively famous in a day.

Tilly was apparently in no rush to come back inside, so I slowly made my way back toward the center of the room where the person—or Shade?—seemed to be. There was a soft clattering noise and I guessed they were setting the meal up on the coffee table rather than the dining table. Perhaps that was the way things were done here?

I lowered myself onto my knees on one of the enormous floor cushions, grateful I hadn't tripped over it, and slowly and carefully inched closer to the table. I could admit, it was quite fun sitting on the floor to eat. I'd never done it before.

"Would it be helpful if I told you what was on the table?"

"Oh, ever so helpful, thank you." I crossed my legs, finding the edge of the low table with my fingertips.

"The Shade diet consists mostly of meat. May I touch your hand?"

I was surprised she asked. Nana had always just grabbed it and put it where she wanted me to feel. "Yes, of course."

I startled slightly as the sharpest nails I'd ever felt in my life rested lightly against my skin, guiding my hand over the tray. "Here is the meat. Over on this side is a dense bread thing that the palace cook has been experimenting with to help supplement your diets. Over here is some fruit from your realm."

"Oh, how lovely. Thank you."

How very welcoming the Shades were—they were really going out of their way to make us feel comfortable here.

"I'll pour the tea for you," Hela said hastily, making quick work of it before guiding my hand to the hot cup. I left it to cool, picking at the meat instead. I hadn't expected to like it particularly—the way Nana cooked meat meant it was always very dry and chewy—but this was quite delicious. "Do you need anything else?" Hela asked.

"No, not at all. This has been very generous, thank you. I feel quite spoiled." I wondered if this is how princesses in fairy tales felt. "Really, you don't need to wait on me. I'd like to pull my own weight and be useful around the place."

I felt her hesitate next to me. "You're refreshingly sweet compared to the courtiers I have to deal with, so I will say these words as a kindness and hope you interpret them as such. You are in a palace now. You're an esteemed guest here, in fact. Meals brought to your room are your due."

"I don't want to get used to such a luxurious lifestyle." Nana would be horrified to see me sitting on my laurels, happily enjoying such a generous portion of food while Tilly romped around outside, as happy as can be. Was this meat safe for her? Perhaps Tallulah or Meera would come back and I could ask them about it. "When will I start working?"

"Working?" There was a shuffling sound of what I assumed was her feet on the bare stone. Did Shades wear shoes? It didn't sound like it.

"Yes. Contributing." I tried to think of a polite way to bring it up. "As I understand it, the Hunters who move here contribute to the power supply of Shades...?"

Hela coughed loudly. Perhaps I hadn't done as good of a job asking politely as I'd hoped. It was just that no one had brought the subject up, and it was making me a little twitchy to not talk about it at all. I'd hoped one of the women would say something yesterday, but they'd both been more concerned with making sure that Tilly and I had all the things we needed from the human realm than discussing work.

"Not all of them. That's not... there's no schedule or anything. Certainly, for now, the expectation would be for you to get comfortable here first."

"I'm glad there's no rush," I admitted. Though, I was also extremely curious still. The hint of that sharp nail on my hand had only made me more so.

What did Shades feel like? What kind of things did they like?

"When you came here, did you think you'd be doing that right away?" Hela asked curiously.

"I did. Is that an awful assumption to make? It seems a little crude of me, now I've been here a few hours and everyone has been unfailingly polite."

Hela laughed. I could sense her relaxing next to me, and I hoped she'd feel comfortable speaking freely. "Not quite the ravishment you thought you'd get on arrival? No, I suppose not. Back in the olden days, that's probably what would have happened by the sounds of it. When you were all the Hunted. King

Allerick's trying to do things differently this time around. Never forget that the power is in your hands. I'll leave you to your breakfast."

I didn't feel particularly powerful as I fumbled my teacup, spilling the hot—but fortunately not burning—liquid over my fingers as I brought the cup to my lips. But then again, the way everyone spoke to me *had* certainly made me feel important. Even the prince had taken a personal interest in my safety and comfort!

Maybe I really could be valued here rather than a burden. If only I could get a message to Lucas to thank him—he might have changed my life more than either of us realized at the time.

I stacked the dishes back onto the tray as best I could after eating, leaving it sitting on the table and feeling my way back around the room to get to the washroom—which was up three steps and circular in shape.

Unfortunately, I didn't have any fresh clothes to change into, so I just cleaned myself up as best I could before heading back down to sit in the squishy dining chair for a moment and catch my breath. Tilly flopped down for a nap at my feet as Hela came in to collect the tray, followed by a morning visit with Meera that made me feel more at ease with everything—especially as she assured me she'd source me some more clothes to wear.

I was feeling quite the lady of leisure when another knock on the door came. Like a grand dowager in my elegant home, receiving guests all day the way the old dames did in the shows Nana used to watch.

"Come in!" I called while Tilly let out a snore. She hadn't seemed the least bit concerned by anyone who'd visited thus far, though I supposed she'd mostly avoided my brothers rather than growled at them. It had never occurred to me before, but Tilly might be a bit of a coward.

I couldn't judge. I was a bit of a coward too.

"Good morning, Iris. How did you sleep?"

"Is that you, Prince Damen?" I asked tentatively. I certainly hadn't expected a visit from him.

"It is—call me Damen, please." He crossed the room in a few steps—how long were his legs?—and took the seat closest to me. His voice was so lovely and friendly that I couldn't help but feel at ease in his presence.

"I didn't expect you to visit again," I said honestly. "You're a prince. You must be very busy doing important things."

"I have no trouble making time for you," he replied smoothly.

"Oh. Okay then." Was that... Was he flirting with me? Was that what that was? Perhaps he was testing to see if I had the capacity for lust.

Surely, princes had better options.

Damen cleared his throat. "Is there anything I can do that might make your transition to life here more comfortable?"

Now, he sounded exceedingly polite. Perhaps he *had* been flirting and I'd reciprocated poorly.

Should I flirt?

I didn't know how to do that. I supposed that I'd never learn unless I tried though.

"Could I touch your hand?"

"You... you want to touch my hand?"

"Yes, please. If that's okay. Only I don't know what a Shade looks like, and it might be helpful to feel." That was a little flirty, wasn't it? While also being a genuine response to his question—knowing what a Shade felt like would make my transition to life here more comfortable.

"Of course." Damen moved closer, dragging the chair with him. Tilly huffed at the scrape of the wood on the stone floor. "You might not like what you find, Iris. We don't feel human."

He almost sounded worried.

"No, I expected as much," I assured him, reaching out my hand, palm up. After a long moment, he placed his hand on top of mine, and I gently began exploring.

Five fingers—that was standard. His palm was a little softer, the back of his hand a little bonier—also pretty regular. The texture of his skin was different to mine, though. Warm and smooth and much tougher. More like leather than human skin.

"Careful," Damen warned as I traced his knuckles. "You're getting closer to my claws."

"Claws," I repeated, pausing. Hela hadn't just had sharp nails, she'd had *claws*. That made far more sense.

"Here." Damen used his free hand to gently clasp my wrist, guiding my movements. There was an odd swooping sensation below my stomach in response to his grip, and I swallowed loudly. "You can touch the top of them. That won't cut you."

I hummed appreciatively, noting how long and tapered they were. Smooth, though. Were all Shade hands like this, or did the prince have particularly soft ones from a more restful life?

"Is there anything else about you that's different from humans?"

Damen made a slightly pained sound. "Maybe a couple of things. Do you, uh, want to feel my face?"

"Would you be okay with that?"

"Not if it was anyone else. But for you, it's fine." Was *that* flirty? Or maybe it was just kindness. Or perhaps it was pity. Actually, that made the most sense. I was blind, and Damen felt sorry for me. "Hold on, I'll kneel so you can reach."

I widened my knees a little so he could kneel more comfortably in front of my seat, and up this close, I realized he smelled quite lovely. I couldn't place my finger on what it was, but it made me think of sunshine. Could someone smell like that?

It was probably inappropriate of me, but I inhaled deeply, trying to take in more of that warm, bright, soothing scent. There was a noise so quiet I thought I must be imagining things, like he'd sucked in air through his teeth.

Damen gently held my wrists, lifting them up until my fingers brushed his jaw, then releasing me to feel around at my leisure. It was very... thoughtful. For some reason, it made my own face feel warm.

Not just my face. The warmth seemed to be traveling down my neck, and if I hadn't been so absorbed in exploring Damen, I would have touched my chest to see if I could feel the heat there.

Much like his hands, the basics of Damen's face seemed to be similar. Two eyes. A nose. A mouth. Everything felt much firmer and more angular than my face felt, but the general shape was the same. I smoothed over his brow with my thumbs, finding a sort of ridge but no eyebrows, and I followed it up on both sides, expecting to land at his temples, but instead going up.

And then up some more.

"My horns," Damen murmured shakily as I followed the swooping curve of them.

"They must be majestic," I replied, lingering a little longer than I probably needed to purely out of curiosity. They were so thick and sturdy. I had the oddest urge to grab them. "Do you use them when you fight?"

"There are specialized fighting styles in different regions that still utilize the horns, but it's not very common anymore. Wealthy Shades often decorate their horns by wrapping them in silver chains and obsidian jewels."

"You're not wearing any of those," I observed, tracing my way down the curve. Surely, princes were wealthy?

"I prefer not to. I have a small crown I wear on special occasions," he added almost sheepishly.

I wanted to feel his hair, so I came down to the base of his horns, wrapping my hands around them gently to get a feel for how thick they were. Damen sucked in a breath, shifting slightly in my grip.

"Sorry," he rasped. "That's... sensitive."

I released him immediately. "I'm so sorry. Did I hurt you?"

"No, no. It didn't hurt," he replied, though his voice sounded a little strained. "You can keep going."

I avoided his horns carefully this time, running my fingers through his hair. Like his skin, the texture was much thicker and smoother than mine, but I hadn't touched a lot of humans to compare to.

His ears were pointed at the tips, and I moved on quickly from those because he squirmed a little as though they were ticklish, following down the thick column of his neck to his shoulders.

I definitely wasn't exploring his face anymore, which was what he'd suggested, and I wasn't going to go any lower. I just wanted to try get an idea of what kind of clothes he wore by touching the collar of his shirt. Did my clothes look strange compared to his? Currently, I only had the one outfit.

"Where's your shirt?" I asked, partly to myself, as I danced my fingers along surprisingly broad, hard shoulders. My shoulders certainly didn't feel like that. Neither had Nana's, and I was very familiar with them from all the shoulder rubs I'd given her over the years.

"Ah. Right. Shades don't wear clothes, strictly speaking."

I snatched my hands back instantly. "You're naked?"

"No, no. We use shadows as coverings," he said hastily. "We can manipulate them, make them more solid or less. Here, feel."

I startled as something soft—far softer than Damen's skin—brushed over my palm before sliding up and curling around my wrist, settling into place like a bracelet. It seemed to swirl in place for a few seconds before disappearing like it had never been there, and I rubbed the spot absently with my fingers, keenly feeling its loss. What an odd sensation.

"So you're covered, but it's not solid the way that fabric is?" I asked, wanting to touch his shoulders again but deciding that was probably a little too bold. I'd been plenty bold already.

Damen cleared his throat. "Yes. Um, you can feel, you know. My chest, if you like. You should be able to feel the faint brush of the shadows as you put your hand through them."

I knew I was taking liberties. Nana had always said how important it was that I keep my hands to myself, even though they were my way of understanding the world. But he *had* offered.

And I was *trying* to flirt. Sort of. I still doubted that a prince had any real interest in me, but I wanted him to know that I was perfectly capable of experiencing lust.

The shadow covering did faintly tickle my skin as I pressed my hand to his chest, but that wasn't the part I was most interested in feeling.

Damen's chest didn't feel anything like my chest. My chest was squishy.

Damen's chest felt like a solid slab of carved stone. There were dips and divots and lines that I was desperate to trace while being acutely aware that going lower was a very bad idea.

I wasn't entirely ignorant—Nana had given me the birds and the bees talk in the most thoroughly off-putting way possible with a lot of emphasis on abstinence—but I'd never touched this much of a man, or a male Shade, in person.

It was better than I expected. My brain was still sensible enough to stop me from being entirely inappropriate, but it was forming some creative what-if scenarios to compensate.

What if *my* hand went a little lower?

What if *his* hands landed on my waist? My hips? My thighs?

What if those claws dug into my skin? What would that feel like? Would I like it?

My daydream was interrupted by Damen's sudden sharp intake of air and the feeling of his horn tangling in my hair as he leaned in closer.

Was he... smelling me?

"Iris," he said, sounding almost pained, carefully disentangling himself from my hair while I folded my hands safely back in my lap. "I should go. I'm not allowed to... Never mind, I should go. Are you going to be okay? I'll come back tomorrow."

He muttered something I didn't quite catch about a month. Perhaps he intended to visit for the rest of the month?

"Of course. Yes."

He tripped over something in his rush to get out of the room, and I was left with a swirling mess of confusing thoughts. Had I scared him off? I had been very enthusiastic in touching him. Hopefully not *too* enthusiastic, though I really did want to know what he felt like. And I'd wanted *him* to know that I wasn't afraid of physical affection.

I found myself touching my own hair and face, my fingers drifting down to my collarbone, comparing the differences between our bodies in my mind.

Damen probably wasn't afraid. He was probably just busy doing princely things and couldn't linger—he'd said he'd come back tomorrow, after all.

Perhaps we'd have the chance to do that again.

CHAPTER 9

I s everything okay?" Andrus called as I jogged past his stationed post at the entrance to Iris's corridor and took a sharp left toward the stairs.

"Everything is fine," I yelled over my shoulder, ignoring the odd looks that I was getting as I made my way toward my room.

My dick was so hard that it hurt, and I didn't think I'd be able to focus clearly on anything until I'd come at least several times.

That interaction had been so... unexpected. I'd decided almost immediately that Iris was the one for me because of her sweetness and gentle nature, and of course, I thought she was pretty.

I hadn't particularly expected any kind of sexual spark to be there—the most I'd hoped for was a comfortable friendship where I could bring her pleasure whenever she was willing.

But Iris had perfumed for me. She'd touched my chest, and her body had announced her desire almost immediately. My cock had been hard and aching since she'd squeezed my horns, but it had begun weeping precum at the smell of her desire.

And I'd stupidly promised Allerick I wouldn't propose to her for a month. I hoped she wasn't offended by me running away—all of my decision-making capabilities had been trickling down from my brain to my cock, and I had to get out of there before I lost hold of them completely.

I should have just asked her to marry me and gotten forgiveness from my brother later. Iris would have a mating mark on her already if I hadn't felt a small smidge of guilt about going against my brother's wishes.

The moment the door to my bedroom slammed shut behind me, I dropped my shadows and gripped the base of my cock, roughly massaging the beginning swell of my knot. Fuck, what would Iris's soft, delicate hands have felt like here? Much better than my rough ones, carefully angled to keep my claws out of the way.

I stumbled over to my bed, collapsing on my back and quickly coating my hand with the lotion on the nightstand that I was growing increasingly familiar with. When was the last time I'd had sex with someone else? I couldn't even remember. With my eyes closed, I could almost imagine Iris's body on mine, her pussy clenching around my shaft instead of my hand.

Had she been seducing me on purpose? I couldn't tell. She'd phrased her requests so sweetly, but her touch had been firm and intentional.

I rolled onto my stomach, gripping my cock tightly in my fist and ruthlessly fucking my hand—far more aggressively than I would ever dare to touch Iris's soft, sweet body. She was so unselfconscious with her body language—my knot had ached from the moment she'd spread her thighs for me so I could kneel between them. There hadn't been a single second of hesitation there.

Would she do the same if she was naked?

Would she have leaned back on that chair if I'd asked her and draped her legs over the sides so I could lick her cunt without my horns getting in the way? I felt certain all the way down to my bones that she would. That Iris would trust me entirely to make her feel good. I would do everything in my power to make sure she never regretted putting her trust in me when that moment came.

No. Iris would never regret giving me her trust. If she gave me the gift of her beautiful, eager submission in bed, then I would show her my gratitude for it every single day. I would *worship* her.

The pressure on my knot was unbearable within minutes, and I hurriedly rolled onto my back, coating my stomach in cum instead of my bedding.

It would be impossible for me to get intimate with Iris without the very real risk of me sinking my teeth into her neck, and I couldn't do that until we'd properly spoken about it. Until I'd *asked* her. Ideally, until I'd proposed to her.

Stupid Allerick, ruining all my plans. This was going to be the longest month of my life.

The eyes of the court followed me curiously as I made my way into the dining hall with everyone else, heading for the table where the ex-Hunters usually sat for dinner. Meera was already helping Iris onto the bench seat, and I shot a pleasant but warning look at one of the Shades, who looked as though they would sit next to her, helping myself to that spot instead.

Iris was wearing a different outfit from the clothes she'd arrived in, which she'd also been wearing this morning. I wondered if someone had raided Verity's supply for her, since the loose warm top and matching trousers she was wearing were both pale pink.

Tilly wriggled under the bench, her tail poking out into the walkway and nose between Iris's feet. If anyone stood on Iris's beast, I might have to make an example out of them. Hopefully, the court knew to watch where they walked.

I snuck one of the plainest pieces of roast meat off the platter in the center of the table and dropped it on the floor for her. Tilly immediately wriggled forward, practically inhaling it with a satisfied lick of her lips.

Well, that was easy. I could win over the dog, at least.

"Hello, Iris."

"Hello again, Damen," she replied immediately, perking up. There was an odd, fluttery sensation in my chest that she instantly recognized my voice.

"How are you?" I watched closely for any sign of awkwardness after this morning, but she didn't appear to be feeling any. *I* was definitely feeling some, having spent most of the afternoon fantasizing about her while fucking my own hand.

"Very well, thank you. I'm excited to be having dinner here tonight. It was so kind of Meera to collect me—and she found me some clothes since I didn't pack any."

"Do you need more?" I asked, straightening. I could coordinate that somehow, couldn't I? Perhaps I could nag Astrid into coordinating it, at the very least.

"We're on top of it," Tallulah assured me, apparently listening in from the opposite side of the table while carrying out a full conversation with one of the courtiers next to her. Her ability to multitask was truly unmatched.

"How was your afternoon?" I asked. A bold question because I desperately hoped she didn't repeat it back to me. *Oh, it was fine, thanks. I spent it wondering if you'd get on all fours on the bed for me and let me lick your pussy from behind.*

I didn't want Tallulah overhearing *that* conversation.

"It was very nice, thank you. I didn't do much—I napped a little, actually." Iris seemed embarrassed about that, though I couldn't see why. I napped all the time. "But only because I didn't sleep well last night. I don't nap usually, I swear," she added hastily.

"Why not? Naps are glorious. Everyone should take them. I had one myself this afternoon." *After several hours of masturbating.*

"Well, that makes sense. I imagine you have a very busy schedule."

Tallulah looked at me with one eyebrow raised as if I was the one who'd put that idea in Iris's head. I hadn't, had I? I was confident I'd never intentionally given her the impression that I was extremely busy.

To my surprise, one of the guards I hadn't seen out of the in-between in years was making his way over to our table, and I loudly encouraged him to join us—partly to shame the courtiers who should have been shamed all on their own by their behavior.

Evrin had been born without horns—which was rare, but it happened. Unfortunately, there was still a lot of stigma attached to it, and many members of the court weren't shy in the ways that they avoided him.

I made a show of standing up and clapping him on the back as a little "fuck you" to anyone watching who thought his lack of horns was contagious.

Evrin had handily taken the attention off me, which was nice of him, though I felt guilty about *why* everyone was staring. It was more unusual to see a Shade without horns than it was to see the prince sitting with the masses instead of at the high table.

Allerick and Ophelia hadn't even noticed. As usual, their attention wouldn't be diverted from each other. They were so obvious about their staring too—I was going to have to pull them aside later and remind them that they were the royal couple and should try to act with a modicum of collectedness in public.

"Sit, sit," I insisted, quickly making the introductions, though apparently they weren't necessary. Meera and Tallulah had met him before, and it appeared that Tallulah wasn't a fan. Interesting.

"Patrolling the in-between sounds like a difficult job?" Meera said to Evrin, valiantly attempting to strike up a conversation while I snuck Tilly more meat. It was only right—I'd seen the bowl of dry, boring food she was subsisting off. A little fresh meat wouldn't hurt.

"It's not difficult so much as tedious," Evrin replied.

Iris tilted her head toward him as he spoke, and I watched, enchanted by the gesture. "Why would it be difficult?"

"It's just darkness as far as the eye can see. It's considered somewhat oppressive."

I'd been so busy staring at Iris that it took a moment for Evrin's clumsy words to set in.

Shit. Of all the people to complain to about the dark being oppressive. I scrambled to come up with something appropriately charming to break the heavy silence, but Iris spoke before I had a chance.

"Endless darkness can be very tedious. I hope they're not all glaring at you for pointing that out. Just because I'm always in the dark doesn't mean others aren't allowed to express their discomfort. It's not a competition."

"Of course not," I agreed clumsily, not wanting to let the silence draw on. If I hadn't been in love with Iris before, I definitely was now.

She'd been sweet, calm, assertive, and compassionate all at the same time. On a good day, I could maybe pull off one of those things.

Fortunately, the conversation moved into safer territory—with the exception of Evrin referencing our idiotic youth, which I didn't think would impress Iris, and I swiftly moved the subject along.

The joy she felt at the very concept of friendship was a heady thing—it perfumed the air around us. It was as intoxicating as that hint of her desire had been, though in a different way.

"What did you do after your nap?" I asked Iris, wondering if she also spent it jerking off like I did. Probably not.

I didn't even know why I was asking, in all honesty. I was usually fairly ambivalent when it came to asking questions about other peoples lives—presumably they did things, and I didn't really see why I had to know about them. But with Iris, I was curious about every single second that I wasn't in her company.

"I spent some time with Meera and Tallulah. They sort of caught me up on everything and how it all works. The king and queen are going to visit tomorrow," she added in a hushed whisper. "Tallulah said I don't need to be nervous about it and that they're really nice."

Was my brother really nice? He was sort of nice. Nicer to the ex-Hunters than he was to me, of course.

I should accompany them for that visit to make sure Iris was comfortable and Allerick wasn't rude. It was really the only solution.

"Is the king your father?" Iris asked, making me almost choke on my wine.

"No, my brother." I cleared my throat. "The previous king was my father. I'm the heir for now, presumably I won't be forever."

I watched to see if Iris would have any kind of reaction to that, but my prospects of ruling—or lack thereof—didn't seem to interest her either way.

Tallulah cleared her throat loudly, and I glanced up to find her looking at me.

"*Stop staring at her,*" she mouthed, frowning.

"*I'm not,*" I mouthed back, though I wasn't entirely confident that was true. There were definitely times when Iris seemed to *feel* me staring, and I always looked away then.

But the fact that I could admire her so openly for long stretches of time was a temptation, and I never really bothered to deny myself those.

CHAPTER 10

Meera had kindly come and helped me get ready for my royal visit this afternoon, picking out clothes and showing Tilly and me the way to the sitting room I was meeting them in.

"I'm a little nervous," I told her honestly.

"I understand why, but you don't need to be," Meera assured me. "Ophelia always does all the talking where the ex-Hunters are concerned, the king is just there for show. And she's very friendly, I promise. They've probably made it seem more intimidating than it needs to be by formally inviting you to have tea with them in a private sitting room," she added disapprovingly.

"Did you not have to do that?"

"It was a group event since a few of us arrived at once, and it was in Elverston House where we were staying so it didn't feel quite so... structured."

I wondered if they were handling me a little more gently than they'd handled the other ex-Hunters. I really didn't want them to think they had to. I wanted to be able to contribute meaningfully the way everyone else did.

"We're here," Meera said quietly, giving my arm a squeeze. She wasn't speaking quietly to avoid drawing attention to us, I didn't think. From what I'd gathered, she was just a very softly spoken person. Her voice was very soothing to listen to.

"Are you coming in?" I asked, a sudden flutter of nerves taking flight in my chest.

"I was going to, but I see Damen is hovering in front of the doorway, waiting for you," she observed, sounding curious about that fact.

"Oh, that's so kind of him," I whispered, hoping there was enough distance between him and I that he wouldn't hear the words. "He's very involved for a prince, isn't he?"

"Not usually," Meera replied lightly, giving my arm a quick squeeze which I took as a warning not to say anything more. "Hi, Damen. I wasn't expecting to see you here."

Tilly bounded ahead, and I heard him ruffling her fur fondly and speaking to her in a low affectionate voice. I was surprised she'd run up to him at all—usually she was content to stay close to my side and barely acknowledged anyone else's existence.

"I thought it might be nice for Iris to have someone she's already met here to make the introductions."

"I couldn't agree more. Of course, I'd intended to stay with her..." It was difficult to pick up on tone with Meera because she had such a reserved way of speaking, but I hazarded that she sounded a little amused.

There was a long stretch of silence before Damen spoke again. "You can come too if you want."

"No, no, that's fine. Iris, if you're content to go in there with Damen, I'll leave you to it." She was definitely amused now. And perhaps a little hopeful? I got the impression that Meera wasn't overly fond of group social situations.

"Of course. I'll be fine with Damen. Thank you so much for helping me this morning."

"You're welcome. I'll come and collect you before dinner? Like yesterday?"

"I would appreciate that. Thank you so much."

She extricated her arm from mine and suddenly Damen's much larger one was there in its place, guiding me forward while I gripped Tilly's lead in my other hand.

"You're not nervous," he said decisively, which confused me for a moment before I remembered Tallulah saying that Shades could read our emotions through scent. That would be an odd adjustment.

I felt a brief flash of jealousy that they had an extra sense for reading people when I was already at a disadvantage being one down, but I quickly squashed the impulse. I wasn't a Shade, I couldn't expect my body to function the way theirs did.

Besides, as Nana always said, comparison was the thief of joy.

"Iris," a friendly, feminine voice said. "Welcome! It's so nice to meet you. My name is Ophelia. This is my husband, Allerick."

There was a sort of grunting sound that I presumed was the husband in question. Did they not use their titles here? It seemed like a very informal way of greeting the king. Then again, perhaps movies had given me an unrealistic expectation of how royalty worked. There had been a lot less pomp and ceremony than I assumed there would be so far.

"And this must be Tilly?" Ophelia asked.

"Oh, yes." Tilly pressed hard against my legs, knocking me a little further into Damen's side. Fortunately, he was as solid as a rock, and steadied me immediately.

"Yes, this is Tilly. She's a little shy, sorry."

"Is she?" Damen murmured. "She likes me."

Ophelia laughed. "I shouldn't be surprised that you've charmed the dog too. Damen charms everyone. Sit, sit, please. We have tea and cake."

"Not *everyone*," Damen muttered as he guided me around a couch until we could sit down, with Tilly on top of my feet. "She's exaggerating. I don't just go around charming everyone I encounter."

"Okay," I replied, a little bemused. Had I missed something?

When the king finally spoke, I heard the resemblance between him and Damen immediately, though his voice was gruffer and less personable. "I wasn't expecting to see you here, little brother."

"Damen has been so kind," I said hurriedly, not wanting him to get in trouble for inviting himself along. "He's really made so much effort to make me feel welcome here."

"How altruistic of him," Allerick murmured.

"Very," Ophelia added enthusiastically. "So helpful of you, Damen."

"I want to make sure Iris is comfortable here," he replied, still sounding oddly defensive. Maybe he didn't get long with his brother? "Here, Iris. A plate of little cakes."

He carefully pressed it into my hands and I set it down on my lap, feeling around with my fingertips. Would they taste like cakes in the human realm? I'd only ever had cake on my birthday or Nana's, it was the most special of treats. Though, after tasting pizza, I couldn't decide what I was most fond of.

"This one is my favorite," Damen whispered, gently nudging my fingers with his knuckles toward something soft. I plucked it up carefully, hoping I wasn't making a mess as I nibbled on the edge of it.

"It's delicious," I agreed, forcing myself to be polite and not shove the whole thing in my mouth. It was creamy but sort of citrusy all at once. So far everything in the shadow realm I'd eaten tasted very similar to the kinds of flavors I would expect to find back home. Not flavors I'd eaten necessarily, since Nana and Clara had always favored plainer foods, but they were things I'd *heard* about, at least.

"How are you finding everything so far?" Ophelia asked, kindly waiting until I'd finished chewing to ask.

"Amazing, thank you. I feel very welcome and taken care of."

"Good, good. We know this is a big adjustment for you, and we really want you to be comfortable here." I waited, sensing that there was more she wanted to say. "I hate to get down to business as it were, but I kind of have to ask about your parents. Did they know you were going to leave? How are you expecting them to react?"

"You don't need to worry about them coming after me," I assured her, feeling silly that their concern hadn't occurred to me earlier. Of course, they were worried that harboring Moriah Nash's daughter would bring trouble to their doorstep. "That would mean publicizing my existence, which is something that Moriah has always been very careful not to do."

"We're not suggesting you go back or anything," Ophelia said softly. "If this is where you want to be, we'll defend your right to stay here no matter who challenges it. We just need to know what to expect, that's all."

"If they thought I was in the human realm, I imagine they'd discreetly hunt me down and lock me back up again—it was why I didn't want to stay there even though I was given the option to escape them. I wanted to come here. They'll never follow me here. If anything, they'll be glad that I've removed the problem from their lives."

The silence extended for a painfully long time, and I wondered if I'd been a little too honest. Maybe I should have come up with a palatable lie rather than giving them such an uncomfortable truth.

"They're fucking idiots," Damen grumbled, breaking the tension.

"I'm sure they did the best they could," I said weakly, because Nana would have been so disappointed with me if I didn't at least *try* to defend them. As she always pointed out, my birth had been a terrible setback for Moriah's career.

"And a Hunter helped you to come here?" Allerick asked eventually. "He contacted Astrid, if I recall correctly."

"Yes—Lucas. My brothers had befriended him. He offered to smuggle me here. Or somewhere in the human realm. Just anywhere away from my family, really."

"This is the same Lucas who reported Verity to the Council when she showed up in the human realm?" Ophelia confirmed, though it was clear by her tone that she already knew the answer.

"It is. But he feels really bad about that," I added quickly. "And he put himself at a lot of risk to get me out. I really hope he's okay..."

"We have a contact in the human realm. I can ask her to check, if you like?"

"Oh, would you?" I asked, immediately relieved. "I would really appreciate that. I just don't want him to be suffering because of me."

Damen grumbled something too low for me to catch, but he sounded distinctly unimpressed. Lucas probably *did* have a bad reputation here because of what he'd done to Verity—maybe I should be a little less overt in my concern. The idea didn't sit well with me, though.

I didn't want to have to hide away pieces of myself anymore.

"There's not much we can do," Ophelia said apologetically. "Verity's mate will likely not be the most understanding if we bring Lucas into the shadow realm—if Lucas even wants to be here."

Mate. It was such an interesting word to use.

"Theon is also my older brother," Damen added, leaning in to speak to me. "And his ability to think things through and assess the possible consequences of his actions is extremely limited."

I nodded in understanding. Lucas likely wouldn't be safe here either.

"Is there anything I should be doing?" I asked tentatively, not wanting to bring up the whole power generation thing again. Perhaps lust was a slightly inappropriate topic to broach over tea and cake with strangers. "I feel very lazy, sitting around all day. Is there some kind of job or something I could do?"

"Not right now. Just get accustomed to the shadow realm first and see what you're interested in. There's no rush." There was an urgency in Ophelia's voice that took me by surprise. I'd vaguely considered that the Shades needed the ex-Hunters who'd moved here more than the ex-Hunters needed them— the idea of being valuable was a large part of what drew me here.

At the same time, I wasn't like the other ex-Hunters who'd chosen to come here. My options were more limited, I was very much reliant on the good graces of the Shades. I didn't want to take advantage of their kindness.

"Why don't I take you around the palace?" Damen suggested. "Give you more of an idea of the place. I know Tallulah and Meera covered the basics, but there's a lot more to it."

"That is so kind, thank you." I bumped him gently with my shoulder before searching my plate for the next little cake to eat. Was cake more delicious than pizza? I couldn't decide. I needed more pizza to be able to truly judge, but I somehow doubted that was a shadow realm food.

"It is *very* kind," Allerick agreed, sounding amused. "*Very* helpful.

You're really going out of your way, Damen."

"Damen has been so generous with his time," I told them. "I'm sure he has much more important things he should be doing—I'm so grateful for all his help."

"I'm sure it's no trouble for him," Allerick said cheerfully.

The king clearly didn't appreciate just how much Damen was doing. I would have to find a discreet way of letting him know how amazing his brother had been when I next got the chance.

We left the eerie silence of the library, Tilly's claws clicking on the stone ground as we headed back through the corridors. It was slightly cooler here, with a faint breeze on my skin. Perhaps we were near a window? My fingers flexed a little on Damen's arm at the sudden realization of how much I must trust him already. It had just been the two of us as he guided me around the palace, and I'd felt completely safe in his company the entire time.

"I think we'll leave the garden for another day," he said, more to himself than anything.

"We should probably head back—I'm sure I've interrupted your routine enough for the day."

He fidgeted slightly, his thick upper arm brushing my shoulder. "Not really."

"Is this your day off?"

"The schedule of a prince is an ever-changing one. No two days are the same."

That made sense.

"Well, I appreciate you taking yet more time out of your day today to show me around. It's been so helpful to get a better idea of how the palace is laid out and how busy it is."

Honestly, just getting the words out was more challenging than I expected. Whenever I thought about how generous Damen was being with his time and attention, it almost brought me to tears.

He gave my arm a gentle squeeze. "I really didn't have any other plans. This has been far more enjoyable than spending the day alone, I promise."

I clearly didn't know anything about royalty. In my mind, there was no *spending the day alone* for princes. But maybe entourages and such were only a movie invention? Nana did say I had an overactive imagination.

"We can probably skip the next room," Damen said. "It's the nursery. The courtiers usually leave their offspring here while they... you know. Socialize. Do court stuff. Whatever."

"Are we not allowed to visit the nursery?"

"I mean, we can if you want. Infant Shades aren't exactly great conversationalists."

"I don't mind that." I'd never really spent any time around young children—with the exception of my brothers, and I was only seven years older than them, so it had been a while.

"Okay..." Damen said slowly. "Would Tilly be okay waiting out here by herself? It might be difficult to keep all the little claws from grabbing her, and I'm sure she wouldn't enjoy that."

"No, not at all," I agreed, touched that he was thinking of Tilly's welfare. "Stay, Tilly. She'll wait here, she's very good."

Damen opened the door, guiding me inside. Whatever the door was made out of, it had done an impressive job at keeping sound out. Immediately, we were greeted by shouting and laughter, as well as a few infant cries.

It was slightly overwhelming since I wasn't accustomed to so much noise. At the same time, there was something almost comforting about it. Bright and cheerful and *lively*. So different from my quiet attic.

"Yara," Damen said, speaking to what I assumed was one of the caregivers. "This is Iris. She just moved here. Are we able to visit awhile?"

"Oh, of course. Please, come in. The children love to meet the ex-Hunters—the queen comes to visit when she has time."

"Let's sit," Damen said decisively, his grip tightening a little on my arm. "There are tripping hazards everywhere. Children are so stressful."

I laughed. "Do you want any of your own?"

"Yes," he replied, his voice slightly strangled as he guided us to sit. We were immediately surrounded by a small crowd of excited children, though I couldn't tell whether they were excited about him or me.

The fact that the prince was in their nursery was obviously a special occasion, but I was more of a novelty from what I gathered. They all spoke very fast—and not always in English.

"I'm going to distract them for a minute," Damen said. "Hold on."

"What are you going to do?"

"A little magic show, of course." He sounded so cheeky when he said it. I wished I could see his face, just for a moment.

I felt him leave my side and then there was lots of ooh-ing and aah-ing from excited children, interspersed by bursts of laughter. At one point, one of his shadows tickled under my chin, and I led the giggles as I squirmed away.

Damen was such a natural, not just with children, but in front of a crowd in general. I couldn't imagine being so comfortable with that much attention.

I startled at the feeling of something pricking at my legs, realizing they must be claws, though much less deadly than a full-grown adult's. They snagged on the fabric of my borrowed skirt, scratching lightly at my skin.

Damen was back at my side in an instant, and I felt as he carefully removed the small hands from my legs. "Sorry, I think she was trying to climb up and sit on your lap."

"She can if she wants to," I replied, lowering one hand in her general direction. She immediately grabbed onto my fingers, and I felt Damen correct her hold so that her claws were away from my skin. After a moment, he helped lift her, and she landed softly on my lap, wriggling back against my torso in her bulky cloth diaper while still holding on to my thumb.

She was a lot sturdier than I expected. Then again, Shades appeared to be much larger than humans, so that made sense.

"She probably can't speak to you," Damen said, his voice softer now. "Or not very well, at least. Shades learn lots of languages—both ones from our realm and from yours. Her vocabulary is probably a bit of a mish-mash of all of them at this point, especially here at court. Infants who grow up in their home region might not learn any dialect other than their home language for many years."

"Hi," I whispered, carefully maintaining my grip on the wriggly Shade on my lap as she turned around and climbed up on her knees, releasing my hand so she could play with my hair. I was a teensy bit nervous at how close her claws were to my face, but Damen was leaning in so close that I could feel his breath warming my jaw. I knew in my bones that he'd intervene before I could get hurt.

"She likes you," Damen observed. "Which makes sense since you are very likable."

There was a strange fluttering feeling in my stomach that I'd never experienced before. "Am I?"

"Of course, you must know that."

I'd never given the matter any thought. My family had mostly seemed annoyed by me, so I supposed, if anything, I thought that I was just an annoying person.

"I haven't spent time around anyone other than my immediate family and a couple of staff who worked there over the years. Lucas was the first person I can remember interacting with outside of our family. I have no idea what kind of person I am."

"A very likable one," Damen said firmly. "Your kindness was the first thing I noticed about you. And your patience and gratitude."

What a lovely picture he'd painted of me in his mind. I knew for a fact that there were moments where I wasn't as kind as I could be, or I forgot to be grateful, or felt impatience. Nana had always made sure to correct my behavior, and I hoped I remembered to do the right thing in her absence.

"But none of what I say matters," Damen continued. "Nor does what your family may have said. *You* decide how you feel about you."

"I like that idea," I replied quietly as the little Shade on my lap brushed the ends of my hair with her claws. I didn't know exactly who I was yet.

But I was going to figure it out.

DAMEN

CHAPTER 11

Today was the day, I could feel it in my shadows.

I almost always woke up feeling lucky, but I definitely felt luckier than normal. My sheets had stayed cool all night. My tea was the perfect temperature when it was delivered to my room in the morning. I managed to make my shadow covering look relatively nice, considering that I was trying to conserve my power by keeping it simple.

It felt like the forces in the realm were conspiring to make today the perfect day to propose, and who was I to argue with them?

Sure, Iris had only been here a week, and that was—in fact—less than a month. But it wasn't like Allerick listened to *me* when it came to his romantic relationship. He'd have been a much better husband from the start if he had, though he liked to pretend that wasn't true.

I'd simply ask for his forgiveness later. All would be well once he realized how happy Iris and I were together.

I met Soren and Astrid in the corridor where they were waiting for me, and we headed to the private drawing room in the royal wing of the palace to meet Allerick and Ophelia for breakfast. I very much liked the idea of loudly announcing to everyone that I was going to be engaged by the end of the day, though, I didn't need their boring doubts and questions spoiling my good mood. I'd simply tell them afterward, once the deed was done.

"Why are you so cheerful this morning?" Soren asked suspiciously.

"Is it so unusual that I'm in a good mood?"

"Not really," Astrid deadpanned. "He's always oddly cheerful."

"Odd for us, not odd for him," Soren corrected. "But he seems different today."

"It just feels like a good day. Can't you feel it in the air?"

"Not really," Astrid grumbled. "One of the new members of the Guard said I was rude. Can you believe that?"

Kind of. I valued my life too much to say that, though.

Breakfast had already been laid out for us when we arrived, though Allerick and Ophelia came in late and harried. At least she'd bathed this time, though her hair clearly gave away what they'd been up to—as did Allerick's jitteriness. He needed to siphon all of the excess power he'd gained from feeding from his wife this morning.

Must be a nice problem to have.

"Good morning, everyone!" Ophelia said cheerfully, taking her usual seat and immediately pouring tea for everyone. "How are we all? What's on the agenda for today?"

"And you think *I'm* unusually cheerful?" I asked Astrid.

Her lips twitched briefly before she busied herself chomping on dried meat in silence, content to let Soren give his boring, detailed report. I admired that about Astrid. She stubbornly didn't partake in things that held no appeal for her.

"What are you going to do today, Damen?" Ophelia asked politely once everyone had finished speaking. Probably to make me feel included.

"Hang out with Iris. The usual."

"She must realize now that you do literally nothing else," Soren pointed out wryly. "I hope she's not still worrying that she's taking up valuable time in your busy schedule."

"I've told her that she doesn't need to worry about that," I replied, a touch defensively. I hadn't *explicitly* said that I do nothing else all day, but did I really have to? It wasn't even strictly true. I visited Theon sometimes. And Orabelle. Occasionally, I followed Allerick around, mostly to antagonize him.

I had hobbies.

"Are you giving Iris a chance to get to know other Shades?" Astrid asked, sitting forward in her seat and narrowing her eyes at me.

"No."

She blinked at me before sitting back in her chair. "Well, at least you're honest about it, I guess."

"You probably should," my brother suggested unenthusiastically. The absolute betrayal—I'd been so supportive of his mystery bride before Ophelia had even arrived here.

"Why? Iris and I are perfect for each other." *Get to know other Shades.* What an offensive suggestion—as if any of these territorial bastards ever did such a thing. "I don't recall being so reticent to give my support when all of *you* were pursuing your romantic connections."

Ophelia laughed nervously, clearing her throat to answer, but Astrid beat her to it.

"Do you *have* a romantic connection? Iris probably just thinks you're being nice to her."

"I've been courting her," I shot back. Slowly. Very slowly. But the intent had been there.

"Does Iris know that?" Allerick asked.

"Whose side are you on?" Astrid and I always butted horns, but I expected better from my brother.

"No one is taking sides," Ophelia said hastily. "We're just talking. We all just want what's best for you and Iris. And if that's each other—well, that's great! Wonderful. Beautiful. And we'll all support you as much as we can to make sure everything goes smoothly."

"Why wouldn't it?" I shrugged. Perhaps it was a little arrogant of me to say, but things usually did go perfectly for me. I knew it was due to luck rather than skill, but my life had mostly been a pleasant and easy run so far. The things that I wanted to happen mostly happened with little fuss. I had very few complaints, except for the Hunters in the human realm, and they seemed to be mostly subdued for now.

There was no good reason why this wouldn't go well for me, too.

Yes, I felt very positive indeed about this. I would propose, Iris would accept, and we would live happily ever after. I was looking forward to it.

Then I would arrive at breakfast tomorrow with my fiancé on my arm and tell all these pessimists who I loved and respected where to shove it.

"Hello, Iris."

She paused whatever she was doing, smiling angelically up at me from her chair in the corner as I came into the room, quickly stopping to unwrap a package of meat and dropping it in Tilly's bowl.

Best to keep the beast on my side.

"Hello, Damen. How are you this morning?"

"Very well, thank you. How are you? What are you doing? Why are you playing with needles? Is that safe?"

Iris smiled up at me and everything bad about my morning immediately dissipated as though it had never been. "I'm knitting. I used to do it with my Nana all the time. Tallulah had all the stuff already and was happy to share it with me, isn't that so lovely?"

"I guess so." Really seemed like the least she could do, but sure.

"I'm making you a scarf," Iris declared. I didn't know what that was or what I would use it for, but I would cherish it all the same. Her first gift to me—hopefully the first of many throughout the course of our union.

"That's very sweet of you. I can't wait to... wear it," I hedged. Was it a garment? That seemed like the most likely option. Of course, it would be looked down upon at court for me to wear a covering made of physical fabric rather than shadow—they would see it as a sign of weakness as generally, only those with a low capacity for channeling power wore garments. However, I would happily tell the courtiers to go fuck themselves if they dared to say anything about a gift from Iris.

She hummed, pleased. "What are you doing today?"

"Visiting you."

Iris laughed softly. "And then?"

"I was intending for this to take up the bulk of my day," I replied, sitting down on the chair opposite her and watching as her fingers seemed to fly, the needles clicking together in the most satisfying way. Though apparently, my words had given her pause, as she stopped for a long moment.

"What did you do with your days before I came to the shadow realm?" Iris asked curiously. For some reason, the question felt like a trap.

"I'm very social. I enjoy visiting with all kinds of Shades and people—I always have. However, I enjoy your company the most," I added in my smoothest, most charming voice. Usually, it was enough to cajole even the surliest of conversation partners, but Iris still looked politely concerned.

"Well, that's very kind," she said eventually. "Of everyone who visits me, I enjoy your company the most too. I find you very easy to be around."

I grinned from ear to ear. This was my moment. This was the opening I'd been hoping for.

"I'm reassured to hear it. Iris, will you put down your needles for a moment?"

She slowly lowered them, setting everything down on her lap and clasping her hands together as I stood up, straightening my shoulders and holding my horns up high and proud. "Sure. What is it, Damen?"

"Iris, would you do me the honor of becoming my wife?"

She frowned, her pretty lips pursed together in the most unsettling way. "Your what?"

I cleared my throat, enunciating the words more clearly this time. "My *wife.*"

Maybe I should have made a speech first. Listed all the things I liked about her. In hindsight, the question may have been a little abrupt.

"Are you proposing to me?"

"Yes," I replied hesitantly. This wasn't going quite the way I expected it to go. I'd hoped that Iris would be more excited and less... well, confused. I definitely wasn't going to include this part in my retelling of events at breakfast tomorrow. Astrid would never let me live it down.

"Oh. That's very unexpected."

"Is it?"

Iris nodded slowly. "Though perhaps I have been misinterpreting obvious signs—I don't have much experience with these things, you see. Before I came here, I'd only interacted with one man who wasn't a family member."

I managed to make some vague sound of agreement, annoyed and slightly jealous at the mention of him despite my gratitude that he'd found a way to get Iris out of harm's way. Did she like him more than me?

"I'm no *man*, Iris."

"No," she agreed. "Perhaps that's why I didn't pick up the signs. I do find your voice very attractive," she added, though she seemed to be talking to herself rather than me.

"Well, that's positive."

"Yes. And I enjoy your company—you're very kind. Charming. Funny."

I puffed out my chest slightly. Why had I been worried? We were back on track. There was nothing to worry about. It wasn't the most enthusiastic acceptance of a marriage proposal there ever was, but the result was what mattered anyway.

"And I like touching you."

"The feeling is mutual," I assured her, wondering if we could do some of that soon.

"But marriage seems like a slightly extreme reaction," Iris said, shaking her head. "Don't you think? We barely know each other."

She... what?

"Are you... are you rejecting me?" I asked, thoroughly failing to keep the disbelief out of my voice. I was the most eligible bachelor in the entire realm! I'd never had any interest in proposing to someone before, but I'd also never envisioned anyone saying *no*.

"That seems like a harsh way of phrasing it," Iris replied with a wince. "It's not so much a rejection as a discussion."

"Iris," I began, dragging a chair close to hers and sitting down. "Please, explain this to me. I don't understand. I love you."

She frowned again. "Damen, you barely know me. You're very nice—the absolute sweetest. I'm sure that if we were to marry, I would enjoy your company very much."

I'm good in bed too, I almost said, containing the words at the last minute. It would be entirely reasonable for Iris to be concerned about that since we hadn't been intimate, and it was tempting to offer her some reassurance that I would take care of her in *all* regards, but I wasn't confident the words would be well received.

"But I'm still finding my feet in the shadow realm. Figuring out who I am and where I belong." She hesitated for a moment. "The freedom I have now... It's more than I ever thought I'd experience in my life."

"You wouldn't be giving that up by becoming my wife, Iris. You would be a *princess*."

She smiled wryly, and I suspected that might have been precisely the wrong thing to say. What was wrong with me? I was usually so suave.

"I'm not princess material—not from what I know of princesses anyway. I don't have any causes to champion. I don't have any knowledge of value to offer. I haven't *contributed* anything. Those things are important to me, Damen. Surely, you understand that feeling?"

Not really, no. I was the crown prince. That was the entirety of who I was and what I did. I didn't champion causes or offer valuable knowledge, and no one seemed to mind. Well, maybe Allerick and Soren, but they complained about everything.

"You didn't misinterpret anything," I rasped, standing and taking a step back. I felt as though I'd been hit square in the chest with a blunt instrument, that my very bones were rattling from the impact. "I misinterpreted things. Or I chose to interpret them in a way that suited my own narrative. I'm sorry, Iris. That was wrong of me."

Her scent soured instantly as she frowned up at me. "I've upset you—"

"No. I mean, that's not something you need to be worried about. My emotions are my responsibility, Iris."

"Will... will you still come visit with me sometimes?" she asked, her voice a little smaller than usual. The pain in my chest turned into something sharper and more acute.

What was this feeling? It was more than just rejection, but I couldn't quite place what exactly was bothering me.

"If you would like that, then of course I will."

"Of course I want that, Damen," she said fervently, the worry clear in her expression. "You're my closest friend."

Some of the tension I was carrying eased a little at that pronouncement. I'd been so thoughtless in proposing—it had never occurred to me that Iris would say no. What if she hadn't wanted to be friends still? I would have lost something I'd come to cherish because I hadn't taken a second to think about the potential consequences of my actions.

"And you're mine," I promised her. "But I am going to leave you to your knitting now—I suspect I won't be very good company today."

"Okay," Iris said quietly. "I hope you'll come back soon."

"I will."

After I tended to my wounds a little first.

IRIS

CHAPTER 12

That... hadn't been how I'd expected my morning to go.

The knitting sat abandoned on the dining table as I crossed the room, my fingers drifting over the piles of clothing until I found the one with the sweaters and felt out the softest, fluffiest one. It wasn't particularly cold today—it didn't seem to get that cold here—but I wanted the comfort of the extra layer of fabric to cocoon me from the world.

Especially since I didn't want to stay here in my room. It was a perfectly nice room, but it was feeling a little claustrophobic now. I hadn't explored on my own yet, but everyone had been so kind—surely they would give me some directions if I got lost? It was a risk worth taking. I needed air.

I needed to... to be somewhere else. Not right here, in this room where that strange interaction had just taken place. It had me feeling jittery and out of sorts. I felt like I'd handled everything wrong. Had I handled it wrong? I probably had.

Damen probably hated me now.

Oh, I wished Nana was here to tell me what to do.

"Come on, Tilly," I whispered, patting my thigh to encourage her over. She huffed a little and yawned loudly and pointedly before eventually making her way over to my side, booping my hand with her wet nose. "Shall we go for a little explore? I think we should. Stay close, okay?"

"Iris, would you do me the honor of becoming my wife?"

A little shiver ran down my spine as I let Tilly and myself out of the room, closing the door behind me. Damen had *proposed*.

Prince Damen.

And I'd said no.

I tamped down the slightly hysterical giggle that wanted to escape. Who on earth did I think I was, rejecting a marriage proposal from a prince? I was a nobody. A burden that even my own family hadn't wanted to deal with. It was absurd that I should say no to marrying anyone, wasn't it? I should be falling down on my knees, grateful that he'd even considered me. That was what Nana would have said, if she could have gotten past the fact that Damen wasn't human.

My head was telling me that I was an idiot and I'd made a decision that I would regret for the rest of my life. But my heart, or my gut, or my intuition—whatever it was—had taken the lead in that conversation. And it had said, loud and clear that it wasn't a good idea. That it was the easy option but not necessarily the best one. He'd said he *loved* me. That couldn't possibly be true, could it? I liked Damen. There was a fluttery feeling in my stomach when I was around him that made me think I liked him in a romantic way even.

But I didn't love him. Not yet.

And even if I did, I wanted to be self-sufficient here. I wanted my life to have *meaning* here. It would be all too easy to let myself just *be* someone's wife—especially if that someone was the prince of the realm. And Damen was incredible—kind, and cheerful, and confident. And I was attracted to him based on what I'd felt when he'd let me touch him.

Maybe I had made a mistake.

No, no. I had to learn to stand on my own two feet first.

"Do you need some help?" someone asked, startling me. "Sorry. I'm Andrus. I'm a member of the Guard."

"Oh, right," I replied hesitantly, trying to decide if I was in trouble or not. The silence lingered for a moment, and he didn't tell me to go back to my room or anything, so I decided to push on. "I was hoping to visit the nursery."

"Really?" he asked dubiously. "You know that there are children there?"

"Yes." I laughed lightly. "It would be a little odd if there wasn't, no?"

He grunted. "I guess we all have different interests. I'll escort you there if you like; it's only around the corner."

Andrus didn't seem very interested in talking, so it was a quiet journey to the nursery, though the noise picked up significantly when we got there. He didn't stick around, but the nursery staff immediately made me feel welcome, guiding me to sit in one of the comfortable chairs. Tilly came in with me this time, despite me instructing her to stay outside. Maybe she didn't feel as confident leaving me on my own without Damen here.

I didn't know how to feel about that.

"This is the quiet corner," one of the Shades said, raising her voice to be heard over the excited chatter of children. I wondered what the loud corner was like. "Is it okay if the children come and visit with you? They were so excited when you came last time—they've talked about you nonstop."

"Of course, yes. I would love that."

"We'll make sure they don't all swarm you this time," she added with a light laugh.

"Hello," a small voice said, tapping me on the arm, careful not to use claws. "Can you see me? My cousin says your eyes don't work."

"That's true, they don't. I can hear you, though." I touched his hand lightly. "And feel you. What's your name?"

"Jonan. What's yours?"

"Iris."

Jonan harrumphed as though he was deciding whether that was an acceptable answer or not.

"Can you make shadows, Iris?" he asked eventually.

"No," I replied, startled. "Can you?"

"Yes. I'm very strong. Feel that?" After a moment, I realized that, yes, I could feel something. It had never occurred to me that children would be able to do that.

"Can all young Shades do that?"

"Only powerful Shades like me," Jonan replied. The tone of his voice reminded me of my brothers, back when they were young. They'd been a little grandiose then—I understood that now—but they hadn't been cruel. That had developed with time. "All the Shades who live here at court can. They're the important ones."

"Surely, everyone is important," I said, pushing back gently. "We all have something to offer. Something that makes us who we are."

There was a shuffling noise, followed by a tapping sound. I hazarded a guess that Jonan had sat on the floor and was drumming his claws on it.

"Did you know that there's a Shade with no horns who lives here? And he came to dinner with all the important Shades and someone said he was trying to court an ex-Hunter. My mother says that's really bad."

"Why is that bad?"

"Because he's broken. Why should a broken Shade get their own ex-Hunter? That's not right. That's what my mother always says."

I swallowed thickly, wondering if I'd made the worst mistake of my life in coming here. Maybe I'd been too ambitious. Maybe I'd been too optimistic. Would the Shades here only ever see *me* as broken?

It probably was a good thing that I'd turned down Damen's proposal. I don't know what he'd been thinking when he'd asked, but it can't have been of the opinions of the wider court. I doubted any of them would want him to be married to a broken ex-Hunter.

"What if that ex-Hunter loves him?" I asked softly. "She probably wouldn't care that he has no horns. You can't choose who you love."

At least, I was pretty sure you couldn't. That's what all the movies had seemed to imply. I was second-guessing everything I thought I knew about love now.

Jonan made a retching sound, mercifully breaking the tense moment. "I'm never going to love anyone. That's disgusting."

I laughed in spite of my flat mood. "I'm sure it's lovely."

"No, I don't think so," he replied decisively. Tilly yawned loudly and I heard Jonan shuffle closer. "What's your beast called?"

"Her name is Tilly. She's a... guide dog," I said hesitantly, remembering what Lucas had said about guide dogs. She guided *me*, did that count? "She helps me get around."

"She has pointy teeth like me," Jonan announced, making me pause.

"You have pointy teeth?"

Damen must have forgotten to mention that in his tour of his face.

"Yup. Want to feel?"

"Jonan!" someone scolded, making me startle. I hadn't realized there was anyone nearby. "Were you going to bite her? What are you thinking?"

"I wasn't!" he objected. "I was just going to ask if she wanted to touch my teeth. That's allowed."

"It certainly is not."

He was quiet for a moment. "Well, why not?"

Tilly rolled over, flopping onto my feet with an exasperated huff, and I did my best not to smile as I leaned back in the chair. It had been a *very* strange day, but a visit to the nursery was the perfect balm for an unsettled spirit.

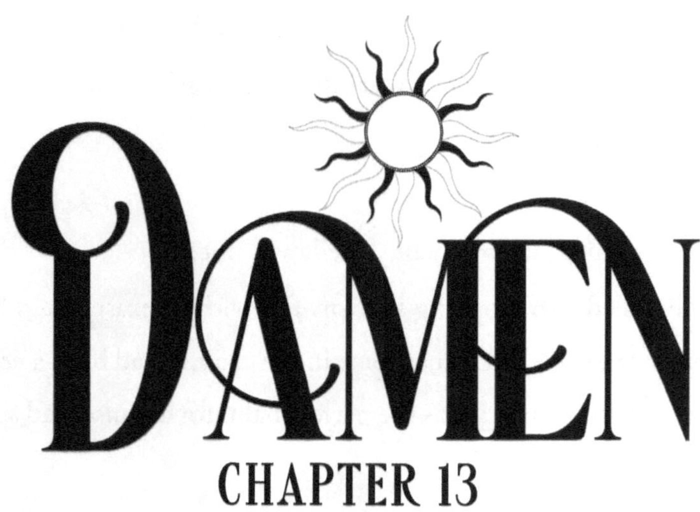

DAMEN

CHAPTER 13

Why are you in my workshop?" Theon demanded, straightening from whatever odd experiment he'd been hunched over to glare at me. "Who let you in?"

"Your mate."

Theon huffed. "She knows I hate company."

"That might be why she let me in," I mused. I wouldn't put it past Verity to deliberately antagonize her mate—he'd been particularly overbearing since their disastrous little jaunt to the human realm.

"Menace," he grumbled affectionately.

All I wanted was a beautiful, happy, dysfunctional marriage like Theon and Verity had. Maybe not quite as dysfunctional, but I wanted to be challenged the way that Verity challenged Theon. She'd made him a better Shade. Or had he become a better Shade because he loved her?

Alas, apparently it wasn't meant to be.

"Are you more pleasant to be around *because* of Verity or *for* Verity, do you think?

Theon shot me a disgruntled look. "I have always been pleasant to be around, which is why Verity chose me."

"I thought you kidnapped her."

"Why she chose me *after* I kidnapped her," Theon amended, incapable of admitting he was wrong.

Why my feet had carried me here while my wounds stung from Iris's rejection, I had no idea. Nothing about Theon projected comfort and sane advice, and yet here I was. Perhaps I just wanted the counsel of an older brother right now, and Allerick had already lectured me once today.

I pulled out one of the low stools beneath his workbench—*why would Theon have more than one if he despised company so much?*—and fiddled aimlessly with the odd implements he kept lying around his workshop.

This wasn't how I'd expected to be feeling this afternoon. I thought we'd be celebrating by now—possibly naked.

Now I felt... flat.

The thing that was sticking with me the most was that she said I couldn't love her. That I didn't *know* her. Was that true? Did I really not love her?

Were these feelings because when I'd met Iris, for the first time, I'd seen a possibility of a future with someone, and I was merely upset that the possibility had been taken away? That she hadn't wanted the same thing as me?

Or was this heartbreak?

As much as I often resented my title, I was the crown prince. Surely, finding someone that I liked enough to marry should have been the easiest thing in the world for me. Maybe I should overthrow Allerick and become king? He hadn't had a problem finding a bride.

Theon sighed dramatically, setting down his tools. "Why are you here? Are you having some sort of crisis? Can Allerick not assist you with this?"

"I thought you'd be wiser counsel," I replied innocently. Nothing could be easier than playing my older two brothers off against each other—they were both so competitive. Allerick tried to be dignified about it now since they were friends, though.

Theon immediately puffed out his chest, a smug grin on his face. "A very astute observation, little brother. So, what is the problem?"

"I proposed to Iris today. She said no."

"Which one is Iris?"

I sighed heavily. "The newest ex-Hunter to come to the shadow realm. You haven't met her yet."

He grunted. "Can you not simply find an alternative bride?"

"Would you have ever considered an alternative bride if Verity had said no?"

Theon scoffed. "What kind of ludicrous question is that? I kidnapped Verity, then put my bite on her neck the day she arrived so she simply could not leave me." He paused for a moment. "Have you considered doing that?"

"Not even once." Theon hadn't actually done that either. At least, not the first part.

He shrugged one shoulder, picking up his tools again. "Well then, I don't know how to help you."

"Come on, Theon," I groaned, slumping over the bench. "When I met Iris... I don't know. I felt like she was the one. I really imagined a future with her."

"Then simply find out whatever it is that's preventing her from imagining the same."

Well, that was easy. Iris had told me that herself. "She wants to find... a purpose in the shadow realm. To find out who she is. She seems to think a princess needs causes and wisdom and other such things."

Theon stared at me. "She's right about that. I like her already."

"She doesn't *need* those things to be a princess," I objected. "I don't have them. My purpose is being the crown prince."

Theon shot me a dark look and I felt a smidge bad about reminding him that I now possessed the title that he'd been given at birth. "In my experience, it's a good idea to have an alternative purpose in life where that particular title is concerned."

I grunted in acknowledgment because he may have a point there. I doubted there was any Shade who could pose a real threat in challenging me for the role—except perhaps Theon, though I was confident he didn't want it anymore. But eventually, I would be usurped. Likely when Allerick and Ophelia had a child, whenever that happened. We had no idea what kind of strength a Hunter-Shade child would possess, but presumably it was significant, given how compatible our kinds were.

And besides that, we were trying to build a new world. One where we lived side by side in harmony. Having a monarch who represented *both* would be powerful symbolism. I wouldn't be the most suitable for the position any longer.

"I don't really have any other talents, though. Being the friendly, charming prince is the only skill I've mastered."

"I was neither friendly nor charming as a prince. Surely you could apply those skills elsewhere," Theon pointed out.

"I suppose so." I couldn't really see how, but perhaps there was a way. I drummed my claws on the bench, acutely aware that Theon's eye was twitching in irritation the entire time. "Do you think Iris's rejection was a forever no? Maybe she'll change her mind once she feels more settled here."

"How should I know? I've never even met her."

I sighed heavily. "I should have talked to Verity about this."

"Probably. You're more than welcome to now. Why don't you leave my workshop and go find her?"

"Fine, fine, I'm going. Thank you for your advice. It was... well, I'm not sure I would go so far as to say it was helpful. I suppose it has given me something to think about."

Theon grunted in acknowledgment as I headed out, running into Verity in the foyer.

"Was he delighted to see you?" Verity asked innocently, a sly smile giving her mischief away.

"You know he wasn't. I wanted to talk to him about my failed marriage proposal, but I see now that it's you I should have spoken to instead."

She blinked at me, silent for a long moment. "You... *proposed*? To who? When? No, wait. Don't answer—we need tea and cake and somewhere comfy to sit first. Please hold, caller."

Verity headed off—a little less energetic than usual after her human-world trip—presumably to send for supplies, and I ambled into the downstairs drawing room, leaving the door open so she'd be able to see me when she returned to the foyer. From memory, this room had been closed up the last time I'd been here, but Verity was working her way around the manor, opening and cleaning out the dusty rooms so they were usable once more.

Lindow had felt like a dying estate before Verity had come here, and she'd brought it back to life with her presence. She'd brought Theon back to life too, in a very literal sense.

Was that *her* purpose? Did everyone need a purpose? All this thinking was making my head hurt.

If revitalizing Lindow and the Duke who resided here was Verity's purpose, it certainly wasn't some grand, unachievable goal. It was localized and defined, and Verity excelled at it. And it had benefitted her too—Verity had a confidence now that she'd never possessed when she lived at the palace.

I wanted Iris to find that sense of confidence in her place in the realm too.

I really shouldn't have proposed.

Fuck's sake. I could never tell Allerick about this. He had warned me to wait a month.

"Okay, okay, Aderith is bringing tea," Verity announced, throwing a fluffy pink blanket at me and keeping one for herself. She sat in one corner of the sofa, pulling her legs up tightly beneath her and wrapping the blanket around her. "Tell me everything."

I relayed the morning's events to her, gratified to finally be getting the reactions that Theon had thoroughly failed to provide.

"Wow," Verity said, sitting back in her seat and taking a sip of the tea she'd poured while I'd been talking. "And after all that... You went to *Theon* for advice?"

"In hindsight, I can see that was a poor choice on my part. But I wasn't in the mood to listen to Allerick and Soren scolding me for not taking it slow and whatever else they demanded."

Verity nodded solemnly. "Very understandable. Absolutely no one wants to hear *I told you so*, no judgment there. What's the plan now?"

"What would you do?"

"If someone rejected my marriage proposal? Leave the whole realm, probably. None of you would ever hear from me again. But you're not as cowardly as I am," she added hastily.

I laughed, helping myself to a cake. Leaving the realm wasn't an option—unlike Verity, I wouldn't maintain my corporeal form once I was out of the shadow realm. I *could* move to a different region—there was family property on my mother's side I could challenge a cousin for.

But if I ran away, Iris might feel bad. She was sweet and kind and good, and I didn't want to make her feel for a single second like she'd done anything wrong.

"I'm not going to do that. I was thinking perhaps that while Iris is searching for her place here, I could do more with mine? Embrace the authority that has been bestowed on me, and such. Be more... involved in things."

Verity nodded in understanding. "Begin your healing journey, totally. I love that for you."

"I was thinking more along the lines of find some form of employment."

She wrinkled her nose. "I mean, I guess you could do that too. Maybe you could be Theon's assistant? The Elders really want him to ramp up his portable-in-between orb production."

"That's very kind of you, but I suspect we would duel within minutes of working together."

"True." Verity nodded, tilting her head to the side thoughtfully. "I can't really see you in a practical job anyway. You've got more of that middle management vibe, you know?"

"No." I only ever understood about half of every conversation I had with her—unlike the others, Verity didn't go out of her way to use references that Shades would understand. I was fairly confident she just said whatever words popped into her head the moment that they appeared there.

"You know—charming and personable and able to present well and talk about maximizing efficiencies, but not really qualified to do anything."

"I can't decide if I should be offended by that or not."

She laughed. "Not everyone can be charming and hold a conversation with whoever they meet—that *is* a talent. Neither of your brothers have it."

I leaned back in the seat, mulling over her words and wondering if she'd let me take this very soft, comfortable blanket with me. She wasn't wrong—neither of my brothers were capable of maintaining a conversation that went beyond a few sentences.

When I thought about Iris's description of having a cause and adding value, my chatty nature didn't really seem like enough though.

"You're overthinking things," Verity observed, watching me closely. "That's a surefire way to drive yourself crazy. And I get it—because I'd definitely be doing the same thing—but you did jump in pretty hot with proposing right away. How did you leave things with Iris?"

"She still wants us to be friends."

"Good. Be her friend. Focus on yourself. Figure out who you want to be. The rest will fall into place when it's meant to."

"You sure about that?"

Verity tipped her chin up confidently. "Of course I am. Trust me, I'm a duchess."

IRIS

CHAPTER 14

Eadlin's little hands landed on my knees right before she started to climb onto my lap. I sucked in a breath of surprise, grabbing her under the armpits and hauling her up before she could dig her claws in for better grip.

"Remember what I said about asking if you want to come and sit on me?" I reminded her gently. "Then I can pick you up and make sure that neither of us gets hurt."

She babbled something to me in whatever Shade language she spoke, immediately snuggling into me. It was probably wrong to play favorites, but Eadlin was definitely my favorite little Shade in the nursery. I think she had been since that very first visit with Damen when she'd played with my hair.

I'd only been visiting regularly for a week, but she was sweet and affectionate, and often came to sit with me to hide out when the other children were roughhousing.

From what one of the staff had said in an offhand way, Eadlin's parents were palace employees rather than courtiers. They weren't explicit about it, but

I got the impression that meant Eadlin wasn't expected to be a very powerful Shade when she grew up like little Jonan would be.

I wondered what that meant for her. She was growing up around future courtiers—would they ignore her someday because she'd be considered beneath them? Surely, the lines of delineation weren't that strict.

"Have you had a good day, Eadlin?" I asked. It felt silly to speak to her in a language she didn't understand, but the nursery staff had insisted that she'd pick it up quickly—Shades seem to have a real natural talent for languages—and that I should keep talking to her.

Eadlin mumbled something, her horns digging uncomfortably into my chest as she wriggled into a comfortable position. Shade mothers must be made of much stronger stuff than I was.

Though, I could adjust, I thought absently. If I had children of my own someday. I'd always liked that idea.

I probably shouldn't have said no to the only person—or Shade—who'd ever wanted to marry me.

I rocked Eadlin gently in my lap, picking up from her lack of chattiness that she must be tired and looking for a soft, quiet place to nap. It was nice to have a specific task to focus on, even if it was just rocking back and forth until Eadlin's breath evened out and her body was still and relaxed.

Despite what Damen had said about remaining friends, he'd vanished for the past few days, and it *hurt.* I was second-guessing everything—every decision I'd made, every word I'd said.

Worse, everyone else seemed to have disappeared too.

Meera had briefly stopped in to drop off more clothes and Tilly's food that Astrid had sourced, but she'd seemed reluctant to talk. Even more than usual. And there had been no more dinners in the dining hall.

It was the worst I'd felt since I'd arrived in the shadow realm. No, since Nana died. Then again, I'd been in a constant state of motion since that morning, and this was the first time I was really still enough to absorb everything that had happened. To just exist and let my mind catch up with all the change I'd experienced.

I kind of wished I was still in motion instead.

"She likes you," a soft voice said. I was struggling to remember who all the nursery staff were—there were so many, and they all seemed to work different shifts. "It's Alyndra, by the way."

"Thank you for reminding me," I replied sincerely, adjusting my hold on little Eadlin. "How are you?"

"I was going to ask you the same question. Your scent is a little off today."

I pressed my lips together, suppressing a laugh. Usually, I was the one picking up nonvisual cues. It was an interesting experience being on the other side of it. "I was just reflecting on my journey here. It's been a busy few weeks."

"I can imagine," she said quietly, fussing with something next to me. It sounded like she was picking up toys. "I hope this isn't too bold of me to say, but I'm always so intrigued by the ex-Hunters who have come here. What must your life have been like to leave everything you'd ever known behind?"

There was sympathy in her voice, and I didn't feel like I'd earned it. I'd had a roof over my head and food in my belly. The attic had been comfortable, if not a little cold when the heating went out. It could have been worse.

"It really wasn't that bad," I hedged.

"Would you have come here if it wasn't that bad? And chosen to stay? Many more Hunters came here with Astrid originally, but they went back because the adjustment to life here was too much for them to handle."

I gave that idea some thought. There certainly had been adjustments, but not *that* many. Even over the past few days where I'd felt a little abandoned—a ridiculous thought—I was never truly alone. Whenever I emerged from my room, wanting to go somewhere, immediately there was someone at my side offering to walk me there. Delicious trays of food were delivered three times a day, with a plate of unseasoned meat for Tilly. My room was even cleaned for me, with fresh sheets seeming to appear of their own accord.

Of course, I'd had Nana to help me before, but the guilt of leaning so heavily on her had weighed heavily on me, especially as she'd aged. Life was far easier for me here.

For the others, I imagined the loss of technology had hit them hard. But Nana had done all of the cooking and laundry, and we hadn't been able to control the thermostat from the attic. There was the television, but hearing so many conversations, being so surrounded by noise and chatter and activity all the time was a more than adequate replacement for passively listening to films.

"So far, every change I've had to make has made my life easier, not harder," I admitted, feeling a little guilty for that fact. Everything had been so smooth sailing for me—I'd even been *proposed* to—and yet I didn't feel like I'd entirely found my feet here.

The process couldn't have gone any smoother, and I didn't have anything to complain about. So why wasn't I content? I remembered Nana saying that I was difficult, and worried that she was right.

"I'm glad to hear it," Alyndra said cheerfully. "So, we just need to find more Hunters like you, and then they won't be intimidated by our way of life and leave?"

I laughed, slightly hysterically. More Hunters like *me*? No one would want that. I was the very worst example of a Hunter.

"I'm sorry to interrupt," a new voice said apologetically. "But you've received an invitation to have tea with Orabelle."

I sat quietly, gently adjusting my hold on Eadlin, not wanting to interrupt Alyndra's conversation.

Alyndra cleared her throat. "Iris, he's speaking to you."

"Oh!" My face heated instantly. "Someone wants to have tea with *me*?"

Alyndra laughed nervously. "Yes. The king's mother. She's, um, perhaps a little less friendly than some of the other Shades you've encountered so far. But I'm sure she'll be nice to you," she added hastily. And unconvincingly. "Yara, is she expecting Iris now?"

"Yes. A member of the Guard is waiting outside to escort you there."

Alyndra carefully lifted a sleeping Eadlin out of my arms, and I felt a little lost without her warm, comforting weight. Perhaps the naptime cuddles had been for both of us. I stood up, patting the side of my leg so Tilly would follow. "Thank you for letting me visit."

"Come back any time you like," Alyndra said, briefly touching my arm. "You're always welcome here. The children adore you."

"Thank you," I whispered, grateful that I had somewhere I could go. Somewhere that I was wanted. I wasn't sure I was actually adding any value on these visits, or that this was the purpose I'd been looking for, but it was a start.

Andrus escorted me and Tilly on the long walk to Orabelle's rooms, careful not to touch me the entire time and speaking as little as possible. He was often stationed near my room and always volunteered to guide me wherever I needed to go, but I also got the impression that he didn't particularly *like* me. Or, at the very least, he was wary of my company.

It made me miss Damen even more.

"Here you go," Andrus mumbled, a door creaking as he pushed it open.

I held on to Tilly's collar, depending on her to lead the way since Andrus hadn't given me any direction. Fortunately, the room seemed to be flat and entirely clear of obstacles—unlike most of the non-corridor rooms in the palace.

"Ah, here she is," a voice said, startling me. It was very clearly an elder female voice, and there was a pang of grief in my chest for Nana.

"Are you Orabelle?"

"I am. And you're Iris. The famous Iris."

I laughed uncertainly. How could I be famous? I only went between my room and the nursery, and barely spoke to anyone.

"Hmmm. What to make of you?" Orabelle murmured. I felt her circling me, taking me in from every angle, and I couldn't decide whether to stay perfectly still or ask Tilly to get me out of here. "You're the one who has my Damen all in a tizzy."

"I don't know about that," I replied slowly, trying to remember who Alyndra said she was. "Are you Damen's mother?"

"In many of the ways that matter, I suppose. He didn't come from my womb, his own mother died on a feeding trip to the human realm shortly after she gave birth."

A lump formed in my throat, and I swallowed past it painfully. How awful for Damen to have to grow up without his mother. How awful for his mother, to have her time with her child cut so very short. Then again, perhaps she'd been a mother like Moriah? It was difficult to reconcile the romantic view of motherhood that I'd always heard about in movies with my own experience of it.

"I'm very sorry to hear that," I rasped.

Orabelle leaned in close enough that the tip of her horn brushed the side of my head and inhaled deeply. She must be much shorter than Damen.

"You are, aren't you? There's no lying about your intentions when you're a Hunter. Ex-Hunter. Whatever you lot call yourselves. There are no polite, empty apologies. When you feel sorry, you smell like it. That must be a strange adjustment for you, being so easy to read."

"Not really," I admitted. "I've never been very good at lying about my intentions. My nana always encouraged me to be kind and polite, and I try to live my life accordingly."

Orabelle hummed again. "Interesting. I've never put much stock in kindness, personally. It seems like more hassle than it's worth."

"It seems like more effort to ruin someone's day than to bring joy to it."

I'd said the words without thinking, and they took me by surprise. Usually, I wasn't so quick to disagree with someone. Especially my elders.

Orabelle snorted. "I can assure you it's not. But perhaps it would be for you—you've got this… inherent *goodness* about you. Like any form of unkindness would require special effort. It's not something I've ever encountered before—I can see why Damen is so fascinated by you. I hear he proposed to you and you told him no."

I winced at the reminder. "It was very unexpected—"

"You don't need to justify yourself to me," she cackled. "He's a headstrong lad with an ego as big as this palace. You've done him an enormous favor, really. It's good for him to have to actually work for something—some*one*—he wants for a change."

I didn't think he was doing that, but I decided against arguing. Damen hadn't visited after I'd rejected him. Clearly, a relationship wasn't something he was interested in any longer.

Which was completely reasonable—I can't imagine how I'd feel if I put myself out there like that and the person I asked said no. Of course, that idea was now off the table.

"He hasn't gone around telling the court that he proposed, just so you know. He hasn't even told Allerick—he knows what a bollocking he'd get for it." Orabelle laughed to herself. "Silly lad. He'll learn. There are lots of secrets at court lately," she added slyly.

"Are there?" It seemed like she wanted me to ask follow-up questions, but my limited social experiences hadn't really prepared me for this.

"Oh, yes. You're one of them."

"*I'm* a secret?" I frowned, running my fingers through Tilly's fur. "But I've been to dinner in the dining hall and everything."

"You'd better sit down." I startled as she grabbed my forearm, dragging me a few steps to a seat. "I'm going to tell you this because I disapprove of the decision not to."

"Okay." I folded my hands in my lap as Tilly lay down on the floor with a long-suffering sigh.

"Three Hunters have come through from the human realm recently with the intention to negotiate some sort of lasting peace with the shadow realm. As no one trusts these new arrivals and they came here shortly after you did, the decision was made to keep your existence a secret from them. Just in case they were sent to collect you."

"Oh." In theory, that was a good thing. I didn't *want* to be found, and I certainly didn't want to go back. And I wasn't opposed to being kept a secret from the new Hunters until we knew if they were trustworthy or not—I was very much accustomed to being treated as a secret.

It stung a little that *they* were being kept a secret from *me*, though. Was I untrustworthy?

"Well, if that's the decision everyone has come to," I said uncertainly, realizing that Orabelle was waiting for a more detailed response. "Then I guess that's the right thing to do. I'm very grateful that they took my safety and wellbeing into account," I added honestly.

"You're not like the other Hunters that gave it all up to come here," Orabelle observed.

"I'm blind."

"I didn't mean like that," she replied dismissively. "You're more... what's the word for it? I'm trying not to be insulting. Damen will be cross if I am."

I had no idea how to respond to that.

"Sheltered," Orabelle settled on eventually. "You're more sheltered. Even the quietest of the ex-Hunters have a sharp edge to them from whatever awful training regimen they put you all through as children. You're missing that."

"Yes," I agreed in surprise. "That's a fair assessment. I never went through Hunter training. I lived in the attic with my Nana and kept quiet and out of sight so I didn't embarrass my family with my existence."

Orabelle was silent for a long moment before letting out a heavy exhale. "And now you're here, hiding away in the nursery. We're going to need a cup of tea for this conversation."

CHAPTER 15

K nock, knock," Meera called, following the staff member in who was collecting my breakfast dishes while I resumed my knitting. "I don't suppose you're free? I'm so sorry—it's been so long since I visited."

"That's okay," I assured her, even if I didn't entirely *feel* okay about it. "Sit down. I'm glad you're here."

It hadn't been that long, really. Technically, I was out of hiding. I'd met the new arrivals—Sebastian and Cora, at least—not the larger wave who'd arrived and were staying in Elverston House. But everyone was so busy lately. Tallulah was mated, pregnant, and had moved away.

Meera had technically moved into the room next door, but she'd been gone for days. Damen had vanished.

It was okay, of course. They were busy. The Hunters had escalated their activity recently, and I could hardly complain that everyone was distracted with that while I sat safely ensconced in my nice bedroom, or played on the floor with the children at the nursery. No one was asking *me* to risk my safety or even to give up my time to keep us all safe.

Frankly, no one had so much as *mentioned* the lust thing. I was beginning to wonder if I'd made it all up in my mind.

"Your hair," she murmured. "It's so blonde now."

"Oh, yes. The dye was just to help me get out of the human realm unseen. Does it look better now?" I asked, touching it self-consciously.

"It's beautiful," Meera assured me.

As Meera told me about the path her quest for revenge had taken her down, I examined my own thoughts and wondered if I was angry enough. Meera's rage had been productive. It had gotten things done.

"Did you have an episode?" I asked absently. "My mother used to have them all the time."

She'd find herself in fits of anger that she simply couldn't seem to break free from. Nana had said she'd been like that ever since she was a little girl.

That kind of anger *wasn't* productive. I'd always worried that the same darkness lurked in me. Genetically, the way my broken eyes had come my way.

Be kind, I reminded myself. *Be kind, be kind, be kind.*

Guilt swamped me at how little I'd been telling myself that recently. I knew that in most respects, Nana would be ashamed of me. Ashamed of the choices I'd made. Of the life I was living. Of how far I'd strayed from the path she'd envisioned for me.

At the same time, I still felt—at least a little—that I was her legacy. I was the project she'd invested so much time and effort into. I didn't want to let her down by forgetting everything she'd taught me.

I was a disappointment to her in so many ways, but *this* I could do right.

"Yay!" Jonan shouted the moment I walked in. "String day!"

"Yarn, not string," I corrected gently, letting him tug me down to sit on the floor with him. A little circle immediately formed around us, with Eadlin leaning against my side and Yara directing the children so they didn't get unwieldy.

While knitting wasn't a Shade hobby, it had apparently been easy enough to have needles made up here that matched mine, and the children were surprisingly patient when it came to learning, despite how small they were. The littlest, like Eadlin, were just here to watch.

"I've been practicing," Jonan bragged. "My mother says I shouldn't because it's a peasant hobby, but I told her that Iris does it, so why can't I?"

"Jonan," Yara gasped, though I quietly wondered if it was mostly for my benefit. From what I'd learned, only Shades who weren't strong enough to form clothes out of shadows bothered with physical garments. It was almost a mark of shame to wear clothing—a knitted scarf was hardly going to be a prized object here.

It wasn't my place to make any kind of judgment on that—I was new here and I didn't know the rules and traditions of the realm. I was just teaching them as a fun skill, and something to keep the children busy for a while and give the nursery staff a break. I'd taught them to loop the yarn in a basic knit stitch, but a few of the older children had gotten good enough to try purl stitches.

There was a commotion by the door, and I wanted to know what was going on but Jonan elbowed me the moment I paused.

"Who's at the door?" I asked him, because I was learning that I needed to work *with* his mischievous nature instead of against it.

"What? Oh, it's the king's mother. I wonder what she wants."

"Orabelle?"

"Are you allowed to call her that?" he asked, his voice dropping to a whisper.

"I think so. We're friends."

"Are you?" It was the most impressed Jonan had ever sounded since I'd met him. "My mother says the king's mother is *very* scary."

"Oh no, that isn't true at all—"

Orabelle's distinctive cackle cut me off. "Not where you're concerned, Iris. You're one of my favorites, you know. His mother, on the other hand..."

"Orabelle," I scolded, worried she was going to traumatize poor Jonan.

"If you'd met her, you'd agree," Orabelle replied unapologetically. There was the sound of a chair scraping across the floor, and she huffed and complained as she got situated close by, apparently making herself comfortable.

Would it be terribly rude of me to ask what she was doing here? If there was one room in the entire palace I couldn't imagine Orabelle wanting to spend time in, it was the nursery.

"Do you want to learn to knit?" Jonan asked her boldly, apparently not put off by the disparaging remarks about his mother.

"Go on then. You teach me. Don't bother Iris, she's helping the other children now."

For all of her rather abrupt ways, she knew exactly how to keep Jonan engaged. He was more than happy to pass on the skills he'd learned, and I got a few minutes to speak with the children who weren't quite as vocal about asking for attention.

"The queen is here!" someone shouted, making me startle as the door opened again.

"What an unrelaxing environment this is for children," Orabelle remarked, as though she hadn't caused a stir herself.

"Oh, I didn't expect you two to be here," Ophelia said, moving over to where we were. "Hi, Iris. Orabelle, what are you doing here?"

"I'm visiting Iris, of course," she replied irritably. "And helping her wrangle these uncontrollable youths."

"The nursery staff do a wonderful job of that and the children are very well-behaved," I added hurriedly.

"Are you teaching them to knit? Can I join?"

There were squeals of excitement at that as Ophelia came to sit next to me and was immediately handed her own set of supplies. I gave up on my scarf entirely as Eadlin crawled onto my lap, probably overwhelmed by the noise. I understood the feeling.

"This is so great," Ophelia murmured. "Do you visit a lot? I haven't been in a while. I've been so busy with other things..."

"Understandably so. I imagine a queen has a lot of duties to attend to."

"Some more pleasant than others," she muttered, her needles clicking together slowly. "You know, it never occurred to me to bring any human realm activities here for the kids to try? I don't know why."

"I wish I had my harp," I admitted. "I think they would love that."

"A harp, huh? You're very impressive."

"She is," Orabelle agreed, making me blush. "Where is Damen? He should be the one showering her with compliments."

"Oh. Um, no." I laughed nervously. "I think that was just a passing thing. That's passed. He hasn't visited in a while."

"What?" Ophelia said sharply. "Why not? Did something happen? It definitely wasn't a passing thing. He's done something, hasn't he?"

"No, no. Not at all."

"He proposed," Orabelle offered. "And Iris said no."

"I don't think you were supposed to mention that," I mumbled, wondering how many parents would be hearing that interesting piece of prime gossip fresh from the nursery tonight.

"I wouldn't have if he'd redeemed himself," Orabelle sniffed. "As far as I see it, he deserves a little shaming at this point."

"Lordy," Ophelia muttered.

"The king is here!" Yara announced, sending the children into a tailspin again. Not just the children. For all my silent complaints about being left to my own devices, this was maybe a little too much interaction all at once.

"Sorry," Ophelia said, raising her voice above the noise. "He's just coming to collect me."

"Nonsense. Son, sit down with us," Orabelle commanded grandly. "What could you possibly be doing that's so urgent that you can't take a few minutes to spend with your mother, hm?"

"That feels like a trick question," Allerick said dryly. "And I'm not going to answer it. What is this activity you're doing?"

Fortunately, Ophelia was able to explain the purpose of knitting while I murmured some quiet words of encouragement to Eadlin that convinced her to at least stop hiding against my shoulder. I was fairly certain that she understood me a little more now, even if she couldn't respond in a language that I could understand.

"This is... nice," Allerick said eventually. "We should perhaps do more things like this. For those who have only ever seen the human realm as a place of death and destruction—though necessary for us to feed—it might be good to see a different side of it. Certainly, Austin's concerts are popular everywhere he goes."

"Iris plays an instrument too," Ophelia added enthusiastically. "It might be a little trickier to get it here—they're quite large. Maybe Sebastian would be willing to help—he's pretty eager to impress at the moment."

She fell silent suddenly, probably realizing she'd brought up the name of one of the new Hunters who I was being very intentionally kept away from.

"Iris knows all about that," Orabelle said dismissively. "Ophelia, when are you going to tell your husband that Damen proposed to her?"

"What? When?" Allerick asked sharply. "Has it been a month since you arrived, Iris? I told him he had to wait a month."

"You did?"

Had Damen wanted to propose right away? That was... romantic. In a fairy tale kind of way. Perhaps a little misguided, but very romantic.

"Doesn't matter," Ophelia replied. "Iris said no."

Allerick was quiet for a moment. "Actually, I know the exact day it happened. He's been in a strange mood ever since."

I sighed at that, a little forlorn. I didn't want him to be in a strange mood.

"Well, what are we going to do?" Orabelle demanded. "He's been licking his wounds for long enough."

They debated among themselves, and I half listened, wondering why they all seemed to think that Damen would be too unmotivated to take action on his own. From what I'd seen of Damen, he was *very* motivated when he wanted to be.

"Can't I go and visit him?" I asked, making everyone fall silent. "I asked if we would still be friends and he assured me we would, but now that I think about it... Well, it might be a little embarrassing for him to have to seek me out after I'd turned him down. Maybe it would be best if I sought him out instead?"

The more I spoke, the more confident I felt in the idea. I wasn't in hiding anymore. It was time for me to be taking more decisive action.

"Of course you can," Orabelle said crisply, breaking the silence. "Allerick will escort you there himself. I would, but my knees hurt and I want to lie down."

"Oh. Well, we don't know where he is. Do we?" I asked as Eadlin climbed off my lap and I stretched out my numb legs.

"At this time of day? He's napping," Allerick replied with absolute certainty.

"I don't want to disturb his sleep—"

Allerick snorted. "I have no such qualms. Let's go."

Tilly trotted along cheerfully next to me, my hand on her collar, as we made our way toward wherever Damen stayed, and I imagined she was delighted to get out of the noisy room. Usually, she was quite fond of our visits to see the children, but they were more excitable than usual with so many additional guests.

It was a quiet walk. Ophelia had accompanied her mother-in-law back to her rooms, which meant I was attempting to keep up with the king—who didn't have his brother's knack for letting me set the pace.

"We're here," Allerick said gruffly, before banging loudly on a door. "Wake up, Damen!"

There was a loud, tired groan from beyond. "What do you want?"

"I have a visitor for you."

There was some shuffling from inside the room, and my face was almost uncomfortably hot as I stood there, waiting for him to open the door. This had been a terrible idea. Why had I wanted to take the initiative? I wasn't a take-initiative sort of girl.

I was a sit-in-the-attic sort of girl.

There was a whoosh of air as the door swung open, and I dug my heels into the ground a little to stop myself from stepping back automatically. *It's fine. This is fine. It's just Damen.*

"Iris. Hi."

"Hi." I was acutely aware of Allerick standing next to me, adding an extra layer of awkwardness to this conversation. "How are you?"

"I'm good." He cleared his throat. "How are you?"

"I'm fine, thank you."

There was a long silence. This had been the worst idea I'd ever had.

"Iris," Allerick began. "Have you visited the courtyard garden in the center of the palace?"

"No, I haven't."

"Damen, why don't you take Iris there?" Allerick suggested pleasantly. "It's a nice walk, and might give her a better feel for the spiral layout of the palace."

"Yes, of course."

There was a long pause, and I wondered if they were communicating silently with their eyes. Eventually, the door closed, and I felt Damen's hand gently touch my elbow. Embarrassingly, I shivered a little at the contact. For some reason, his touch had always felt different to anyone else's. Better. More... more like home.

"I'll leave you to it," Allerick announced, already striding away. I truly couldn't make heads nor tails of the king. His tone was very gruff and a little intimidating, but the words he said tended not to be.

"Did he drag you here?" Damen asked ruefully as we started walking.

"Not at all. I asked if I could visit."

"You did?" He sounded surprised.

"Yes." My face heated. "I hope that's okay. I've really missed your company, Damen. And maybe you haven't missed mine, and that's fine—"

"I have. I have missed your company, Iris."

"—but I just wanted to reach out first so that you knew that when I said I still wanted us to be friends, that I meant it."

He noisily blew out a breath. "I know. I know that you meant it. And I meant it too, when I agreed. My ego was just a little bruised, that's all. Theon says it's good for me."

I winced. "I'm sorry—"

"Please don't apologize. Let's go back to how things were, okay? How have you been?"

I contemplated the question. "Before we go back to how things were, I need to tell you off first."

Damen laughed quietly. "Go ahead."

"I had tea with Orabelle, and she told me about the Hunters visiting the realm and how everyone had decided to keep them away from me. I understand the logic, Damen. But it stung a little to be left out like that."

He tucked my hand more securely into the crook of his arm. "I'm sorry, Iris. You're right—that wasn't the right decision. We'll do better next time. *I'll* do better next time. You shouldn't be the last to know about decisions that impact you directly."

"Thank you," I murmured, the wind immediately disappearing from my sails. I hadn't expected him to be so... agreeable. To actually listen to me and apologize and want to do better.

It was comforting in a way that I didn't know I needed.

"What else did Orabelle say?" Damen asked suspiciously.

I laughed. "When I had tea with her? Or when she came to visit me at the nursery earlier?"

"At the *nursery*?" Damen spluttered. "Those poor children. Sounds like we've got a lot to catch up on—start at the beginning."

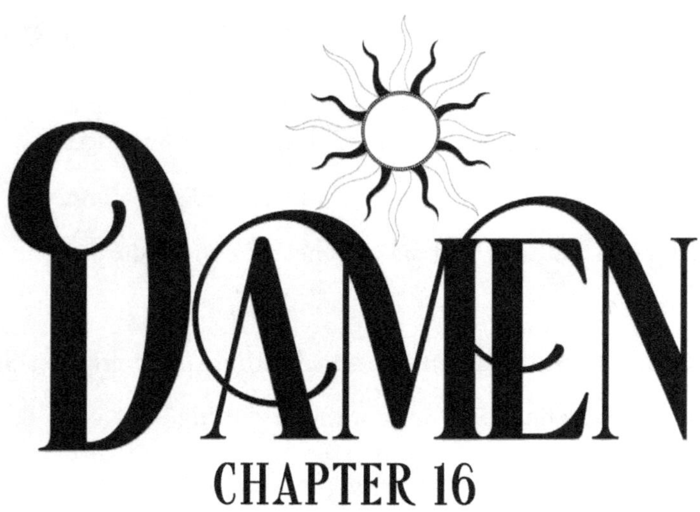

DAMEN
CHAPTER 16

"Where are you going?" I asked Soren, running into him and Astrid in the foyer. "Can I come?"

He narrowed his eyes. "Why?"

"Maybe I can help."

He shot me an alarmed look while Astrid snorted. "No, thank you."

"I want a job," I sighed, slumping my shoulders. "Why is that so hard? Why can't someone just give me one?"

"Do you know how to do anything?" Astrid asked.

"Of course I do! I'm very approachable. And I was a great scholar—ask anyone. I was far more accomplished in my studies than Allerick or Soren."

"That's true," Soren agreed. "Though, too undisciplined to go any further with it."

I briefly entertained the idea of getting back into it now before dismissing it almost immediately. I didn't want to spend my time buried in dusty old tomes, working away alone and in silence, even if the contents of those books were interesting.

Though Ruvyn seemed to enjoy his life at The Itrodaris just fine. Maybe I should ask him about a career in academia.

"Can I join the Guard?"

"No. You don't have the discipline for that either," Soren replied easily.

"Where is all this coming from?" Astrid asked. "Are you bored or something?"

"I'm on my healing journey."

She rolled her eyes. "You've been spending too much time with Verity."

"Verity has compassion for my struggles."

Astrid side-eyed me like she was about to say something truly mean before seeming to think better and pursing her lips shut. Probably something about me not having struggles, which wasn't an entirely unreasonable assumption.

Aside from my irreparably broken heart, my life was mostly quite comfortable.

"Tallulah was hoping one of the ex-Hunters could accompany her to the negotiating session today, but I think everyone was otherwise engaged. And some of them are more adept at navigating those conversations than others—I think you'd be particularly good at it, even though you're a Shade," Soren suggested.

"Sure. I can do that." It didn't sound particularly stimulating, but I was good at talking. I was confident I'd have no issue with it.

"We'll be running our first training session today with some of the new ex-Hunters," Soren volunteered, apparently realizing he hadn't answered my question. "It would be a supremely bad idea for you to help out with that— they're nervous enough already."

"They're training with you?" I asked, surprised.

"Mostly with Astrid and Meera," Soren replied. "It was Meera's idea. She thought that some of the more skittish ones might gain confidence if they knew how to defend themselves."

That made sense. Was that something Iris would be interested in doing as well? Everyone knew about her now. She could explore more freely if she wanted to. And she'd definitely be safe in Astrid's hands.

"Go ahead," Soren told Astrid quietly. "I'll catch up with you."

Oh dear.

He came to a stop in the corridor, clasping my shoulder to keep me in place.

"You have a very serious look on your face," I teased, trying to lighten the mood.

"I'm worried about you, Damen."

"That is wholly unnecessary."

"I don't think it is. It's very unlike you to be so restless."

"I can't win," I complained. "You're all on my case when I do nothing, and now when I try to do *something*, it's a problem too. I can't do anything right."

Soren blinked at me, dropping his hand. "That's not how I want you to feel at all, Damen. I think it's great that you're trying to be more involved around the palace. But you seem restless in your... spirit," he finished, seeming a little frustrated as he struggled to find the words. Emotional talks weren't Soren's strong suit, and I appreciated that he was trying.

It made me pause and consider my answer a little more carefully, rather than giving him a glib response to get this conversation over and done with. "I do feel restless in my spirit. But I'm working on it."

I'm working on *me*. I wanted to be a Shade worthy of the sweetest, kindest woman in the realm, as well as a Shade worthy of the title I held.

The path to get there wasn't quite as linear as I'd hoped it would be, but I was confident I'd find it.

Soren nodded once. "Okay. Will you tell me if you need help?"

"Do you want me to?"

"Of course." He hesitated. "You're like a younger brother to me as well, Damen."

I grinned and he scowled at me like he already regretted saying it. "I have always considered you one of my older brothers. You are all of a similar temperament."

"Yes, yes," he said impatiently, though not unaffectionately. "You'd better get going if you want to sit in on that meeting. It's starting soon."

"On my way!" I called over my shoulder, already heading for the stairs. Interesting. I felt buoyed in a way that I hadn't just a few minutes earlier. Perhaps there was something to be said for serious, emotive conversations.

"Damen!" Tallulah said in surprise, standing by the meeting room door with Evrin, his hand resting lightly on her waist. "Are you joining us?"

"I thought I might, if that's okay."

"Of course. I don't know how interesting you'll find it," she added apologetically. "At the moment, it feels like every conversation is just going in circles."

"Well, perhaps I can be of use in that regard." I shrugged. "Or I'll make it worse. Let's find out, shall we?"

Sebastian, the representative from the Hunters Council, stood as we entered, and I was gratified to see that he looked a little less smug when I walked in, if for no other reason than Verity was a close friend of mine and she deeply resented having her former fiance existing in the same realm as her.

A very reasonable position to take.

"Well," Sebastian began awkwardly after we'd taken our seats. "I suppose we have to address recent events. Things have... shifted."

Tallulah sat back in her chair, watching him with an entirely neutral look on her face. If it was a negotiating tactic, it was a good one. Sebastian was immediately flustered.

"Everyone I was reporting to was arrested."

"Report to yourself?" Tallulah suggested mildly. "If you believe in what we're doing here, then why not keep going? You can always present an option back to the new leadership—Harlow Miles."

Sebastian scowled. "*Harlow*? She's not a leader."

"She's the one currently leading," Tallulah countered.

"That's an interim measure. She's not qualified," Sebastian snapped. I leaned forward in my seat, resting my forearm on the table, and he immediately straightened, looking contrite.

"Let's all keep calm here, shall we?" I suggested mildly. I hadn't liked this prick before, and I liked him even less now. Since Meera had wiped most of the players from his board, he'd been walking around the palace smelling like stress, and it was deeply unpleasant.

Sebastian inclined his head stiffly. "Of course."

"As far as I can tell, you don't have anywhere near the sway that you used to. In fact, I'm not confident you've got any authority left at all—the people who hired you are imprisoned now, are they not?" I asked, because I wanted to make him squirm a little.

"No one has replaced me," Sebastian said defensively. "Or even suggested the idea."

"Perhaps not, but that doesn't really matter if they don't respect your word, does it? We could come to whatever arrangement we like, and it might all be for nothing because you're no longer recognized as a figure worthy of respect."

Perhaps I shouldn't have come along to this—I was probably making Tallulah's job harder.

She didn't seem mad though as she leaned back in her seat. "I did ask you to bring Harlow along to this meeting," she reminded Sebastian.

"Harlow is some kind of... tech expert or something," Sebastian shot back, clearly ruffled. "She isn't qualified for this."

"Neither am I," Tallulah pointed out. "But I have the trust of the people and Shades that I'm working on behalf of. You don't have that, Sebastian. Not anymore, not with a whole new set of faces in charge. Harlow has stepped into that vacuum, has she not?"

This appeared to be a sore spot for Sebastian since his scent soured even further, and he shifted uncomfortably in his chair. He didn't know that Harlow was our contact and had been given advance notice that everything was going to fall apart, making it easy for her to take up the mantle. Undoubtedly, Sebastian would have done the same if anyone had warned him that a position was opening up, but wisely, no one had.

His intentions seemed somewhat more pure than the Councilors we'd dealt with before—I suspected he really did want to find a solution that would last and wasn't overtly exploitative of the Shades. However, he clearly still believed in the *superiority* of Hunters, and we couldn't afford to forget that.

Sebastian sighed heavily, massaging his temples. It was the least composed I'd ever seen him. "I'm not even sure why I'm here, to be honest. Everything has fallen apart, and I guess there's some comfort in the familiarity of being here, you know? The landscape back home has changed so much that I don't recognize it—I don't recognize my place in it anymore—so I keep coming here because at least it feels like I'm doing something. Like it isn't all completely hopeless."

I gave Tallulah a pointed look because we had strayed well beyond my area of expertise now. I could, and would, happily tell Sebastian that he was a loser, and no one trusted him, but I wasn't equipped to deal with the emotional fallout that followed.

She narrowed her eyes slightly at me before composing her expression into something kind and understanding for Sebastian. "You're in a really unique position right now, Sebastian. You could be at the forefront of change right now. You could be a decision-maker rather than just a spokesperson. It's crazy to me that you're not seeing the opportunities that are available to you right now rather than the ones you've missed. You could shape the future of both realms, and you're sitting here, wondering what to do now that you haven't got overlords giving you specific instructions."

"They weren't my overlords," Sebastian muttered, his face an interesting reddish color. She'd embarrassed him, but it had been effective too. He was clearly giving the matter some thought. "Perhaps we should call it for today's session. I mentioned to Cora that I'd spend some time with her this afternoon."

"Did you?" Tallulah asked, raising an eyebrow. I tried in vain to copy the movement, even though I knew Shade facial features weren't as moveable. It just looked like such a fun gesture to make.

"She's been socializing a little more," Sebastian continued. "Obviously, she's had a hard time of it, but I think she wants to find her place here regardless. She's trying to befriend Jade."

From memory, Jade was one of the new ex-Hunters who'd moved into Elverston House, and was not the most approachable of sorts. But perhaps she was like Theon—once you got past that hard exterior, you would find the most loyal of friends. Would Iris like to meet them? She'd been sheltered a lot since she arrived—too much, actually—but she couldn't be hidden away, confined to socializing with the infants in the nursery, forever.

I experienced a feeling that might have been jealousy, even though Iris had already rejected me. In my stupid head, I still wanted her all to myself.

He nodded at us both as he stood, quietly excusing himself. There was really no need for Sebastian to stay in the shadow realm since he had the use of a portal to travel back and forth as needed. Maybe he just preferred it here?

I might feel a smidge bad for being so hard on him if he genuinely enjoyed living here and wanted to stay.

Tallulah and Evrin looked as though they were having a cute moment together—must be nice—so I headed out of the room, contemplating finding my brother. I didn't think it was fair to leave these conversations resting on Tallulah's shoulders when the circumstances had changed so drastically. She needed more support.

"Hey!" Tallulah called, her bright red shoes clicking against the stone floor as she rushed to catch up with me, Evrin easily keeping pace with her steps. "Thanks for that. That was really helpful."

I slowed so we could head toward the main foyer together, giving Tallulah a chance to catch her breath.

"I'm glad my presence there was useful."

"*Super* useful. I mean, I've got it under control," she added hastily, seemingly worried that I'd question her competency. "But Sebastian responds better to authority figures, and you're a prince. That's just the truth of the matter. Can you come along to the next meeting?"

I glanced at her, trying to determine whether or not she was in earnest.

"Yes. I could. I was going to suggest to Allerick that he should be attending."

She frowned up at me, planting her hands on her hips. In many respects, Tallulah reminded me of a particularly strict nurse I'd had growing up. She was prettier and more colorful, but equally as intolerant of my bullshit.

"Why can't you do it?"

I opened my mouth to respond before shutting it again. Why *couldn't* I do it? I had the time. I didn't really know what I was doing, but Allerick was probably making it up as he went along at least half of the time. Why not me?

"There's no reason I can't. I'll be there."

Tallulah beamed, and I looked over her head to find Evrin smiling proudly at me too.

"Stop it," I said to both of them sternly. "Those are the most patronizing smiles I've ever seen."

"We're just so proud of you," Tallulah sighed dramatically, clutching her chest. "You'd be such a force to be reckoned with if you believed in yourself, you know."

With that, they walked away, hand in hand and disgustingly cute.

Believed in myself? I believed in myself. Didn't I?

I was great. I was funny and charming and strong. That was *all* I was, but I *believed* that I was all of those things.

Tallulah didn't know what she was talking about. I believed in myself just fine. It was everything else that was the problem.

IRIS

CHAPTER 17

"Do you want to come for a walk outside with me?" Meera asked. "I know you like to go to the nursery in the mornings, but just if you wanted a little change of scenery..."

"I would love to, thank you." She hovered as I got myself ready, leashing Tilly since we were going outside. I doubted she'd bolt, but it never hurt to be careful. "Are we going somewhere in particular?"

"I started a vegetable garden at Elverston House. I need to go tend to it, but I thought you might want to come. You know, get to know the grounds a little more. Maybe meet some of the new ex-Hunters if they come out? They're... shy."

"They're *all* shy?" I confirmed, sliding my feet into my shoes. Meera was shy, but I wouldn't describe any of the others that way. I had thought of her as an anomaly among Hunters.

"A lot of them weren't properly included in the Hunters. For a variety of reasons," Meera said awkwardly.

I frowned, turning over the words in my head.

"Are they... like me?"

Meera was silent for a long while. "They are people who have limited participation within the Hunters for a variety of reasons."

They were the rejects. The outcasts. I'd heard about them. Nana had always reminded me how lucky I was that Moriah let me live at home, instead of being sent to wherever they were. Or ending up in service at someone else's home, the way Clara had. Since the first time I got here, I felt truly nervous at the prospect of meeting someone.

What if they resented me because I hadn't been sent away like they had? Nana said the places they went to were horrible, and made me repeat how grateful I was that Moriah shielded me from that.

"Maybe I could meet them later?" I suggested nervously, smoothing down the itchy fabric of my skirt. I was feeling sort of nauseous at the thought.

"Of course. Sorry. I didn't even... I didn't even think. Um, we could walk around the palace gardens if you like? It's right here in front of us."

"Sure. Yes. It's nice to get some fresh air." I had the small courtyard attached to my room, of course. But that was sort of Tilly's domain now.

"Okay. Well, this is the garden. The palace is circular, you've probably noticed the corridors curving inward, right? They spiral toward the center. The garden has a similar layout, lots of curving garden beds with paths in between. If you follow it all the way until the end, you'll get to the barracks where the Guard stays. Elverston House is down a path to the right."

I nodded, a little surprised at how descriptive she was being.

"We're standing in front of the main portal," Meera continued. "It's right outside the palace. Sebastian uses it to get to the in-between, then he uses the open portal on the human realm side to get home."

"Okay," I said slowly. It wasn't that what Meera was saying wasn't interesting, I supposed, but it was odd for *her* to be the one saying it. She usually barely spoke at all, and today she was rambling. Did she feel bad about bringing up the new ex-Hunters in Elverston House? I wasn't upset with her or anything, just nervous about meeting them for the first time. "Is everything okay, Meera?"

She exhaled shakily. "No, not really."

I reached out clumsily, bumping her elbow before resting my hand on her forearm. "What's going on? Is this about your trip to the human realm? Did something else happen?"

"Yes." She cleared her throat. "I need to tell you about it, but I was trying to make sure you had a pleasant morning first."

"I think I'd rather just know," I said gently, taking my hand away and wrapping my arms around my waist.

"Okay. Okay." I listened as Meera paced a few steps in front of me. "*Yourparentswerearrested.*"

"I'm sorry, I didn't catch that."

She made a slightly pained sound. "Your parents were arrested. They were mixed up in all the shady financial stuff that the rest of the Council were involved in. I don't know what will happen exactly—I guess the charges will be different for everyone depending on what they did. But the Council has been taken over by Hunters who are working with the Shades. Whatever happens, your parents' careers are over. They've been effectively ousted."

"Okay."

"Okay?" Meera repeated dubiously.

"I'm not quite sure how to feel yet," I admitted, hugging myself a little tighter. Moriah was the only mother I had, but she'd resented my existence my entire life, and locked me away where she didn't have to look at me.

She'd given me Nana and kept me from being sent somewhere worse, and I *wanted* to be grateful but I still struggled with my gratitude where Moriah was concerned. I knew how privileged my brothers' lives were, and it was difficult not to feel the tiniest hint of bitterness that my life had played out so differently.

The idea of Moriah in jail didn't bring me any joy, but a small part of me wondered if she'd appreciate what my life was like, confined to the small, cold attic. That wasn't a kind thought, though. Nana would be horrified.

"I'm sorry," Meera said awkwardly.

"You don't need to apologize," I assured her. "Presumably, it was their own actions that landed them in this mess. I've certainly overheard enough through the vents to know that whatever they were doing, they were very secretive about it."

Regular Hunters business was always discussed around the dining table—usually with drinks and food and boisterous laughter. Anything related to finances was conducted in hushed whispers in the library, and I never caught the details of those conversations.

"Iris," Damen said suddenly, making me jump. "What's wrong?"

"Nothing," I replied automatically, not wanting to burden him with my problems.

"I can smell that something is wrong," he pointed out gently. "Talk to me."

I don't know why I did it. I had no idea if anyone else was around—he could have been walking next to someone and in the middle of a conversation. But I walked forward anyway, reaching for Damen in total confidence that he'd meet me halfway.

"Hey," he murmured quietly as I walked headfirst into his chest, his arms immediately wrapping around my shoulders. The moment his chin came to rest on the top of my head, I exhaled, some of the stress melting out of my body.

Since the moment I'd arrived in the shadow realm, I'd associated Damen with comfort and support. In spite of the recent awkwardness between us, he still felt safe to me.

He felt like home.

Was that a normal way to feel about someone you didn't know very well? Maybe I should have married him.

"Talk to me. Is everything okay?"

I gave the question some thought. "No. But I feel much better now."

He squeezed me a little tighter. "What do you need?"

One stray tear escaped at the question. He'd asked it like it was the most natural thing in the world.

"Meera, would it be horribly rude of me to head back inside now? I'm so sorry—"

"Please don't apologize," she said hastily. "I can't emphasize enough how much you don't owe me an apology. We can talk later. When you're ready. I'll leave you guys to it."

I listened as her footsteps retreated, wondering idly if she was going to her vegetable garden now. That seemed to be her place of peace, and it sounded like she needed it.

"Do you want to go back to your room?" Damen asked.

"Yes, please."

I waited in place for a second for him to speak to someone else, but it appeared that we were alone. Instead of linking our arms together like he usually did, Damen draped his arm over my shoulders and tucked me tightly into his side.

"I'm okay, really," I assured Damen, not wanting him to worry. "Meera was just telling me that my mother was arrested and her career at the Council is over, and I suppose I don't know what to make of that."

He squeezed my shoulder sympathetically.

"Did you know?" I asked, suspecting that information wasn't news to him based on his silence.

"Yes," he admitted guiltily. "Trust me, I wanted to tell you yesterday more than anything. But Meera asked that she be the one to break it to you—she feels terrible about it."

I mulled it over and decided I didn't feel upset about it the way I had when everyone had hidden me away from the new Hunters without saying a word. I didn't begrudge Meera wanting to be the one who told me.

"It's okay if you're mad at me about that, Iris."

"I'm not mad. It's fine. I don't want to complain—"

"Complain," Damen interjected firmly. "Complain to your heart's content. Talking about something that's weighing on your mind doesn't make you ungrateful. Having a bit of a whine from time to time to those who you trust and those who care about you isn't a poor reflection of your character. Or, at least, I hope it's not since I whine almost constantly to everyone about everything."

I laughed. "You do not. You're just saying that to make me feel better."

"I swear to you, Iris," Damen began solemnly. "I am the whiniest Shade in the entire realm. You just haven't seen it yet because I've been trying to impress you."

His words made me feel all soft and squishy on the inside. "I have always been very impressed by you, Damen. I'm sure everyone is, even the ones you whine at."

"We'd have to ask my brother about that—I'm sure he'd have an opinion on it," Damen replied wryly. "He has an opinion on everything."

"He loves you," I chided gently. "That was very clear from speaking to him yesterday. He cares about you so much."

I could make a direct comparison there. My brothers absolutely didn't feel that way about me.

"He's not so bad," Damen admitted begrudgingly. "Can't we go hang out in my room instead? It's bigger and there's still an outdoor area for Tilly. We can lounge around and I'll read us a book."

"You'd do that?" I asked, my voice wavering slightly.

Damen turned toward me, his jaw brushing the top of my head as he inhaled deeply. "Of course. Today is going to be a relaxation day—I'm excellent at those. I'll send for tea and cake. You with me?"

"I'm with you."

"That was nice," I murmured, lying back on the sofa in Damen's room as he finished reading a story about a Shade who lost his shadows. It was clearly a children's story—the moral being that he needed to believe in himself—but it was lovely to listen to, regardless.

It reminded me of listening to fairy tales when I was young and Nana used to read to me. There was more about the shadow realm that was similar to life in the human realm than wasn't. It seemed baffling in hindsight that the Hunters Council had been able to villainize the Shades so effectively when they really weren't so different from us.

"There's still a little while before dinner. Should I run you a bath? That might make you feel better. And my bath tub is nice—yours is wholly inadequate for relaxing in. Of course, I would stay out of the room," he added hastily.

"You would do that for me?" I asked, surprised. Not that Damen hadn't always been generous with me, but this felt different.

Intimate.

The attraction to Damen—to his voice, and the feel of him, and the way he treated me—had always been there, but I'd done my best to squash it down and I was pretty sure I'd been succeeding at it. I didn't understand the nuances of romantic relationships, but even I knew that once someone had proposed to you and you said no, things got a little more complicated.

But his easy kindness this afternoon had been weakening my resolve. And the idea of being naked in his space...

There was something sort of territorial about it, though I couldn't put my finger on exactly what that was.

"Iris. Your scent," Damen groaned.

"What about it?" Why did my voice sound like that? Like I was out of breath even though I was just sitting still?

"It's... intoxicating. Your desire is the most addictive scent I've ever experienced in my life."

My desire? Somehow, it had never occurred to me that Shades would be able to smell *that*, though of course it made sense since they could pick up our other emotions.

"Does it make you uncomfortable that I'm aroused?" I asked curiously, trying to establish if I was being inappropriate or not.

"That's not quite how I'd describe it," Damen rasped. Oh good, his voice sounded just as strained as mine did.

"How would you describe it then?"

He groaned. "Iris, you're killing me. I'm trying to behave myself. You don't want this from me."

"What don't I want from you?"

"Sex. Intimacy."

I frowned, thinking back on our conversations. "When did I say that?"

Damen was silent for a long moment. "I guess you didn't. You said you didn't want to get married."

"No, that seemed like a rather dramatic step to take when I'd just arrived," I agreed. "But I never said anything about not wanting sex. I'd love to have sex. I came here thinking I'd be having sex all the time." I paused for a moment, giving it some thought. "I've never done it before though, so I might be bad at it."

"*Fuck*," Damen whispered, sounding almost pained.

"Should I not have said that?"

He laughed, though it was strained. "I would prefer you not say it to anyone else. I find I am *very* jealous where you're concerned."

I frowned. "I wouldn't say that to anyone else. I feel safe with you, Damen. Only you."

"Good." He exhaled loudly. "Will you allow me to bring you pleasure, Iris? It would be the greatest honor of my life."

That seemed a little extreme, but I wasn't going to complain. "Of course. I would love that."

Did that mean we were going to have sex? Surely that would mean that he would experience pleasure too, and he made it sound like it was just a me thing.

"Will you lie on my bed for me, Iris?" Damen asked. His tone was polite, but there was a rumbly edge to his voice that I hadn't heard before. It seemed to creep down my body, settling somewhere just south of my belly.

"Yes," I whispered, sucking in a breath of surprise as he scooped me off the couch before I could stand and carried me over to the bed like I weighed nothing, laying me out on it like I was something precious to him.

There was the faint sound of Tilly's paws clicking against the floor as she made her way outside of her own accord. I was quietly grateful for that—I didn't want to traumatize my dog.

"Can I lift your skirt?" Damen asked. So gentlemanly.

"Yes, you may."

I shivered as the air hit my bare thighs and Damen's claws drifted gently over my skin, right up to the elastic edge of my panties. His breath seemed to hiss out between his teeth as he inhaled, and I fervently hoped that he liked what he was seeing. Arousal wasn't a foreign feeling for me, but *seduction* was a game I had no idea how to play.

When I'd listened to characters flirting in movies, they mostly sounded quite sure of themselves, and I didn't know how to replicate that.

"Can I take these off you?" Damen asked, a faint tinge of desperation in his voice. Maybe he didn't mind that I wasn't sure of myself.

"Yes," I agreed again, hooking my thumbs in the waistband and lifting my hips slightly to shimmy them down, bumping his nose as I did so. "Oh! I'm sorry."

"Don't be," Damen growled. "I'm hoping my face gets very well acquainted with this sweet pussy, Iris."

"That sounds... very nice," I stammered, allowing Damen to take over pulling my panties down my legs.

Pussy.

I hadn't ever heard it called that before, but the way he said it sounded... sexy. Reverential and filthy all at once.

Once the fabric was out of the way, Damen made short work of settling himself between my thighs, hitching up my legs and encouraging me to drape them over his shoulders where they'd be out of the way.

My heart pounded in my chest at how exposed I was. How vulnerable. But that didn't feel like a bad thing when I was with Damen. If anything, it heightened my desire.

I was vulnerable and I was at his mercy, and I had complete and utter faith that I was safe and taken care of.

"Iris..." Damen groaned, the claws of his thumbs oh-so-gently tracing the crease of my thighs. "How am I going to stay away from you?"

"You don't have to."

"I do, though," he murmured, dipping his head and pressing his lips to one thigh, then the other. "I have no self-control where you're concerned. A little would never be enough. I'd want *everything*."

That also didn't sound so bad. Maybe I'd been too hasty about the marriage proposal.

Before I could say as much, he was gently opening me up to him with his thumbs, and something that could only have been Damen's tongue swiped my sensitive flesh.

I nearly jumped out of my skin. His mouth was hot and wet, and his tongue was rougher than I expected it to be—far rougher than mine was— and it was *good*. I'd certainly hoped this part would feel pleasant, but it was a hundred times more than that.

"Damen," I gasped, my hands reflexively reaching for him and finding his horns. He groaned hoarsely as I secured my grip, not squeezing too hard but just... keeping him in place.

If he proposed to me after this, I was certain I'd say yes.

"That's it, Iris. Hold on to me. I'm going to make you feel so good."

I already felt wonderful, but Damen meant what he said. He got to work like pleasuring me was his sole purpose in life, moving his tongue in one direction, then another. Circling, teasing, applying more pressure. Every motion seemed to be a test—I could *feel* his attention on me as he focused on my every reaction, studying it and repeating whatever proved most effective.

"Ready to come?" he asked with absolute certainty, though based on my own silent fumblings in bed each night, I was pretty sure I wasn't anywhere near that.

"You sound very sure I will," I said instead, not wanting to upset him.

"Oh, I am. Do you *want* to come now?"

"Yes, please." I was never going to say no to that—it was the best stress relief in the world.

"Then lie back and let me work," Damen replied cockily. And while I'd been *aware* he'd been studying, I hadn't appreciated just how closely.

With just a few movements of that clever tongue, I was gasping and trembling, desperate for release though he kept me hovering right on the edge until I felt like I'd die without the release. His pointed teeth lightly scraped my skin as he sucked on my sensitive nerves, and I was done. I came with a pleading strangled sound I'd never made in my life, the desire coursing through my body so strong I felt as though I'd choke on it.

"Iris..." Damen growled, prying my thighs apart. I hadn't realized I'd been clenching them around his head, the smooth underside of his horns pressing against my skin. "You are exquisite."

That was... wow. I'd brought myself pleasure before but it had never been like that. There was always an underlying tension whenever I did it—was I being too loud? Was this something I should be doing at all? All of those inhibitions had disappeared with Damen.

He made me feel so incredibly safe in all things, but this in particular.

"You're incredible," he murmured. "You're *delicious*."

His teeth scraped lightly over my hip as he moved up my body, but I was too languid to react.

"*You're* incredible," I slurred, panting like I'd been running. What did penetrative sex feel like? If it was half as good as that, then I'd been underestimating it all these years.

There was a brief rumbling sound that filled the air, a vibration that ran through Damen's body before it immediately stopped.

"What was that?" I asked in wonder.

He cleared his throat. "A purr. I've never done that before."

"Is it a bad thing?"

"No. No, it's a very good thing. But that's why we should stop," Damen murmured regretfully. "Before I do something I can't take back."

"Don't disappear," I said hastily, hating how desperate the words sound. "Don't leave. I'll keep my hands to myself, I promise."

"It's not your hands I'm worried about."

"You'd never do anything I wasn't expressly comfortable with," I replied, entirely confident in that. "Could you just... hold me a little? Please?"

Damen made a pained sound, immediately moving up the bed and lifting me into his arms, adjusting us so that we were comfortable. I rested my head on his hard chest, my legs tangled with his strong ones. It shouldn't be comfortable—he was so firm beneath me—and yet it was. His skin was warm and his arms circled me like he could shelter me from anything and everything.

"You should never have to ask me to hold you, Iris. You certainly shouldn't have to beg. I'm sorry."

"You have nothing to apologize for," I assured him firmly, squeezing him a little around his middle. Everything about him was so *solid*. Did it bother him that I wasn't built the same way?

He carefully ran his claws through my hair, detangling the strands with an astounding amount of gentleness. If anything about me bothered him, Damen didn't let on.

"What do you miss the most about the human realm?" he asked quietly.

I hummed thoughtfully, rousing myself from the verge of sleep. I'd never been so comfortable in my life.

"Probably not as much as you'd think. I miss knowing where everything is, I think. The attic I shared with Nana was very small, and over the years we'd made it just right for me to get around. I've mostly gotten the hang of my room, but it's still a little disorienting."

"We'll talk about how to improve the layout tomorrow when you're not so tired—I should have thought of that."

"I'll adjust, Damen. You don't have to do that for me."

"I want to, Iris. I want you to be happy here. What else do you miss from the human realm?"

"Pizza," I laughed. "I only had it once but it was the most delicious food I've ever eaten."

"I'm not familiar with it, but I'll ask Astrid to collect some on her next visit to the human realm."

"Oh, please don't! I'm sure she has far more important things she needs to do when she's in the human realm."

"Not at all," Damen replied confidently. Even though he was the more knowledgeable one of how all of this worked, I somehow doubted that was true. "Anything else I should ask her to retrieve? Don't be shy, Iris. Verity sends Astrid with entire lists of items to collect."

I wouldn't be doing that. Verity probably added a lot more value to the realm than I did—it was only right that she could make requests in return.

"That's all," I assured him. "Astrid is already fetching Tilly's food, which is so very kind of her."

Besides, there was nothing else I missed—nothing except Nana, and there was no bringing her back.

Even then, the more time I spent here, the more complicated my relationship with Nana felt. Despite her reminders for me to be kind, sometimes it felt as though she hadn't always been very kind to me. At the same time, my company had been forced on her when Nana had been too old to be of any value to the Hunters anymore. Moriah had basically assigned me to her care as a way for her to earn her keep—it wasn't a job she'd wanted.

But she'd also been kinder to me than anyone else in my family.

She'd given me Tilly. She'd given me an education, to the best of her ability. She'd read me stories when I was little and encouraged me to use them as an escape from reality, the same way she had.

It all made missing her a complicated prospect.

"Are you okay?" Damen asked drowsily. "Your scent is a little... cloudy."

"I'm okay," I murmured, stroking my thumb over his skin in slow, soothing circles to help him sleep. "I'm happy. Happier than I realized, I promise."

CHAPTER 18

A strange sound woke me up. A sort of impatient huffing noise that belonged nowhere near my luxurious bedroom. Fortunately, I caught myself before I startled, because if I had, I'd have knocked Iris clear off the bed and on top of Tilly, who was the source of the annoyed sounds.

She'd slept here last night? I hadn't meant to fall asleep—we hadn't even had dinner. Then again, I shouldn't be surprised that I had. Holding Iris had been such a relaxing experience, no wonder I'd drifted off.

Tilly huffed impatiently, giving me the most pitiful expression I'd ever seen. I'd never closed the door last night, so she was able to get out at least. She was probably hungry.

What was I meant to do now? A member of staff would be arriving at any moment with my tray of tea. I didn't want anyone seeing Iris in a state of undress except me.

As carefully as I could, I extricated myself from Iris's surprisingly tight grip around my arm and slipped out of bed, intending to intercept the staff at the door.

"Oh. Good morning," Iris said, sounding as surprised as I'd felt when I'd woken up.

"We fell asleep," I said quickly, standing awkwardly next to the bed. What was I *doing*? I was never flustered like this.

Then again, I didn't usually have the most intensely intimate experience of my life—without even coming—with someone I'd proposed to and been rejected by. And that I very much still had feelings for that were absolutely not reciprocated.

I didn't regret anything we'd done last night, but I did question the wisdom of my choices just a little. This wasn't going to help me move on.

I didn't want to move on.

Iris smiled, and it was a little softer and lazier than her usual smile. Her hair was a tangled mess, and there was a pink patch on her cheek where she'd been lying on it, and everything about her was a little more rumpled than normal.

It was adorable. I wished I could see this sight every morning when I woke up.

"I should go. Tilly must be starving."

Tilly sighed loudly, apparently in agreement.

"Do you want to stay for breakfast? I can ask that they send a bowl of plain meat up for her."

"You would do that? That would be so nice."

It was really the least I could do, and I hated how grateful Iris sounded for it. She deserved to be spoiled. I should have been doing a better job of that—even if it was just as a friend.

A friend who knew how good her pussy tasted, but a friend nonetheless.

"I'll go arrange our meal, then be right back," I promised. "Do you need anything before I go?"

"I can manage." Iris smiled, and I leaned in, instinctively pressing my lips to her temple before I let myself out of the room. I noted that Iris didn't assume that she was interrupting anything this time, so I supposed she'd realized that I didn't really do anything with my day.

Or I hadn't, in the past.

Then again, the more involved I was becoming in things, the more I wanted to do. There was something surprisingly satisfying about... making stuff happen. It had never occurred to me that it was something I'd enjoy. It was just that I also enjoyed my afternoon naps too. Was it too much to ask to have both?

I jogged down to the kitchen, deciding to take some initiative and get things done myself.

"Calix," I said cheerfully, wandering into the kitchen while he sharpened his carving knife, looking as though he was contemplating throwing it at my head. "Might I make up a breakfast tray to share with a friend this morning?"

"As in, *you'll* make up the tray?" he asked dubiously. "Don't you usually send your staff down for that?"

"I'm trying something new."

"Why?"

"Can I not try something new? Is that such an odd concept?"

Calix narrowed his eyes at me for a moment before a slow smile took over his face. "You're trying to impress someone. Finally found an ex-Hunter to lavish your attentions on, hm?"

I grumbled out some vague sound of agreement, pulling one of the wooden trays off the shelf and heading for the counter of breakfast dishes that were surplus to the dining hall's requirements.

"I'm surprised you actually *need* to impress anyone. Surely, the title does all the heavy lifting for you? From memory, the king made an appallingly little amount of effort to woo his wife."

"Yes, well, I tried that approach already and it didn't work out for me."

Calix snorted. "I like her already. And I'm impressed that you haven't given up at the first hurdle—I admire your perseverance, Your Highness."

The honorific sounded sarcastic, but I would expect no less from Calix.

I piled the tray up as high as I could, making sure to grab food for Tilly, before heading back upstairs.

Iris had washed and dressed in the clothes she was wearing yesterday in my absence, and was standing in the doorway that led out to the balcony. Her pale hair blew around her face in the breeze, and my shadows reached for her of their own volition. She looked like mine. She felt like mine.

How could she not be mine?

"Breakfast," I announced croakily, setting the tray down on the table.

Iris felt around for the wall, though I was already in motion to go and collect her.

"I wish I had a cane," she said a little wistfully. "Nana never wanted me to use one, but I think it would come in handy sometimes."

"A cane?"

"Yes, it's like a stick, I guess. To help me get an idea of whether there are obstacles in front of me."

I paused, mid-step. "Hold out your hand for me."

She immediately did as she was asked, so trusting and sweet. I formed a shadow baton in my hand the way we always did for combat training, and shaped it to be a little longer so Iris could easily reach the ground with it. It wasn't as solid as a stick, but I funneled enough power into it that it was solid and would reverberate if she struck something with it.

It really seemed like the least I could do. After all, it was thanks to Iris that I was feeling so energized this morning.

If I'd fed so well based on just licking her pussy, I couldn't imagine how much power knotting would fuel me with. I shuddered as I closed the gap between us, depositing the makeshift cane into her hand.

Do not think about knotting.

"What is this?" Iris asked, her fingers closing around it as she tested the weight in her hand. "It's so light."

"It's an extended version of the shadow batons we use for training. Try it—you should be able to feel it if you tap it on the ground."

She carefully adjusted her hold on it before tapping it on the ground. It didn't make a noise, but her eyebrows shot up as she felt the sensation.

"Unfortunately, it requires proximity. It'll disappear if I'm not nearby," I added apologetically. "Perhaps it will do as a temporary solution, though? Until Astrid can source you a proper one?"

"It's amazing. *Thank you.*" Iris tapped the ground again, tentatively making her way toward me. I stayed in place as she gently knocked the side of my foot, just so she could get an idea of what an obstacle felt like. "Is that you?" she asked.

"It is."

"Oh good." I caught her just in time as she threw herself into my arms, laughing as I scooped her off the ground and carried her to the small dining table.

Iris pressed her lips to my collarbone, clinging onto me tightly. "That is the most thoughtful thing anyone has ever done for me. Thank you, Damen."

That settled it. I was just going to have to do more thoughtful things. That couldn't be the best that Iris had ever experienced—it was unacceptable.

I dished up her food, explaining where everything was on the plate, before serving Tilly and then myself.

"Ophelia was telling me about the instrument you played in the human realm," I said, pouring us both tea. "It sounds very impressive. I don't think we have anything like that here."

Iris's lips twitched. "I don't think harps are very common in the human realm anymore either. It was already sitting in the attic when we moved in. We had a video player—I don't really know how to explain it, honestly. But Nana found harp video lessons that I listened to over and over again for years. My technique is probably terrible, but I found it very soothing."

She said it so nonchalantly, like it was nothing impressive at all.

"That's so amazing, Iris. I'm not sure you realize how incredible you are. I don't tell you enough how incredible you are. I'm going to work on that."

"You really don't have to," she said, her face coloring as red as Ophelia's hair. It was quite delightful. As was her scent—which was a sweet mixture of joy and what I assumed was embarrassment.

"I think I do. Have you had many people in your life praising your accomplishments?" She shook her head. "Then I'm going to be the first—or at least, the loudest. I can tell you, it's very rewarding. I'm praised constantly for doing very little, and I enjoy it immensely."

Iris laughed. "You're just modest. You probably have a list of accomplishments a mile long."

There wasn't a trace of dishonesty in her face. She wasn't hinting at anything, or trying to discreetly push me into being a specific model of Shade or prince that she had in her mind.

It was a little unsettling to realize, but Iris might have just... believed in me. Exactly as I was.

There was a knock on the door, making us pause our meals.

"Who is it?" I called, wiping my hands on a napkin.

"It's Soren. Are you up? You didn't come to breakfast."

Iris immediately looked worried. "Oh no, did you have plans already?" she whispered. "I'm sorry, I didn't mean to interrupt them—"

"I asked you to stay for breakfast," I reminded Iris gently, giving her hand a quick squeeze. "And I didn't miss anything important. Do you mind if Soren comes in? I can go outside and speak to him if you'd prefer."

"Oh no, that's okay. I don't mind."

Good. I didn't say it because I wasn't entirely proud of the thought, but I wanted someone to see Iris in my space. To see us together. I wanted some kind of external validation that we were... involved.

Or whatever it was that we were.

"Come in!" I called.

He threw open the door impatiently, marching in clearly ready to complain about me skipping breakfast before stopping and observing us in silence for a moment. "Sorry to interrupt."

"Hi Soren," Iris said shyly.

"Hello Iris."

Tilly trotted over and flopped down at his feet, immediately rolling onto her back and exposing her belly.

I didn't know what that symbolized but it felt vaguely traitorous of her. Was I not the one who was constantly feeding her meat?

Soren lazily flicked a few tendrils of shadows from his fingertips to rub Tilly's belly, making her tongue loll out happily, and I felt even more betrayed.

Later, I was going to give her the best belly rubs ever so she remembered that I was her favorite Shade.

"Tallulah sent a message to you at breakfast," Soren told me. "She said Sebastian will be bringing Harlow Miles along to today's meeting, and wanted to verify that you would be in attendance again."

He sounded surprised by that. Apparently he wasn't going to talk me up at all in front of Iris and impress her with my newfound diplomatic skills.

"Of course," I replied. "It's starting soon, I think. I should probably head that way."

"I can head down to the nursery," Iris volunteered, pushing her plate away.

"Finish eating first," I instructed, not wanting to rush her. "And you don't have to. You could come with me? As you pointed out, we've made a lot of decisions for you in who you meet and interact with, and that wasn't fair of us. Of me. And I think it would be valuable for Harlow to meet you."

"I'd like to meet her too," Iris agreed with a gentle smile. "And the new arrivals in Elverston House. I'm a little nervous about meeting them, but I think I should."

I looked at Soren, who nodded slowly, looking at me as though I'd grown another set of horns. "I'll see if any of them are interested in coming up to the palace for a visit. I believe Jade has been working her way up to it."

That seemed to be as good of a starting point as any. Jade was the ringleader of the newbies.

Soren excused himself, and I took a few moments to get ready while Iris finished her meal.

It felt... *easy*. Having Iris in my space felt like the easiest thing in the world. It felt like she belonged here.

We were friends. She understood me. I liked to think that I understood her. There was a *connection* between us, and the physical chemistry had been undeniable.

I straightened my spine, looking at myself in the mirror. I'd moved too quickly by proposing, I understood that now. But maybe that was the beginning of our path instead of the end of it.

Maybe, in time, there would be a second chance for us.

Maybe, I could figure out how to get Iris to fall in love with me.

IRIS

CHAPTER 19

Damen walked next to me as we made our way to the meeting room, with Tilly on my other side, but I insisted on using my new shadow cane to navigate as best I could by myself.

I wanted to stay glued to Damen's side forever so the shadows would never dissipate.

And maybe for some other reasons too.

The events of last night kept replaying in my mind, and I had to force myself to think about *anything* else so that my scent didn't give me away. I'm not sure I would have minded it if only Damen could pick up on my desire, but the idea that every Shade I walked past could smell when I was aroused was a slightly mortifying prospect.

Fortunately, I had a lifetime's worth of experience in masking my emotions.

"Are you sure Tallulah won't mind that I'm here?" I asked Damen, fidgeting a little with the itchy fabric of the skirt I was wearing from yesterday.

"I'm confident. Do you like that outfit? You seem uncomfortable."

I forced myself to stop fidgeting, not wanting to seem ungrateful for the clothes I'd been given. "Sorry."

"Iris," he sighed affectionately. "Stop apologizing. If you don't like it, we can get you some different clothes. We should have already—those are all Verity's things, aren't they?"

"How could you tell?" There was an odd, unpleasant sensation in my gut that might have been jealousy.

"The color. Verity only wears pink."

Oh, right. That made me feel a little better. What was I jealous about anyway? Verity was happily mated to Damen's brother, from what I could recall. I hadn't actually met him yet. Or if I had, he hadn't said anything. I had heard such mixed things about Theon from everyone, I had no idea what to make of him.

"We're here," Damen said unnecessarily, because Tallulah's squeal of excitement had already alerted me to her presence.

"Are you a hugger?" Tallulah asked.

"I'm not sure. We could try?"

I laughed as she pulled me into a firm hug. The only person I'd hugged for comparison was Damen. Tallulah was a lot softer, and her hair tickled my nose.

It was probably inappropriate of me to notice, but her breasts seemed to be a lot bigger than mine. Were mine abnormally small? I'd never been self-conscious about them before but I might start now.

"I'm so glad you could join us. Iris, you've already met Sebastian in passing—he's here today, and my mate Evrin is here too. I'd like to introduce you to Harlow Miles. She's been our contact in the human realm for a while now, and she's stepped in as interim leader at the Hunters Council."

"Hello," I said politely, expecting a Hunter vaguely in the image of my mother to be standing in front of me.

"Hey."

She certainly didn't *sound* like my mother.

"Let's go sit down, shall we?" Tallulah said cheerfully.

Damen rested a hand on the small of my back, gently guiding me into the room and into a seat, managing to help me into it in a way that felt entirely natural and gentlemanly. It wasn't that I was opposed to accepting help or didn't think that I sometimes needed it, but Nana's insistence that I should be more than capable of doing everything on my own was a difficult lesson to unlearn.

"I was hoping we could start off today with a bit of a catch-up on what's been happening in the human realm," Tallulah began. "The king and queen really wanted to be here for this conversation, but sadly, they had commitments in other parts of the realm today. King Allerick sends his assurances that both myself and Prince Damen are fully capable of acting in his stead in this regard."

Damen jolted slightly next to me, as though the words were a surprise to him. I couldn't understand why they would be—Damen who was nothing but thoughtful and patient and the first to lend a hand, seemed as though he could be trusted with anything.

"Cool," Harlow said easily. I really wanted to ask Damen how old she was because she sounded *very* young, but I wasn't sure I could do it without anyone else overhearing. "Basically, a few of us have sort of taken over when the old guard went to jail. As I'm sure you're all aware, there are regional councils— we're just one. However, we're the most influential one since we won the bid to handle the Shade negotiations. Obviously, there's been a lot of pressure from the other councils who are trying to swoop in and take over because they don't like the direction we're going in. Sebastian has been doing a great job at holding his ground on that front—he's been offered millions of dollars to go and work for some of them."

"You have?" Tallulah asked, surprised. "And you're not interested?"

Sebastian cleared his throat. "I took on board what you said last time about being in a position to effect real change. That's not an opportunity that can be bought. Besides, I don't need millions of dollars in the shadow realm."

"Do you want to stay in the shadow realm?" Damen asked dubiously.

"Yes. Perhaps I haven't always done a good job at showing it, but I do really like it here." He cleared his throat nervously. "I'm actually seeing someone. I think she could be the one, you know?"

There was a long silence.

"...Cora?" Damen hedged.

"What?! No." Sebastian sounded appalled. "She's, like, nineteen. I'm not even sure she likes men? I'm dating a Shade. Cosima."

"That's amazing," Tallulah gushed. "So you're going to stay here?"

"If the option is available to me," Sebastian replied uncomfortably.

"I don't see why it wouldn't be." Damen stretched his arm over the back of my chair. "I don't think you'll be invited to any parties hosted by the Duke and Duchess of Lindow, but other than that, I'm sure you'll fit in just fine."

"I can live with that," Sebastian agreed.

"So we're in agreement that if Hunters want to move here, they can?" Harlow confirmed.

"As long as they're respectful of our realm, sure," Damen replied. "It's probably best for them to do a test run of sorts the way Sebastian did to make sure they like it and they get along with everyone. But yes. We'd like to fuel the power stores... that way. Rather than the old ways."

"In Elverston House," Tallulah added. "Where Meera and Verner are acting as dorm parents of sorts."

"That seems reasonable," Harlow agreed. "Feeding is the big issue we need to come to an agreement on, though."

"Yes," Tallulah said. "While there's a preference to have more ex-Hunters in this realm to keep the energy stores filled... that way." She cleared her throat, and I could have sworn Damen snickered quietly next to me. "We appreciate that the likelihood of being fully self-sufficient is remote at this stage. It's a big realm, there are a lot of Shades to feed. They're going to need to be able to supplement by visiting the human realm."

And scaring humans.

I fidgeted a little, struggling with the morality of that notion having grown up being repeatedly told how awful it was.

"It would be our preference that Shades returned to the human realm to feed. At least some of the time," Harlow added.

"That's your preference?" I asked, surprised. I hadn't actually meant to speak—I didn't feel qualified to add anything of value to this conversation—but the words had come out unbidden.

"Sure," Harlow agreed. "Fear isn't inherently a bad thing. The kind of fear that Shades instill when they feed is like a warning bell in the back of your mind, reminding you to be aware of your surroundings, to assess your risks, to not be reckless. You'd be surprised at how eerie the effects are when that suddenly disappears from society overnight."

I hadn't thought about it that way. No—I hadn't been *taught* about it that way. The kind of fear Harlow was describing didn't sound that bad. The way Nana had described it, the human victims were writhing on the floor in agony, trapped in an endless loop of horror within their own heads.

"I appreciate how dangerous it is for you guys there, even if our region is a strict safety zone," Harlow was saying.

"Is that the intention?" Damen asked.

"Yes. I'd like to reassign the existing patrols for that purpose. To keep those who don't agree with our new policy out of our area."

"Because you can only make promises for your region," Damen surmised.

Harlow hummed. "Correct. Whatever agreement we come to is a pilot run of sorts. We're going to use it to demonstrate to other regions what is possible when we work together instead of against one another."

Sebastian cleared his throat. "We thought of it as the beginning of an alliance of sorts. One between us that, hopefully, more and more regional councils will join over time. We'd want you, Damen, and Tallulah to be involved, of course. And perhaps some other representatives of your choosing, as well as more from the Hunters side."

Damen leaned in close, his horn catching in my hair. "Do you think this is middle management? Verity says I have a very middle-management vibe."

I considered everything I knew about middle management from films and TV shows, trying to decide whether that was a flattering assessment or not. "I think that means you're good at talking."

Damen made a solemn noise of agreement. "I am excellent at that."

"Okay," Tallulah mused. "So, we're going to do this? Just us for now? A small but mighty test run."

Harlow laughed. It was a pleasant, raspy sound. "Why not? There's been endless talking. Endless agreements. *Broken* agreements. Let's actually *do* something. It feels small in the grand scheme of all the history between our kinds, but hopefully it's a gentle river that leads to a mighty ocean, you know?"

"Sure," Tallulah agreed, amused. "That's a nice way to think about it. Will you join us for dinner in the dining hall later, Harlow? Meet a few more of us?"

"I would love that. Lead by example and whatnot. I've totally cracked this management thing, right?"

Damen leaned in again to whisper in my ear. "Sebastian is trying so hard not to comment on that, his face is actually going a little purple."

I pressed my lips together to avoid laughing, while giving Damen's arm a gentle squeeze of gratitude because I appreciated him sharing that with me.

"Great," Tallulah was saying to Harlow. "We can show you around a little as well in the meantime. Visit Meera's vegetable garden, show you some of the self-sufficiency things we're doing. Iris, do you want to come with us?"

"Not this time—but thank you for the offer." It was very sweet of her to ask, but I was still in yesterday's itchy clothes, and I desperately wanted to get changed.

"I'll walk you back," Damen said cheerfully, sliding his hand into mine as we stood, careful not to catch my fingers with his claws. It was odd, but the gesture made me blush. Why did holding hands feel so intimate? We almost always linked arms when we were walking around the palace.

Somehow, this felt like a level beyond that, though.

"I hope that wasn't too boring for you?" Damen asked as we headed away from the group, Tilly in tow.

"No, not at all." I paused, trying to decide whether to be honest or to make an attempt at seeming normal. In the end, I settled on honesty. "Things that probably seem boring to you are all novelties to me. I've spent my life doing nothing, only experiencing *anything* vicariously through TV shows. It felt very exciting and important to be part of an official meeting."

"I can definitely take you to more of those. I'm going to make a list of places I want to take you," Damen declared. "Ranging from boring and mundane, to fancy balls. How does that sound?"

"Dreamy," I admitted.

"Want to go down to the kitchens and learn all about how they wash dishes for the whole court? It's a romantic proposition, I know. I'm really pulling out all the stops for you, Iris."

I laughed, giving his hand a gentle squeeze. "I know you're teasing, but I actually would find that very interesting."

He shrugged, the movement dragging my arm up and down with it. "Then, we'll go. Do you want to stop and change first though? You keep fidgeting with your skirt."

I wanted to melt into a puddle on the floor at how attentive he was.

"Yes, please."

"Okay. Quick conversation stop, though. There are a couple of people who look like they're waiting to meet you."

"Oh. Who?"

"Cora, who came to the shadow realm with Sebastian and her brother who we do not speak of, and Jade, the youngest and most intimidating of the most recent crop of ex-Hunters. As far as I know, this is her first trip inside the palace walls. Good morning, ladies. How are we today?" he said, turning his attention toward them as we approached.

"Good, thank you," one of them replied nervously. "I'm Cora. This is Jade. We wanted to say hi."

There was an awkward pause before Damen gave my hand a soft squeeze. "They're talking to you."

"Oh! Hi. Sorry. It's so nice to meet you both."

"It's nice to meet you," Jade replied. Her voice was a little deeper and more deadpan than Cora's was. "You're such an inspiration to all of us over at Elverston House."

"Me?"

"Absolutely. There are a few ex-Hunters at Elverston House with disabilities, and all of us were the lowest rung on the Hunter hierarchy for some reason or another. We were all sent here as sacrifices, and fortunately, it's turned out well for us, but you... You *left*. We've only heard about your story since we came here, but it's fucking badass."

I shook my head, laughing nervously. "You must have me confused with someone else. I did leave, but one of the Hunters helped me. He did all of the heavy lifting."

"He handled the logistics," Damen corrected swiftly. "Making the choice to walk away from the only life you'd ever known and into a different world by yourself is the badass-ness they're referring to."

"I believe the correct term is badassery," Jade corrected.

"Human languages are so nonsensical," Damen complained.

"Could I meet some of them?" I asked tentatively. "Maybe visit you guys sometime?"

I was struggling to make sense of Jade's words in my mind. I wasn't anything impressive. Lucas had been the one who'd made this happen.

Maybe they didn't know about my privileged upbringing and that I'd never been sent away like many of them undoubtedly were. They probably wouldn't like me after that.

"We would love that," Jade replied sincerely. "Let's make that happen, okay?"

"Okay," I agreed, staying quiet as everyone said their goodbyes.

Damen sighed dramatically, adjusting his hold on my hand so it was more secure. "Now everyone is going to start telling you how impressive you are, and it won't be special when I do it."

"It's still the most special when you do it," I assured him with a laugh.

"Don't ever forget it. As I'm sure you've figured out, I'm very selfish."

If Damen was selfish because he didn't want to be second in my affections, then I hoped he never changed.

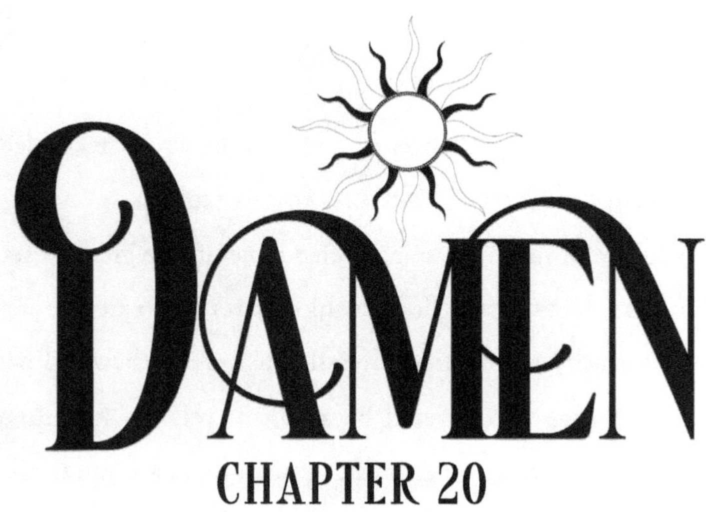

CHAPTER 20

I waited for Iris to dismiss me the moment we arrived back in her room, but she invited me in, suggesting that I sit while she washed up and found something to wear.

So... were we spending the day together? Was she in love with me yet?

I'd miscalculated last time, but I wasn't going to make that mistake again. The next time I proposed, the timing would be exactly right. I crossed the room to let Tilly out, pausing mid-step with my foot hovering over a cushion.

"Iris," I called. "Isn't this room horribly difficult for you to navigate?"

"Um," she replied from the washroom, her voice pitched a little higher than usual. "It took some getting used to, that's all."

Everyone who had been in this room and not offered to fix it was a wretched person-or-Shade, myself included.

"What can I do to make it easier for you? Surely, these floor cushions are a liability."

"They're not great," she admitted, voice muffled slightly—was she drying her face?

Was she naked in there?

No. Focus.

"Could you drag them over by the wall, maybe?" Iris added. "I don't want to lose them completely, they're very comfortable to sit on."

"Of course." I lifted the small coffee table off the ground, setting it up by a window, and dragging the floor cushions over to go around it. That way, she'd feel the warmth from outside when she sat here by the window.

The floor rugs were layered because this was the first floor and the ground was stone and cold to the touch. I pulled them around until they were in a single layer and less of a trip hazard. I didn't feel great about it still—I wanted them secured to the ground somehow. Even better would be *my* floors, which were smooth wood.

Could I suggest Iris move into my rooms instead? Was it too soon?

She emerged in loose trousers and a matching sweater—in pink, of course.

"More comfortable?"

Iris nodded. "I prefer loose, flowy dresses—maybe I'm just used to them because that's what Nana would always get for me. But these are comfortable too."

Loose, flowy dresses, I noted. I could make one of those out of shadows, but that was an enormous act of trust. Even more so for Iris, who wouldn't be able to see if the shadows disappeared.

"What did you think of Cora and Jade?" I asked.

"I liked them," Iris said enthusiastically. "They sounded quite young."

"Is that a good thing or a bad thing?"

"I wonder if I'll find them easier to relate to in some ways. When Meera or Tallulah talk about their jobs, or Tallulah talks about things that happened at college, I feel a little... behind, I suppose. Like I haven't done all the things that I was meant to do."

Iris said it like it was a mere observation instead of one of the most devastating sentences I'd ever heard. She was on a roll with those today. Not intentionally, of course. She was just relaying her experiences.

But the experiences had been terrible, and I needed to rectify them immediately.

"What would you like to do? I can make it happen. Do you want a job? You're already practically working in the nursery—we can arrange compensation—"

"Oh no, please don't. What would I even use money for? Unless I have to move somewhere else, I guess."

"You have a home here for as long as you want it," I said firmly. "You'll never *have* to leave the palace. And, of course, you will never need to pay anything to live here—no one else does—but you should have your own income. And you're giving so much time to the nursery, if you enjoy it and you'd like to keep doing it, it would be very easy to turn it into a job. But only if you wanted to," I stressed, not wanting to put any pressure on her.

"I quite like the idea," Iris said after a short pause. "If only to have that experience of *work* that I never got to have in the human realm. And I can't imagine anything else I'd rather do—spending time with the children is so rewarding. Thank you, Damen. That's really thoughtful of you."

It would have been more thoughtful if I'd thought of it sooner. Why hadn't I thought of it sooner? That's what I should have been doing instead of trying to find more productive uses for my time.

Then again, maybe I could do both. It would cut into the several hours I'd allocated for naps each day, but I could probably spare it.

"I'm afraid it's probably harder to replicate some other human-realm experiences. We do have a higher education facility, but from what I know of the human realm, it's very different from yours," I said regretfully, meeting Iris halfway as she came down the few steps into the main room and lightly touching her arm so she knew I was close.

The Itrodaris was basically a silent mausoleum where Shades drifted between stacks of books, never speaking or looking one another in the eye. I wouldn't wish it on anyone who got any modicum of enjoyment out of conversation.

Really, Allerick should have enjoyed it there a lot more than he did.

"That's okay," Iris reassured me, patting my arm. It wasn't a gesture anyone else had really done for me, and it had come to be very comforting for me. "I don't want to relive a life that I *could* have had. I just want to enjoy the life I have now."

"I intend to make sure of that."

"You already do, Damen. I don't know what I would've done here without you, do you know that?"

"You'd probably be fine," I replied, a little disheartened by that fact. Iris was brave and kind and resourceful, and she didn't need me at all. As demonstrated by the fact that we'd spent some time apart and she'd promptly made herself a beloved fixture at the nursery without any help from me.

"No, I don't think that's true at all. You were so unfailingly kind to me, right from the moment I got here. It really gave me faith that I'd made the right decision."

"You did." From what I knew of her life in the human realm, Iris had definitely made the right decision. "Shall we go learn about dishwashing and other miscellaneous palace administration before dinner in the dining hall? It can be a day of the most mundane exploring you can imagine."

"Promise?" Iris laughed.

"I promise. But let me tell you about the changes I've made to your room first. How strongly do you feel about those drapes around your bed? They seem like an obstacle you could do without."

Iris's scent sweetened into something so perfect, I wished I could bottle it and keep it forever.

Better yet, I'd keep the source.

We successfully toured much of the palace before my brother rudely summoned me to report back on how the meeting had gone. Iris assured me that she wanted to visit Meera after their awkward conversation yesterday, and we parted ways for—at most—an hour before dinner.

It really seemed like a wholly unreasonable amount of time to be apart, though, perhaps the worst part was that I doubted Iris had really noticed my absence.

In any other romantic endeavor, it would have been an absolute deal breaker that I liked them more than they liked me. My ego wouldn't be able to take the blow.

I found I didn't mind following Iris around like a lovesick fool, though. She never made me feel bad about it.

"Damen," Ruvyn called, slipping through the crowd to catch up with me in the entry hall as I filed in for dinner with the rest of the court. "You're not going to dine at the high table tonight?"

No, my future wife isn't sitting up there yet.

"Not tonight. We have a special guest from the human realm joining us. Usually, she'd sit up at the top table, but I suspect Harlow would find that to be a miserable experience. Why don't you come and sit with me and the ex-Hunters?" I asked. "I wasn't expecting to see you back at the palace so soon."

"We did say the next time we saw each other would be when you visited me," Ruvyn remarked dryly. "But we both know that will never happen."

A feeling I wasn't accustomed to settled into my gut. It might have been guilt.

"I'll visit," I promised, wondering if Iris would like to join me. If it was anywhere else, I assume she'd want to just for the experience, but I wasn't sure how she'd feel about the silence at The Itrodaris. Sound meant even more to her than it meant to others.

"It's okay," he replied easily. "There's no rush. In all honesty, I came back here purely for my own curiosity. I want to spend more time with the ex-Hunters. My recent findings about them have been… intriguing, to say the least."

"Have they? Perhaps you should present them at court. We've got the bones of a plan in place now for relations between the shadow realm and the human realm going forward. It might be a good time to understand a little better what that relationship was in the past."

"Present my findings?" Ruvyn asked, surprised. "No one has ever asked me to do that before. Not at court, at least. Usually we all just present our findings to each other at The Itrodaris."

"Is it something you're interested in?"

"Well, yes. Of course—it would be an honor."

"I'll see what I can arrange then," I replied absently, mulling over some options.

"You will?" Ruvyn asked.

I glanced at him. "The doubt in your voice is incredibly bad for my ego."

"It's just not really your thing, you know. Arranging stuff. Especially unprompted."

I opened my mouth to object but closed it again, realizing I couldn't.

"It's nice," Ruvyn commented. "You're really coming into your own, Damen."

Why, yes. Yes, I was.

Iris was already seated with Meera, and I gestured for Ruvyn to follow me over to their table. Harlow was sitting on Meera's other side, and Ruvyn and I took the bench opposite next to Tallulah and Evrin while Meera whispered in Iris's ear.

"Hi, Damen," Iris said immediately, smiling in my direction.

"Hi, Iris," I replied softly, pressing my leg against hers under the table. She immediately moved her other leg in close, intertwining them. "My friend, Ruvyn, is here. He's visiting from The Itrodaris—that education institute I was telling you about. Ruvyn, this is Iris, Meera, Tallulah, and Harlow. You've probably encountered Evrin in the in-between, no? Harlow here is our human-realm guest."

"Nice to meet you," he said gruffly. I'd forgotten how uncomfortable he was when talking to others. Ruvyn was great company, but he took a while to warm up.

"Where's Verner?" I asked Meera, glancing around the room.

"He's gone to Lindow to try and convince Theon and Verity to join us for dinner. Judging by how long he's been gone, I'm guessing Theon is hesitant to come along."

I frowned. "That was an entirely unreasonable mission to send Verner on. I should have gone—I'm excellent at cajoling Theon into pretending he doesn't actively despise everyone."

"How did your meeting with your brother go?" Iris asked, beaming at me from across the table. Was she as happy to be reunited as I was? I wished I was sitting closer. Beneath her, would be ideal.

"Oh, fine. He was happy to hear about the progress we'd made this afternoon and how the plans are coming along. Harlow, it would probably be useful to meet him after dinner."

"Coming into your own," Ruvyn repeated under his breath, sounding impressed.

"It's kind of intimidating, you know," Harlow remarked. "Meeting royalty."

"I'm royalty. You don't seem very intimidated by me."

"Is your brother like you?" Harlow asked.

I snorted. "No, not at all."

Harlow looked around the room. "Everyone here is, like, fancy, right?" Her gaze fixed on Ruvyn. "Are you a Shade duke or something?"

"I'm not a duke." He frowned. "I'm a scholar. My brother is the duke."

Her eyes widened slightly. "I was joking. Are you guys still running the feudalism OS here?"

"I don't know what that means," I admitted.

"Neither do I," Meera said, her lips twitching slightly as she looked at Harlow.

Ruvyn cleared his throat. "The shadow realm more closely mirrors the human realm at one point in your history, but we didn't have the wars and revolutions the human realm had, which tend to overhaul society at a more rapid rate. Change here happens slowly, though it's faster now than it ever has been."

I stared at Ruvyn, wondering if I'd ever heard him speak so much.

"But there must have been some level of change in the realm when the Hunt*ed* left," Harlow pointed out, leaning forward and looking intently at Ruvyn. I expected him to shy away from such direct conversation, but he was staring right back.

"It appears that much of that information—the whats and whys of their leaving—was scrubbed from the historical record. We can only speculate why."

"And what do you speculate, scholar?" Harlow asked, blinking up at him.

Were they...

Were they flirting?

Was I witnessing a strange, intellectual, and very public form of foreplay?

Iris had her lips pressed tightly together as though she was trying not to smile, her head tilted to one side to listen. Meera was glancing between Harlow and Ruvyn with every word spoken.

"I theorize that our Shade ancestors expunged the records out of shame. Because they looked back on that sordid part of that history and regretted their actions. Though, in trying to hide what they'd done, they only made life more difficult for their descendants to achieve any kind of reconciliation."

"And what about their descendants?" Harlow pressed. "What about Shades now? Have they learned from their ancestors' mistakes?"

"I am confident that Shades now would treat the descendants of those

Hunted *very* well," Ruvyn replied smoothly. The faint scent of desire drifted across the table, making Ruvyn straighten while I did my best not to inhale any of it. Only Iris's desire smelled appealing to me.

"Damen," Iris whispered, leaning across the table. "Tilly is getting restless. Would you mind walking me out—"

"Of course not." I jumped to my feet, immediately striding around the table to her. Somehow, this history lesson had turned into a conversation that felt inappropriate for me to be part of, and I usually reveled in inappropriateness. Maybe it was just that I knew Ruvyn was lonely, and if there was even a slim chance of him and Harlow connecting, I didn't want to get in the way of that.

"Thanks, guys," Meera muttered, shooting me an unimpressed look as I ushered Tilly out from under the table.

I gave her what I hoped was an apologetic smile. "I'll tell Verner to hurry up if we run into him."

Iris tucked her hand into the crook of my arm so easily it felt like it was meant to be there, holding on to Tilly with the other as we made our way out of the dining hall.

I'd sort of assumed that Iris also just wanted an excuse to escape the awkwardness, but Tilly was actually restless. The moment we were on the palace steps, Iris let her go and she shot into the garden, peering at us through a gap in the bushes as she did her business.

"Poor girl," Iris said guiltily. "We were inside a lot this afternoon. I didn't give her a break."

"I should have thought about it too. She seems fine now, though," I assured Iris. "Did you want to head back in? We can walk Tilly in the garden if you prefer. I can send for some dinner from the kitchens later."

"Are you sure? You don't want to join the others for dinner?"

"There will be plenty more dinners in the dining hall. One every night, in fact. I've barely missed any since childhood."

"Well, I'm sure Tilly and I would both appreciate a walk around the gardens, if it's not too much trouble."

"You're never any trouble, Iris," I assured her, inspiration striking me. "There's a covered walkway on the edge of the palace gardens with flowers that only bloom at night. The smell can be quite heady," I warned, though it was nothing compared to the scent of Iris's happiness.

"That sounds amazing, I'd love to go there. Thank you, Damen."

She was so effusive in her gratitude. It made me want to do better, to be better. To be more openly and enthusiastically grateful for all of the beauty and comfort in my life that I'd taken for granted.

"That was an interesting conversation at the table," I commented once we were in the privacy of the gardens. There were some members of the Guard on patrol, but they discreetly gave us space.

"Oh, yes. Harlow likes Ruvyn very much, I think."

"Yeah?" I glanced down at her, stupidly surprised at her astute observation. I should have known by now that Iris was always paying attention. "I think Ruvyn likes her too."

"That's sweet," Iris sighed, smiling to herself. I wished I could crawl inside her head and find out what she was thinking. "Have you ever been married before?"

That's what she was thinking about? I nearly choked on my own tongue. "No, never. I'm guessing you haven't?"

She laughed. "No, definitely not. I suppose I'm wondering how it all works here—how common it is. Giles wasn't my biological father, you know. Well, no, you don't know. I've never really talked about it."

I tightened my arm, pulling her in a little closer. "Did your father die?" I asked, thinking of the way Orabelle had taken me in after my mother died in childbirth.

"No, no. Well, not as far as I know. My blindness is due to a genetic condition—from what Nana told me, after my sight had already gotten really bad, my dad admitted that his brother had experienced the same thing. Moriah divorced him, feeling deceived, I guess. I don't know whether he wanted to take me with him or not, but Nana said Moriah wasn't willing to risk him telling people that she was my mother, so she kept me instead and sent him away. She's a Councilor, so she could do that kind of thing." Iris paused, tilting her head back thoughtfully. "'Nash' isn't really my last name, but I was never told any other, so I just started calling myself that in my head. The twins are much younger than me, born after Moriah eventually remarried."

What a horrible childhood Iris had been given. Made to feel like a dirty secret right from the very beginning, hidden away and ignored, and eventually replaced with children that her mother had wanted more.

"That's awful. I'm so sorry you went through that. Was Giles kind to you?" I asked, hoping that it was at least slightly less terrible than her mother.

"He wasn't cruel. He never came up to the attic, and seemed mostly content to just ignore my existence. I only heard from him when the twins would sneak up and he'd have to come and fetch them."

"Were they kind to you?"

Iris hesitated. "I didn't know any different then. At the time I would have probably said yes—that they were as kind as they could be, and that it wasn't their fault that I was such a burden on my family. Now, I'd say no," she added hastily before I could express my outrage at that response. "I suppose I still struggle to hold them entirely at fault for it. One thing I've learned from visiting with the little Shades in the nursery is that being afraid of anyone or anything that's different from yourself is a skill that can be both learned and unlearned. The twins were conditioned to hate me, and they did it very well. I feel sorry for them that their hearts are filled with so much anger."

"I feel like I want to murder them," I volunteered.

Iris's mouth turned down in a faintly disapproving way, but nothing in her scent indicated alarm. "I'd prefer you didn't do that."

"Then I won't," I sighed. "Your wish is my command."

Iris breathed deeply before spluttering slightly. "Are we at the night flowers? Wow, that is *strong*."

"It is," I laughed. "If you came here during the day, you wouldn't smell anything at all."

"That's so interesting," Iris murmured, breathing more shallowly this time as we stepped under the arched walkway where flowery vines bloomed overhead. "Will you describe it to me?"

"During the day, there are giant leaves overhead with large, heavy flower buds drooping down. Now, they have opened—the flowers are probably as big as your head. In the past they were gray, but since the ex-Hunters started moving here, color has returned to the realm. The one above us right now is red."

I swallowed tightly, feeling briefly overwhelmed. I couldn't have even imagined the shadow realm looking like this—so bright and abundant. It hadn't even been a possibility that we'd known to dream about.

"Is it strange for you to see all the color here now?" Iris asked perceptively.

"In a good way," I said hastily. "Sometimes, it feels quite surreal. The garden now looks very different from the garden of my childhood."

"What was it like growing up here?" Iris asked, inhaling deeply with each step, her head turning this way then that as she followed her nose.

"Good, I suppose?" I'd honestly never given the question much thought. I wasn't sure anyone had ever asked me before—it was very much assumed that growing up in the palace would be a comfortable experience.

"Did you attend the nursery?"

I laughed. "I wasn't supposed to. My father was a hard man—a much more difficult king than Allerick is. He didn't want us to mingle too much at court, he'd prefer we only associated with the *right* kinds of families. Soren and Allerick are close in age, so that worked out well for them. I mostly trailed around after them, begging for their attention. They seemed to alternate between being annoyed with me and extremely overprotective of me." Not much had changed on that front. "Occasionally, when I was feeling mischievous, I'd sneak into the nursery to play with the other children. I think Orabelle knew—she'd always whisk me away before my father realized where I'd gotten to."

"She's very sweet," Iris said. *Orabelle*? I doubted that she'd ever been described as *sweet* in her life. "Was she a sort of mother figure for you? I had Nana for that, I suppose. It wasn't quite the same. She wasn't very... nurturing."

It hurt my heart to think of a young Iris feeling so alone in the world, locked away where no one could see her.

"Orabelle isn't very... warm," I settled on, struggling to find the right word. "But she's fiercely caring. My father had many children by many different females, and none of them had an easy time of it. Some were cruel in their attempts to elevate their own children above the others. I don't blame them for it, that's the environment my father created. But I'm glad Orabelle wasn't like that. She took me under her shadows, and encouraged Allerick to spend time with me even though I was young and annoying."

Tilly sneezed loudly, looking up at me with the most forlorn expression I'd ever seen on her face.

"The smell might be a little potent for Tilly," I laughed, bending down to scratch her ears.

"Oh! Her nose is much more sensitive than mine. Shall we head back?" Iris asked, giving my arm a squeeze.

No. Let's stay out here forever. I can find a part of the garden that doesn't smell as strong for Tilly.

"Of course."

CHAPTER 21

I'm so excited you're here," Cora gushed as I stepped into Elverston House the next day. "Would it be horribly inappropriate of me to ask if I could hold your arm and bring you into the drawing room? The floors are super uneven."

"No, that's very helpful. Thank you."

Meera had brought me here, but had been waylaid in the garden by someone asking questions about the weeding. And I'd mostly come because I wanted to get to know Cora and Jade anyway. I'd never really had friends before, and I didn't know what the signs were for finding potential ones, but I just had a feeling where the two of them were concerned. Or maybe it was wishful thinking. Maybe it was my insecurities talking because I knew how far behind I was in life experience compared to Ophelia, Meera, and Tallulah, who were all closer to me in age.

I guess I wouldn't know unless I tried, though. I was going to make an honest go of befriending Cora and Jade.

The air was chillier in Elverston House, I noticed. And our words echoed a lot more—perhaps there were less soft furnishings in here to mute the sounds?

"We're in the middle of renovations right now," Cora was saying. "It's kind of a mess, but it'll be nice when it's done. Meera and Verner have been so amazing—they coordinate everything. All of the rooms that had been closed will be opened up so new Hunters can come and stay here when they arrive."

"Do you think you'll move here when the renovations are done?" Jade asked, startling me at how close she was standing. "It'll be less hazardous then."

"I think I'm pretty set up where I am," I said apologetically, not wanting to differentiate myself from them even more.

"That makes sense," Cora replied, gently guiding me to an armchair as Tilly came to a stop alongside it. "Meera mentioned you've been spending time in the nursery too. Easier to do that if you're only down a corridor rather than in a totally different building."

"So how come we've never heard of you?" Jade asked, skipping the small talk. "The Nash family is pretty famous."

"Well, yes. But I'm something of a liability," I pointed out gently.

"Right. But if anyone could get away with it, Moriah Nash could. Other famous families have kids who aren't Hunter material. Sometimes, like Austin Thibaut, they make them famous. Those rich families do whatever they want."

"That's not a great comparison," Cora said mildly. "The only thing that prevented Austin from a career in the Hunters was himself. He *could* have fit the mold, if he'd wanted to. No offense, Iris."

"None taken," I replied faintly.

"I guess so," Jade grumbled. "I'm sorry you had to be imprisoned in your mother's house, Iris. That must have sucked."

"I thought you might hold that against me," I admitted. "That I'd gotten to live at home. I know other exiled Hunters aren't so lucky."

"Was it a nice home life?" Cora asked, sounding doubtful.

"The group homes can suck," Jade added. "But we all had each other, you know? We were all in it together. The worst part was that we worked long as hell hours for pennies and were told we should be grateful to have a roof over our heads. It was exploitative as fuck."

"I didn't work. I just... stayed in the attic."

"All the time?" Jade asked, horrified.

"Sometimes, if we were certain no one was going to visit the house, I could walk the paths around the property with my nana and Tilly."

"Did you ever go anywhere else?" Cora pressed.

"Not until a spontaneous trip to Utah—my nana died, they didn't know what else to do with me. And then here."

They were quiet for a long moment.

"That sucks, dude," Jade said with a whistle. "I mean, the labor camp group home also sucked, but at least I got to have a gas station hot dog sometimes, you know? Break up the monotony."

"You must be so glad you came here," Cora added.

"Oh, absolutely. It was the best decision I ever made," I said decisively. "How about the two of you?"

Cora laughed. "I never had any doubts that it would be a good choice."

"I was sent here as a human sacrifice, but it's all worked out in the end," Jade deadpanned. "I like it a lot more here than the human realm."

"This might be a little forward of me to bring up since we just met, Iris, but oh my gosh. The way the prince looks at you." Cora sighed dreamily. "It's the talk of the court."

"How does he look at me?"

"Like you're his center of gravity. Like the sun rises and sets with you. Like nothing in the world matters but your happiness. If my future Shade wife doesn't look at me like that, I don't want her. Right, Jade?"

"I'd prefer a husband," Jade replied, her tone giving nothing away while my heart seemed to be thudding out of my chest. "Despite my best efforts in the human realm, I remain chronically attracted to dick only. But right now, I'd prefer no one. Commitment is a horrifying concept."

I latched onto the idea of talking about their romantic lives rather than mine. I had no idea what I was doing, and I was increasingly worried that my behavior was unkind. Cruel, even. I'd already rejected Damen's marriage proposal. Was it wrong of me to continue the physical relationship we were developing?

"You shouldn't rush if it's not something you're interested in. Have you been... dating, Cora?" I asked, fumbling around for the word I wanted. It seemed like such a human concept, and I wasn't really sure what the norm was here.

"Courting," she corrected gently. "And no. When my brother was alive, he really hated the idea. And then he died and was, you know, a traitor or whatever and even the Shades who'd been kind of interested in me backed all the way off."

"Want me to talk to them?" Jade asked sharply. "Anyone who thinks you're anything like your brother is a fucking idiot, and I'll tell them that myself."

"That's really okay," Cora replied hastily. "You don't have to do that. I'm going to prove with my actions that I'm trustworthy, even if it takes a little longer to convince everyone. This is my home. I want to build a reputation that lasts."

"What if they never change their mind about you?" Jade asked, voice laced with suspicion.

In some respects, Jade reminded me of Nana. Nana had lived through incredibly hard times, and she'd always expected the worst. When I was young, I hadn't understood why she'd lash out over everything—even good things— but I got it a little more now. Even when something was good, she didn't expect it to last. She hurt *it* before *it* hurt her.

It hadn't made her easy to live with, but at least I understood.

"They will," Cora replied confidently. "If Astrid can turn things around, then I definitely can. And me proving myself will hopefully make it easier for new ex-Hunters who come to this realm with good intentions—even if their families didn't have the best track record. We set the example here, right? What we do *matters*. I want to be a good role model."

Both Jade and I were quiet, and I wondered if she was reflecting on Cora's words or if she was intimidated by them. I was somewhere between the two.

Perhaps it was just my ego talking, but I wanted to matter. I'd spent my entire life so far being invisible—I wanted the next few decades of my life to mean something. I wanted to make a difference in the lives of the children I interacted with in the nursery. I wanted them to see that it was okay that I was different from them. That different wasn't a bad thing.

I wanted to be truly a part of life at the palace, so that when new ex-Hunters came here, they saw what that could be like.

And I'd already started. It was a buoying feeling to realize that I was already building those foundations, and they had the potential to form something strong.

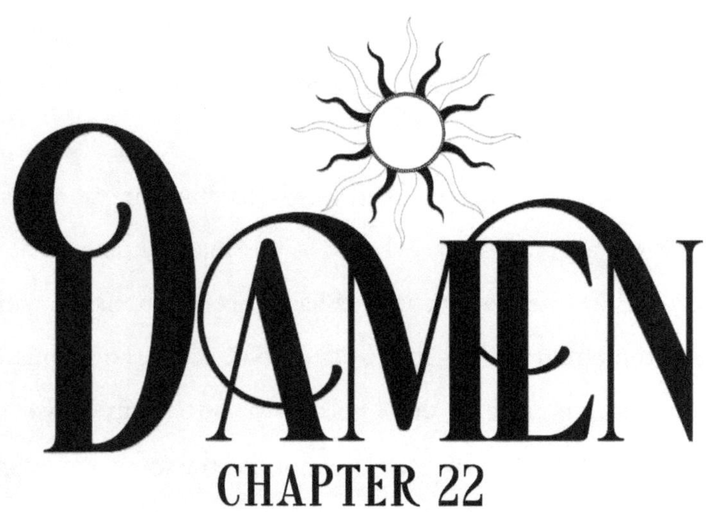

CHAPTER 22

Iris was in a strange mood when I went to collect her for dinner the following night—but strange in a good way. More settled and confident than usual, with her shoulders pushed back and her head held high. The last remnants of the strange color she'd added to her hair had washed out, and her natural bright, pale hair gleamed with a silvery sheen in the orb light.

Regal. Iris looked regal.

She'd have made a majestic princess, if that had been something she'd wanted.

Maybe someday. Don't give up hope.

"How was your day?" I asked, sitting on the end of her bed and rubbing Tilly's side as she trotted over to lean against my legs.

Iris paused in the middle of brushing her hair, pulling it all over one shoulder in a way that showcased the smooth column of her neck to perfect advantage. I scrunched my eyes shut, doing my best not to look. That was a temptation I didn't need.

"Illuminating," she said after a long moment. "Each day that passes, I dream a little bigger. I suppose, when you don't know what's possible, *everything* feels impossible. The more I learn what *could* be, the more tempting it is to reach for it. Does that make sense?"

"Perfect sense," I agreed, her words forcing me to assess my own complacency yet again. I knew what was possible. I knew what it was to have power—I'd been born into it. But had I been responsible with it? Had I considered the opportunities it provided? Not really. I'd dismissed that as Allerick's domain, and nothing that I needed to concern myself with.

"Damen?" Iris asked sweetly. I memorized the soft way that she said my name, wanting to replay it in my mind before I went to sleep each night.

"Yes, Iris?"

"You know that thing you did the other night with your tongue?"

I almost choked on said tongue, not having seen that question coming for even a moment.

"Yes," I rasped. "What about it?"

She chewed thoughtfully on her lower lip. "It was really fun."

This woman would be the death of me.

"It was, wasn't it?" I hesitated for a moment. "Would you like to do it again?"

"Only if you would. Or we could do something else that's, you know, fun."

"Do you have any requests?" My cock was so hard that somehow it was hard to talk. My dick was the only part of my anatomy that was functioning correctly right now.

"Well, no. I don't really know what the options are. I've never done any of this before, as you've probably figured out."

Was that a trap? Should I answer that?

"Why don't you lie back and let me take care of you?" I asked, an idea springing to mind. A very sensory idea that I thought she'd enjoy.

"Okay." There was no hesitation, no shyness. She stripped off her clothes as if it was the most natural thing in the world, and I closed the distance between us, savoring the feel of her naked skin under my palms as I scooped her up and carried her to the bed—now free of the heavy drapes. Not because I thought Iris couldn't get there on her own, but because I thought I'd die if I didn't touch her.

If Iris wasn't blind, I'd still be trying to get my hands all over her at any given opportunity if she'd let me. At least this way, I could pretend I was being polite and helpful at the same time.

I set her down on the bed and she propped herself up on her elbows, legs stretched out long.

"Iris," I rasped, drinking her in. She was so relaxed in my presence, and while everything about her was beautiful, that might have been the most beautiful thing. Iris was comfortable around me, and it was an honor I would continue to work every day to be worthy of, no matter what happened between us in the future.

"What is it?" she asked, her hair rippling like silk as she tilted her head to the side.

"You're like a dream."

Her face flushed the most divine shade of pink. "Does my body look very strange compared to yours?"

"Different, but not strange. You're very... delicate." I trailed my claw down her thigh, watching as her skin pebbled in my wake.

"And delightfully soft." My hand—enormous compared to hers—easily wrapped around the top of her thigh and I gave it a squeeze, admiring the gentle give of her flesh. Shades weren't built that way.

I shifted so that I could grab both of her legs, massaging them slightly as I worked my way down to her ankles. Iris's thighs parted slightly, her back arching as I took my time easing the tension in her muscles. Had she ever had a massage before? I had been remiss in not giving her one.

"So dainty," I murmured, tracing my claws over her feet. Iris giggled immediately, snatching them away.

"That's not fair. Are you ticklish?" she laughed.

"No," I replied, baffled, trying the gesture again but more softly this time.

"Stop! That's worse."

I stopped instantly, folding my hands in my lap. "I'm sorry. Does it hurt?"

"No, no, not at all. It tickles. It just makes me laugh."

"Your body is such a delight," I sighed, thrilled that I had discovered something new. "Does this tickle?"

I summoned two extra limbs made of shadows, directing them to twine around Iris's legs briefly before brushing against the soles of her feet.

She kicked out again with a surprised laugh. "Are those your shadows?"

"Yes. Do you like them?"

"Very much." She was quiet for a moment, her scent blooming into something sensual and intoxicating. "What else can they do?"

A shiver ran down my spine. "Anything I want them to do. Anything *you* want them to do."

"Will you keep... exploring me with them?"

My knot throbbed fiercely. "Tell me if I do anything you don't like."

"I will," Iris said, nodding her head eagerly.

I directed the shadow limbs back up her legs, teasing her inner thighs for a moment before sending them over her hipbones instead, lingering at her ribcage and only faintly brushing the underside of her breasts.

It wasn't much movement, I didn't want to push her too quickly while we were trying something new. Yet, it seemed to be providing more than enough stimulation. Iris writhed closer, whining slightly as I kept the tentacles just out of reach of wherever she wanted them to go.

Occasionally she'd rub her thighs together, trying to relieve some of the ache between them, before letting them fall open again and giving me a magnificent view of her glistening pussy. My mouth watered at the feast she was laying out for me, but I forced myself not to partake just yet. I wanted to savor this moment.

"Can you put your shadows inside me?" Iris asked. I nearly swallowed my tongue.

"Yes," I choked out. "Would you like that?"

"I can't get pregnant that way, right?"

I muffled a groan against my fist, imagining Iris round with my baby. "No, no. Not from a shadow tentacle. You need my cum for that."

"I wish I could have your cum," Iris sighed dreamily.

"It'll be all over your ankle in a minute if you don't stop talking like that," I growled, giving the base of my cock an aggressive squeeze—whether to help it along or stop myself from losing control, I couldn't quite decide.

She hummed thoughtfully. "That would be okay, wouldn't it?"

"Iris," I groaned, lying down on the bed between her legs, half draped over them, my hips thrusting lightly into the mattress of their own accord. I had a far better view of her pussy from here, which wasn't helping with my intention not to entirely humiliate myself. "Are you teasing me on purpose?"

"I think so, yes. Something about the idea of you losing control, of being absolutely desperate for me... It's very appealing."

"I *am* absolutely desperate for you. Always." I inhaled deeply, hoping I could embed the scent of Iris's desire deep within my soul and keep it there. "Now spread those thighs so I can fuck you with my shadows."

She did so with a faint whine, and I used my hands to push her ankles up, flattening her feet against the mattress.

"Look at you," I murmured, my gaze transfixed. "That pussy knows who it belongs to."

Iris made a muffled sound of agreement, wriggling down the bed, trying to get that aching, needy pussy a little closer to my face. I tutted at her impatience, using my hands like shackles on her ankles to hold her in place.

"Are you rushing me, princess?"

I hadn't meant to call her that. But I wasn't mad that I had.

"Yes," Iris complained. "Because you're taking so long."

"So greedy," I sighed in mock disappointment before kissing the inside of her knee so she'd know I wasn't serious. There wasn't a single thing on this earth Iris could do that would disappoint me. She owned me, body and soul.

My tentacles swirled around her nipples, tightening and releasing, and I formed a third one, letting that one brush between her thighs.

"Oh!" Iris startled before flopping back onto the mattress with a moan as I toyed with her clit. "You can make more?"

"As many as I like." Especially with her desire already feeding me, making it easy to wield my shadows. The power I got from her was like nothing I'd ever experienced before. "You're going to come for me like this first," I instructed, sending more power to the thin strand of shadow stimulating her clit, making it more solid. "If you want a tentacle in your pussy, you're going to have to earn it, princess."

She made a garbled response, already grinding down on my shadows as best she could with my hands pinning her ankles in place and another set of shadow limbs ruthlessly toying with her nipples.

Go slowly, I reminded myself. *Don't get carried away.*

Iris would look beautiful with my shadows crisscrossing her torso, pouring down her throat, collaring her neck…

Slowly.

Perhaps, someday, she would allow me that privilege. I couldn't bear the thought of it belonging to anyone else.

"Damen!" she gasped, digging her heels into the mattress as she came with a beautiful cry, writhing to get closer and farther away all at once. I was trying to be a more productive citizen, I really was, but the idea of spending every moment of my day in bed with Iris had a lot of appeal.

Bringing her pleasure sounded plenty productive to me.

"That's it, princess. Aren't you good? Are you going to spread those legs a little wider for me or do I have to make you?"

She paused for a moment, breathing heavily. "Make me."

My cock wept with precum, forming a wet patch on the bed beneath me. I wanted every drop of my cum inside Iris, but I managed to retain just enough of a hold on my sense to remember that I couldn't fuck her.

Two more tentacles appeared, wrapping around Iris's thighs just above her knees and pushing her legs further apart. I let myself indulge in one quick taste, moving up the bed to slowly swipe my tongue through her flowing arousal, stopping at her clit and toying with it roughly with my tongue.

"Damen," Iris whined. "You said you'd fuck me if I came."

Whenever I thought I had the upper hand, she'd go and say something like that and I was lost. Had I ever heard Iris say *fuck* before? How was I meant to seem cool, calm, and collected now?

I couldn't even formulate the words to respond. I moved back so one tentacle could keep circling her clit, then sent another, thicker one to tease her slick entrance.

"Is this what you want?" I rasped.

"Yes. *Yes*. Please."

"Well, then. Let's see how well you take me."

Iris exhaled shakily as I pressed forward, taking my time and letting her body get used to me. Unfortunately, there was no sensation in my shadow limbs—I couldn't *feel* her cunt tightening around me. But it was certainly nice to see it, and to hear the exquisite sounds that Iris was making.

I paused for a moment. "How does that feel, princess?"

"Good," she whispered, arching her back and lifting her hips. "Different. I like it. Can you go in a little more?"

"Of course." I filled her a little more, thickening the tentacle so her pussy stretched tight around it.

"Oh yes," Iris moaned, fingers grabbing clumsily for the blanket beneath her. "That is *good*, Damen. I can't even imagine how good it would feel if it was your cock inside me instead."

"Minx," I chided affectionately, all but humping the bed now. "You wouldn't be able to speak in full sentences if my cock was inside you right now."

I focused on thrusting the tentacle in time to the rolling movements of Iris's hips, building up slowly, slowly, slowly. As of its own accord, my hand had wrapped around my cock, and I fisted my shaft roughly, staring at the pretty picture Iris made for me.

There was no way I was going to make it back to my room before I came this time.

"I'm going to come. It feels different this time," Iris whimpered. "There's a kind of pressure."

"Let it happen," I soothed, rubbing her thigh with my free hand. "Let go, Iris. I've got you."

She arched her back, mouth open on a silent scream before sucking in a desperate, greedy gasp of air.

"That's it," I encouraged raspily, entranced by the sight. "You're amazing, Iris. You're so beautiful. Fuck, you're incredible. *Fuck*. I'm going to come."

I didn't stand a chance. I finished all over my fist, moving my hand down to massage my swollen, achy knot.

Iris frowned. "I thought you were going to come on me?"

This woman was going to be the death of me.

This time, when I woke up next to Iris, it was with a sense of purpose.

She was deep asleep, and I quietly crept out of bed, letting Tilly outside and filling her water bowl before slipping out into the corridor and heading upstairs.

"Astrid," I called, jogging to catch up with her and Soren as they made their way to the breakfast room. "Can you procure me a pizza from the human realm?"

It was time to escalate things.

Iris *needed* to fall in love with me. It was imperative.

Astrid closed her eyes, exhaling heavily. It was an improvement on how she usually responded to anything I said—we appeared to be making progress.

"That is such an impractical request, Damen," she said eventually. "Why do you want a pizza? We have all the ingredients here—just make one. Or command someone to make it for you. I don't know how this works."

"No Shade will know how to do it," I pointed out. "And I want to surprise Iris. Do you think any of the ex-Hunters would know?"

Astrid shrugged, though my explanation seemed to have won her over at least a little. "Tallulah probably knows how to make dough."

"Right. I'll ask her then." I was slightly deflated by that idea, only because Tallulah didn't actually live at the palace anymore and I would have to wait for her to arrive. Could I visit their house and demand she come and make dough for me? Evrin probably wouldn't like that.

Astrid looked at me for a long moment. "Or Ophelia might be able to help you, I guess. She can cook."

"Perfect!" I brightened immediately, leading the way to the breakfast room where my sister-in-law was stirring a cup of tea.

"Sister, I require your services this morning. Will you help me make a pizza for Iris?"

"Um, sure. I mean, I guess we have all the ingredients, right?" She looked at Astrid for confirmation. "Meera's tomato plants have done really well, I'm sure I could make a sauce."

"Do you know how to do that?" Astrid asked dubiously.

"How hard can it be? Mash the tomatoes up until they're a saucy consistency. I'm sure I can figure it out."

Perhaps this wasn't a good idea. Maybe I should have insisted Astrid go to the human realm and purchase one.

"This is all sounding very romantic," Ophelia added enthusiastically. "Are you wooing Iris now? She deserves to be wooed."

Was that what I was doing?

"She doesn't want to marry me," I pointed out.

"She didn't want to marry you *then*. You did ask very early on," Ophelia chided gently. "Iris had an even steeper learning curve than the rest of us in adjusting to life here. Once she's had time to find a new normal, who knows what she'll want to do?"

I grunted in agreement, wanting this conversation to end. Everyone was staring at me and this wasn't the kind of attention I enjoyed. I liked when everyone was laughing at my jokes, not giving me vaguely pitying looks as they remembered that time I proposed and she said no.

The fact that Soren and Astrid didn't look at all surprised by this news just added insult to injury. Now everyone knew about my failed proposal.

"Can we get started now? I want to make Iris breakfast."

Ophelia suppressed a smile. "It's not really a breakfast food. Then again, roasted meat isn't either and I've gotten accustomed to that, so why not?"

Allerick frowned as she stood. "I was hoping we could discuss what the mood around court is after the negotiations yesterday. I know some of the information has already leaked."

"No secrets at court." I shrugged. It had been that way our whole life.

"There are some concerns," Soren admitted, piling food onto Astrid's plate. "Mostly around placing our trust in the hands of Hunters to both keep their word and to patrol the area while we feed. Understandable concerns."

"Have you heard anything that worries you?" Allerick asked him.

Soren shook his head. "No, I don't think so. If this was a few months ago—when Ophelia first arrived here—then yes, I would have been concerned about the rebels using this information as justification for further violence. But, for the most part, the ex-Hunters are a fixture here now. Certainly at court, and increasingly in the wider realm. The energy stores have been decreasing, yes, but at a vastly slower rate thanks to them. And they've all made a concerted effort to adapt to life here. There's a level of trust now that makes this plan feasible."

"Great, sounds wonderful," I interjected. "Can we go now? I want to make Iris's breakfast."

Allerick snorted. "Go on then. It's nice to see you out of sorts like this. I believe it's doing you wonders."

"I'm so glad you're enjoying it," I snarked, annoyed that I'd given him grief about his relationship too many times in the beginning to be offended that I was getting it back.

"Come on," Ophelia said affectionately, leading me out of the room. "Let's go pester Calix in the kitchen."

"I wouldn't be doing this if you weren't here," I admitted. "He's nicer to the ex-Hunters than he is to me."

"Calix? Oh, he's a big ol' softie. You're all so dramatic."

The softie in question flipped his carving knife in his hand like it was made of shadows as we walked in, impatience written all over his face.

"What do you want?"

"We're going to make a special human realm treat for Damen's lady love," Ophelia announced, clapping her hands together once and bouncing on the balls of her feet. "Can you spare us some bench space?"

"No."

Ophelia rolled her eyes. It was a very human gesture and it never failed to make a small shudder of revulsion run down my spine. Fortunately, Iris never did it.

"Caliiiiiix," she whined, dragging out his name. "Don't be mean. Levana would be so disappointed in you."

He gestured dismissively at a small patch of the counter, though I could have sworn he laughed as he turned away.

"Perfect. There's a small cupboard of ingredients that Astrid's collected up—let me grab what we need. Ooh, look there's already a tomato sauce here. I wonder if Tallulah made that. She mentioned that she was going to start preserving stuff."

"Do you know what you're doing?" I asked as Ophelia set down an assortment of unfamiliar ingredients on the bench, looking less certain of herself with each one.

"Sure, I do. I've made dough before. There was definitely flour and water involved. And yeast—we have that. I don't remember the exact amounts, but I can eyeball it."

"I have lost confidence in this venture," I told her solemnly.

"What's this you're making then?" Calix asked moodily, peering over her shoulder.

"It's like a soft flatbread," she explained. "To put toppings on."

He grunted, stomping off without another word. Such a charming fellow.

"This is flour," Ophelia explained, pouring a liberal amount of the white dust into a bowl. "And I guess I'll just like, tip some of the yeast on top…"

I should have just woken Iris up by licking her pussy. That would have been a far more romantic gesture.

"And then, um, I'll just add some water and mix it with my hands until it feels doughy. Yes! How hard can it be? They made dough in the olden days without stand mixers and internet recipes. I'm sure I can figure this out."

"Who are you trying to convince here?" I asked.

"Everyone within hearing distance," Ophelia assured me, slowly adding water to the bowl of white powder.

She worked in silence for a while, and it did seem to be making... something. It didn't look appetizing, but it definitely looked like...

Something.

"I don't think I got the yeast measurement right," Ophelia muttered.

"Here." We both jumped as Calix slammed an oval-shaped flatbread down in front of us. "Use this. I've been trialing different bread recipes."

"You just *had* this the whole time?" Ophelia asked, outraged.

I concurred fully, but I was too afraid of Calix to say anything.

"I wanted to see what you'd come up with," he replied with a rasping laugh before striding away.

"I'm telling Levana on you," Ophelia complained, shaking her head. "Okay. We've got a base. We've got sauce. There's definitely cheese in the ice pits, and Meera has basil in the garden. Let's do this."

Far later than I wanted to be, I made my way back to Iris's room with a tray of whatever this concoction was, regretting all of my decisions since the moment I'd woken up this morning. I could have stayed in bed with Iris. What was I thinking?

"Can I come in?" I asked, knocking on the door.

"Damen? Yes, of course."

"Is everything okay?" I asked, finding her sitting fully dressed on the bed, gnawing a little nervously on her lip while Tilly snoozed at the end of it.

"It's fine. I'm fine. I'm glad you came back."

I paused for a moment. "Did you think I wouldn't?"

"I don't know. I wasn't sure. You weren't here when I woke up…"

"Oh, princess, I'm so sorry. I wanted to surprise you with a… gesture. It was an incredibly bad idea in hindsight. I don't think anyone should let me have ideas, in all honesty."

Her scent and expression brightened immediately, and I vowed never to leave her asleep and alone again.

"You wanted to surprise me? What's that smell?" Iris asked, her nose twitching in the most enchanting way as she turned her head from one side to the other.

"I made you pizza."

"You *made* it?"

"With Ophelia's help," I amended. "In truth, it looks extremely unappetizing to me. There isn't even any meat on it. I'm not quite sure what the purpose of this dish is, but I'm hoping it will bring you some joy."

Iris laughed. "Okay, okay, let me try it. It smells like it's going to bring me joy. What did you put on it?"

"Ophelia said to tell you it's a Margarita pizza because those were the ingredients we had. But also that it isn't a Margarita pizza because she didn't have the right cheese."

"Well, I've never tried one of those, so even better."

I helped Iris get comfortable at the small dining table in her room before sliding the tray with the entire pizza on it in front of her. As much as I wanted to make Iris happy, I would not be putting the strange, floppy meat-free creation in my mouth.

She felt around for the edges, gingerly picking up a piece and lifting it to her mouth for a bite. It was probably a good thing she didn't know how blatantly I stared at her—I couldn't look away. Her bright, blunt teeth were so dainty and charming. And her face was so soft and expressive—sometimes in ways that I wasn't entirely sure she was aware of.

If Iris didn't like the pizza, I was fairly confident I would know instantly based on the look on her face.

She nibbled on it tentatively before relaxing and taking a bigger bite, giving me a smile that didn't entirely convince me that she was enjoying it. "Thank you, Damen. It's very good."

"Are you absolutely sure? It doesn't look good."

Iris pressed her lips together, trying not to laugh. "It really is! The texture is a little different from what I had last time, but I'm guessing we don't have all the same ingredients here. I do really like it—won't you try some?"

"Absolutely not. I have a plate of roasted meat here—wouldn't you prefer that?"

She shook her head, still hiding a smile. "No, thank you. I'm glad you're eating too, though. Have you had a busy morning?"

"Pizza making was my whole morning," I admitted, which didn't sound very impressive on reflection, given how sad the creation on her plate looked. "Do you have plans for today? I was going to visit my brother Theon. You could come along, if you wanted to?"

Her scent sweetened into something so syrupy I felt like I could taste it. "You'd take me along to meet your brother?"

"Of course."

"That means a lot to me, Damen. To just... not be hidden away. That means a lot, thank you."

"Of course," I replied slowly, a small glimmer of hope bubbling in my chest. Maybe Ophelia was right. Maybe there was a chance that Iris would be mine someday.

"While you were pizza making, Yara stopped by and asked if I could help in the nursery later since Alyndra had to visit home," she said, looking faintly guilty about making plans.

"Good," I said firmly. "I'm glad they're seeing you as a reliable source of help, that's amazing. My brother isn't going anywhere—he barely leaves Lindow. You can accompany me another time if you want to."

The tension in Iris's shoulders eased immediately, a relaxed smile on her face. "I can't wait."

IRIS

CHAPTER 23

You must be Iris," a cool, elegant voice said as I stood up from the ground, brushing off my trousers at the end of the day. "I'm Oleta. Jonan's mother."

Ah.

Hopefully, my face was being cooperative and not giving away my lack of enthusiasm at meeting the Shade I'd heard so much about.

That wasn't kind of me.

Then again, based on what I'd heard of Oleta, she wasn't particularly kind either.

"Jonan talks about you nonstop, you know," she continued, not waiting for an answer. "He's very enamored with you."

"He's a wonderful child."

Oleta was quiet for a moment. "I suppose. He's very chatty."

She said this like she wasn't wholly convinced it was a good thing.

"He's very enthusiastic and always willing to try new things. He's really enjoyed the knitting we've been doing—he even taught Orabelle how to do it."

"I didn't realize he'd spoken to her directly," Oleta replied in hushed tones.

"Oh yes. Jonan was really the only child she interacted with while she was here."

"I see. And the king's mother was, er, interested in what you were doing? This... knitting thing?"

"Orabelle is a friend of mine," I assured her.

"Right. Interesting. I didn't know that. And there are some... whispers that you and Prince Damen are courting?"

I let the silence linger just long enough to be uncomfortable—a trick I'd learned from Moriah. "I'm sorry, what does that have to do with Jonan?"

"Nothing, nothing," she said hastily. "I'm just being curious, that's all. Jonan talks about you so much, and all of your... quirks. And now I hear that you're connecting with all kinds of influential Shades at court. One doesn't know what to think."

Ah, I think I got it now. Based on what she knew about me from Jonan, she wanted to dismiss me as beneath her notice. But because of the friendships I'd formed, she was worried that might not be in her best interests.

"I suppose you'll have to make up your own mind," I replied sweetly as Jonan came bounding across the room, relaying his day at the top of his lungs to his mother.

I didn't think I was quick to anger—or even annoyance—but this conversation had me feeling distinctly negative.

The two of them left, the nursery clearing out for the day as parents came by to collect their children. Eadlin's parents were nearly as quiet as she was, but they were very pleasant to be around. I could see where she'd gotten her sweetness from.

"Thank you so much for helping today, Iris," Yara said, moving around me as she collected up wooden blocks. "The prince mentioned that you might be interested in working here on a more permanent basis? As an actual employee?"

When had Damen even found the time to say something? The way he prioritized the things I said and actually tried to make them happen made my chest ache in a good kind of way. If I thought too much about the pizza he'd made me, I'd burst into tears.

It hadn't actually tasted very good, but it was just so *thoughtful*.

"Only if that's okay," I replied hesitantly. "I appreciate that I don't have formal work experience or training or anything."

"None of us did when we started. We've just learned along the way and you will too," Yara reassured me. I could hear the smile in her voice, and it was a very soothing sound. "The children adore you, they'll be so happy to hear you're sticking around. And you've really added something special to the nursery, you know. This might be treasonous of me to say, but I was *sad* when the queen's schedule got busier and she couldn't visit very often anymore. I'd have been devastated if it was you."

I hurriedly swiped away a rogue tear, embarrassed that I was getting weepy over her words. It was just so nice to be... *wanted*.

"Though that might still happen," Yara added affectionately. "It seems to me like you might be on your way to becoming a princess, in which case your schedule will undoubtedly pick up."

"Oh." I laughed awkwardly. "I don't know about that. But regardless, I *want* to be here. I'd never give this up."

"Good. Are you heading straight to dinner in the dining hall? I can walk you there if you like. I don't eat here myself—the king has said I'm welcome to, but I prefer to return home to my family."

She told me about about her much younger brother as we headed down to the dining hall, and the aging father who lived with her and spent his days gardening.

"You should come visit," Yara suggested shyly. "It's not as grand as the palace, of course. It's just a small home—"

"I would love to visit, Yara. Thank you. That's such a kind offer."

"It would be my pleasure. My family has already heard so much about you—they'd love to meet you. Anyway, I'll leave you here now. The prince is heading your way."

Oh good. I'd missed him today, which seemed silly since we'd spent so much time together recently. It just never quite felt like enough.

Yara laughed. "I don't need to ask if you're happy to hear that—your scent gives you away. Have a nice evening, Iris."

"You too," I replied, my face hot.

"You're delightfully red today," Damen said, gently touching my cheek with his knuckle. We were surrounded by Shades in the busy corridor, and I was surprised that he was touching my face so easily in front of the crowd. Pleasantly surprised.

It felt territorial in a way I didn't hate.

"How was your day?" I asked, not wanting to explain *why* I was red in the face.

"Fine." Damen took my hand, though I felt him bend down to greet Tilly, quietly cooing at how pretty she was. My heart could barely take it. "Theon complained about my presence, but he'd complain if I didn't visit too, so I'm not worried. Oh, and I have more clothes for you—one of the staff delivered them to your room."

"For me?"

"Yes. I mentioned to Verity that you had a penchant for flowy dresses and she had an abundance of spare ones on hand. Don't feel guilty—I can see it on your face. She has a whole room devoted to clothing, and Astrid has been busy sourcing items for Elverston House. It may be a while before she can get you anything new."

"I'll just borrow Verity's clothes until then," I replied, chewing on my lower lip. It really did feel like a big imposition, and I hadn't spent much time with Verity to develop a friendship with her.

"Sure," Damen replied, a little too casually.

"Is it busier than normal?" I asked, noticing that the noise levels were much higher than usual. We usually filtered into the dining hall pretty easily, but we seemed to only be taking a step or two at a time today, with bodies pressed in all around us. Tilly was glued to my leg, and I scratched her between the ears in encouragement. I supposed the Shades who lived here must be getting used to her now since there were a lot less *oohs* and *aahs* than usual.

That was quite a nice feeling. She was becoming a fixture around the place too.

"Yes," Damen agreed, suddenly sounding nervous.

I elbowed him gently in the side. "Are you not telling me things again?"

"It's not like that," he replied hastily. "The worry is for me this time, not you. I mentioned to Ophelia that it might be nice to have Ruvyn come in and present his findings from his research on Shades and the Hunted, and she made it happen a lot faster than I expected. And I guess the news may have spread... There are lot of Shades here from noble families who don't actually reside at court. Calix is probably shitting himself at the sudden surge of extra mouths to feed," he muttered, sounding faintly guilty about that.

It wasn't like Damen to be so unsure. I wanted to wrap myself around him and cuddle those doubts away, but I wasn't sure he'd appreciate that in front of all of his peers.

"I'm sure Calix knows you couldn't have predicted there'd be so much interest." Wasn't this all ancient history now? I supposed I was interested in what had happened in the past, but I'd mostly been focused on what the future held.

"It's more popular than I expected. Ruvyn and some of his colleagues at The Itrodaris have been uncovering and translating old documents that haven't been seen before now. Apparently, they were looking in the wrong places before but they have a better idea of where to find things now."

"That sounds like a good thing," I replied, trying to figure out what the odd tone in Damen's voice was. It wasn't quite distress, but there was a note of discord.

"I guess it only occurred to me just now that whatever he has to say might be difficult to hear, and I'm the one who suggested it so I feel responsible. I'm not used to doing anything that has stakes. It's a lot more pressure than I realized."

I hummed in agreement, pressing my lips tightly together so I didn't laugh at his bewildered tone.

"You're smiling," Damen chided affectionately, bumping me lightly with his shoulder. "Did that sound very spoiled and princely of me?"

"A little," I admitted. "But I think it's wonderful that you're pushing yourself out of your comfort zone. And maybe whatever Ruvyn has to say *will* be difficult to hear, but that doesn't mean we shouldn't hear it. No good ever comes from hiding from the truth—that's what Nana always used to say."

She'd always said it in a muttered, unhappy sort of a way, though. And mostly when she was mad at Moriah. In hindsight, I wondered if she hadn't been referring to me. In her own way, she'd stuck up for me as best she could.

"I hope all the Shades in the crowd are as wise as your Nana."

"You should probably hope they're a little wiser than that," I admitted, knowing that for all Nana's mostly good intentions, she'd hated change and hated Shades even more.

Damen laughed, giving my arm a gentle squeeze. "You've got a real talent for cheering me up, you know."

"Do I? You seem cheerful most of the time as it is."

Damen hummed. "You might be right. I might be cheerful most of the time—that's just my temperament, the same way that my brothers are always surly and miserable. Maybe what you make me feel is *happy*. That's something different."

There was a fluttering feeling in my stomach, and I imagined my scent was broadcasting something sickly sweet and interesting for everyone to pick up on and analyze.

"Was Allerick supportive of all of this?" I asked, feeling suddenly flustered and wanting to change the subject.

"Yes," Damen said, sounding surprised. "I guess I always knew that he thought I could be more industrious with my time, but I didn't really expect him to be so supportive of it when I did. Maybe I didn't give my big brother enough credit."

I gave Damen's arm a gentle squeeze.

Our quiet moment of conversation in the chaos came to an end as Shades greeted Damen, though a surprising number seemed to recognize me now and wanted to say hello.

"Would you mind terribly if we sat at the top table tonight?" Damen asked once we were already in the dining hall.

I blew out a long breath. "You couldn't have mentioned that when were standing outside?"

"I probably should have." He squeezed my arm lightly. "I don't think I can get out of it—Ruvyn is technically my guest and he's going to be up there. But I can walk you to where Meera and Verner are sitting if you like, and meet you afterward."

That was a very thoughtful offer. But I didn't want Damen to be the only one who was being thoughtful all the time.

"Would you feel better if I sat with you?" I asked.

"Of course, but—"

"Then I'll sit with you." I paused for a moment, taking a steadying breath. "Just don't let me embarrass myself, okay?"

"Never," Damen replied fervently. "You never have to worry about that with me. We were technically supposed to wait until everyone was already seated before making our grand entrance, but that felt like a little too much pressure for your first time on the dais. We'll just head up now while everyone is busy finding seats and let Allerick and Ophelia do the formal stroll."

"Will they mind?"

"Probably not. I don't much care either way. Come on, Tilly," Damen said, securing my arm in his grip and leading us up the length of the room. There were conversations all around us, as well as bouts of raucous laughter, and the clinking together of goblets. Damen knew everyone, and he made a point of introducing me to every Shade he spoke to. It was the first time I considered how much of his social life he'd been giving up in order to spend time with me.

"Okay, four steps up," Damen said quietly, holding my arm tightly. "Want a cane?"

"Yes, please."

One made of shadows materialized in my hand immediately, and I impressed myself with how gracefully I navigated the steps.

"You're going to be seated between me and Ophelia. Ruvyn will be on my other side, Allerick on Ophelia's other side. Usually he sits in the middle, but Ophelia wanted to sit next to you and apparently the queen gets to do whatever she wants so now he's sitting on the end."

I giggled quietly, not wanting to draw any more attention to myself than I had to.

"Is everyone staring at me?"

"No," Damen lied.

"That was very unconvincing."

"They're simply admiring your beauty." I went to nudge his ankle with my foot, but bumped into Tilly's side instead. She adjusted her position with a long-suffering sigh, half draped over my feet as if to keep them in place.

"Tilly is very relaxed," Damen remarked. "There's no equivalent beast in the shadow realm—everything we have is far more... wild. Theon and Verity have a cat. Her pet from the human realm. He is perfectly adequate, I suppose, but far inferior to Tilly."

"Tilly is in a league of her own, but I always wanted a cat."

Damen sighed. "I'll add it to the list."

"That wasn't a request!"

"You don't make requests. I have to use my initiative—and it's *very* out of shape."

I shook my head. "It seems to be guiding you just fine."

The noise died down to a respectful murmur as the king and queen made their entrance, and Damen informed me that Ruvyn was following along behind them looking terrified. I knew how he felt. At some point, I'd grabbed Damen's hand under the table and was clinging on for dear life, though I couldn't even remember when I'd done it.

"Hi, Iris!" Ophelia said cheerfully, pulling her seat back and lightly touching my shoulder as the noise levels rose back up again. "I'm so glad you're here. How are you?"

"Nervous," Allerick replied for me.

Ophelia tutted. "It's bad manners to comment on someone's scent like that, Allerick. You know better."

"It's fine," I assured her. "I probably wouldn't have answered honestly anyway.'"

"I'm going to introduce Ruvyn now," Damen told me, carefully extricating his fingers from my iron grip. "I'll be right back."

I nodded, feeling slightly bereft without him even though he was only standing up next to me. When had I gotten so needy? Worse still, I didn't even want to change. Not really.

"Settle down!" Damen called out, a smattering of laughter following his words before the room went quiet. "We've got a special guest today—an old friend of mine and full-time scholar at The Itrodaris. Ruvyn has come to share the new developments from his ongoing research into the history between Shades and Hunters. Or, rather, the Hunted as they were known then. Thank you, Ruvyn."

Damen sat back down, picking up my hand again and linking our fingers together to rest on his thigh.

He had a very nice thigh.

It was distractingly strong.

Don't think about that, the king can already smell you.

Ruvyn cleared his throat, and his nerves were palpable, even from here. My impression from movies was that being an academic wasn't exactly the same as being a public speaker. Perhaps Ruvyn was more comfortable with the former than the latter.

"Um, I would like to thank Prince Damen for inviting me here today," he began uncomfortably. "My name is Ruvyn. I am one of the scholars at The Itrodaris who has been studying the recently uncovered Torlen Papers—so named for the family estate where they were discovered. These records are many centuries old and were housed in a private library at the Torlen Estate. They have kindly donated them to The Itrodaris for study and preservation. To date, these are our most extant records of the relationship between Shades and what were then known as the *Hunted*. They also point to some evidence of when and why the relationship deteriorated."

Ruvyn paused for a moment as murmurs of interest broke out among the crowd, and his voice sounded a little more steady when he spoke again.

"The translations are still a work in progress, however, I can share some of what we've found so far." He cleared his throat. "From what we understand, the Hunted mostly resided in Mistwood, Bremrus, and Bolsfort. Now that we've started looking in those parts of the realm, we've seen a significant increase in the evidence we have available."

The words meant nothing to me, but they clearly did to the rest of the hall.

"What am I missing?" I asked, leaning in closer to Damen. There was a surge of noise in the room as everyone spoke over each other, and while I couldn't make out the words, some of them definitely sounded heated.

"Um," Damen began, sounding more uncertain than I'd ever heard him. "It would appear that the parts of the realm that had the most Hunters are the parts of the realm with the Shades who... er, with the Shades who have the least capacity for channeling power," he finished awkwardly.

The least capacity... Like the weakest Shades? That sounded logical enough. Hunters couldn't do what Shades could do. If they'd had children together, then it made sense to me that the shadow-wielding abilities of those children might be diluted in comparison to their Shade parent.

But no matter how much I thought it through, it was clear that I wasn't getting the full picture because I didn't understand why everyone was suddenly so agitated.

"One theory is that the residents of these areas share more traits with the group we now call the Hunters due to their shared lineage."

The noise level in the room increased while Ruvyn valiantly tried to regain their attention.

Share more traits... As in, they were more human? I thought of little Eadlin, curling up in my lap whenever she was overwhelmed while young Shades like Jonan wildly flicked shadows everywhere.

That wasn't to say that she'd *never* have shadow magic of her own, but from what I gathered, it wouldn't be as powerful or present in the same way that Jonan's would.

"So, you're saying the Hunters dilute our bloodlines?" someone in the crowd called out. "They make us weaker?"

"Shit," Damen muttered.

"Shit is right," Allerick agreed dryly.

Okay. I understood the issue a little more clearly now.

"Should we say something?" Ophelia asked hesitantly. "Will it make things worse if I talk right now?"

"It would be very unwise for anyone in this room to take issue with my wife," Allerick replied darkly.

"What does this mean for the realm?" someone else yelled, their tone slightly more hysterical.

"I'm not quite sure why they're so upset," I admitted quietly to Damen, though it was Ophelia who answered.

"There are some Shades who feel that the opinions of those with less ability to channel power are less... relevant. I guess there had been an assumption based on how compatible Shades and Hunters are—with the mating bites and so on—that any children we had would be, well, *strong*. They might be having some buyer's remorse about their Hunter queen now," she finished with a nervous laugh.

"Do not for a second believe that attitude is going to be tolerated in my court," Allerick replied smoothly, though his voice had an edge to it that I'd never heard before. "I'm going to say something—"

But Damen was already standing, releasing my hand again as he cleared his throat. It wasn't a grand gesture, but the seriousness in his tone was obvious, even from that. The fact that Damen usually wasn't so solemn probably helped—the room fell eerily silent in an instant.

"Who of you took a walk around the gardens today?" Damen asked casually. "Doesn't have to be the palace gardens—any will do from what I've heard."

There were a few strained murmurs.

"Did you enjoy the colorful flowers? The green leaves? Things we never thought would exist in the shadow realm?"

Silence.

"Who fed from the energy stores today?" Damen asked. How did he make his tone casual and steely all at once? "I know plenty of you did. We've been wholly dependent on them for a while now. Very kind of our ex-Hunters to keep those topped up for us."

The silence grew a little more tense.

"Mistwood, Bremrus, and Bolsfort provide almost all of the food in the realm. The ex-Hunters are currently providing almost all of the power. If anyone is laboring under the impression that *we*—the courtiers—are the valuable ones here, I would urge you to do some serious self-reflection on what it is you think are you contributing to the world. We're not fighting any battles against one another. Our physical strength and the strength of our connection to the shadows are meaningless when we're in the human realm—an equalizing arena where every Shade is vulnerable. What makes you superior, hm? Stand up and tell me now if you have an answer, I am more than willing to hear it."

A shiver ran down my spine, and I wouldn't have been surprised to find that I wasn't the only one.

"I thought not," Damen said lightly after a long moment where no one responded. "Ruvyn, thank you for coming and sharing your findings with us. Everyone else, enjoy the meal that has come courtesy of the food-growing regions of the shadow realm and shut the fuck up. If I hear a single muttered complaint about weakened bloodlines, it will be followed by a duel. Let's put those so-called superior skills of yours to the test."

And with that, he sat down, dragging a platter loudly across the table and leaning in to load up my plate first.

"Cheers to that," Allerick drawled—sounding almost pleased by his standards. There was the quiet clink of goblets, and I wondered if Ophelia had raised hers in toast. Her breathing had gotten very shallow over the course of Damen's impromptu speech.

"How are you feeling?" I asked Damen, giving Ophelia a moment with her husband. "That was very brave of you."

"Do you think so?" I heard him swishing the wine in his cup. "It didn't feel brave. It felt obvious."

I could pinpoint down to the exact second the moment I fell in love with Damen, and it was right then. There was no doubt in my mind any longer, no hesitation. I knew it all the way down to my bones, and it was the best feeling in the world.

If only I hadn't already rejected *his* declaration of love. I blew out a shaky breath, absently chewing on a piece of meat despite the fact that I'd lost my appetite.

What was I meant to do now?

DAMEN

CHAPTER 24

A re you okay?" I asked Ruvyn, pulling him aside after dinner. Astrid had cornered Ophelia and was whispering urgently to her, with Iris standing close by, offering what looked like soothing words to the both of them. I imagined that if someone was going to feel panicked by the asshole comments some courtiers had made at dinner, it would be Astrid. She was primed to see danger everywhere, and rightly so. "I'm sorry, that didn't go as I'd hoped."

Ruvyn looked contemplative. "No? I think it went about how I expected."

"And you had no qualms about doing it anyway?"

"I'm a historian. It's not for me to pass judgment on the events of the past, merely to establish what those events were to the best of my ability, acknowledging that I can never be truly impartial because I'm shaped by the world around me. Sometimes, the things I find in my research are unpleasant. That doesn't make them untrue. If only I was a more charismatic speaker," he added ruefully. "I expected their response and yet, I wasn't able to counter it successfully."

"Leave some talents for the rest of us, Ruvyn. That you were able to translate those ancient texts is a far more impressive ability." If he could have blushed, he might have. "Will you return to The Itrodaris now? You're more than welcome to join me for a drink."

He looked past me, scanning the room. Specifically, the spot where the ex-Hunters always sat.

"Looking for someone in particular?" I teased.

He started guiltily, shadows rippling in embarrassment. They were hearty-looking shadows too, almost like he'd fed *very* well recently...

"A slightly smaller crowd of ex-Hunters than the last time you were here," I observed, allowing myself a little fun before putting him out of his misery. "I believe there'll be a larger group here in a couple of days though, to finalize the new arrangement between the Shades and the Hunters."

"That's nice," Ruvyn mumbled.

"Isn't it just? I hope you'll come back and say hello. To me, of course. Who did you think I was talking about?"

He narrowed his eyes. "You're so irritating. Why is that sweet woman even remotely interested in you?"

I perked up. "Do you think she is?"

Ruvyn scoffed. "I think that's obvious to everyone, though I can't imagine what she's thinking. From what I overheard at dinner, she's sweet. Courteous. Helpful. Kind. Curious about the world, and driven to participate within it."

"Are you saying I'm not those things?"

Ruvyn didn't even dignify that with an answer, he just stared. And that was fair because I certainly hadn't been any of those things in the past, but I was trying to do better now. Iris had made me realize how indolent I'd been, and I didn't want to be *that* Shade anymore.

Iris had never demanded I be better. Being in her presence made me want that for myself.

"I'm working on it," I muttered, suddenly feeling a little embarrassed at how I'd reveled in my ennui for the past decade, proudly boasting about how uninterested I was in everyone and everything while others worked hard around me, striving to be better.

"I can see that," Ruvyn said after a long moment, watching me a little more closely than I was accustomed to. "And I'm glad for it—you've always had the talent and the ability, Damen. Just not the drive to see it through. And now you do. I'm going to return to The Itrodaris now—this has been more than enough conversation for me for the day. Enjoy your evening."

As soon as he was gone, I made my way back to Iris, wanting to check in with her after what had been a rather tumultuous meal. Of all the nights to invite her to sit at the top table with me.

Though, she'd handled it perfectly, because of course she had. Iris was smart and adaptable, and never shied away from any challenge sent her way.

"But Shades value strength, everyone knows that," Astrid was telling Ophelia. "Someone is definitely going to have a problem with the king of the shadow realm mixing genes with a weak Hunter."

Soren grimaced where he stood next to his mate. I suspected he'd had the same concerns but intended to keep them to himself in order to spare Ophelia's feelings. Her sister had no qualms about telling her the truth.

Allerick's shadows flickered in irritation. "If they have an issue with me, they can challenge me for my throne."

"No one is going to challenge you—you're the strongest," Astrid pointed out, shaking her head slightly before returning her attention to Ophelia. "Make sure you don't go anywhere unescorted for the next little while. Or forever."

"I won't, I won't," Ophelia replied, a little bemused. Probably because Allerick was hovering behind her and Levana, her own personal guard, was standing nearby. Ophelia was almost never alone. Still, the reminder was worthwhile.

"Iris, are you ready to go?" I asked, touching her arm.

"Yes, I think so." She turned toward my voice, smiling softly up at me. I was probably imagining things, but her smile looked a little different tonight. More affectionate and more unsure all at once.

It was probably just Ruvyn's words. I'd ask her about it when we were alone.

"I'll walk you back," I offered, tucking her hand securely into the crook of my arm before giving Tilly's head a quick scratch.

Allerick looked as though he was going to object—probably wanting to discuss the evening's development, but Ophelia shushed him, gesturing for me to go. She really was my favorite sibling.

"Is your friend okay?" Iris asked as we made our way through the corridor, filled with Shades clustered in small groups, discussing recent events. Wisely, they all fell silent when I was in earshot.

"He is. He'd already considered the likelihood of such a reaction."

"Then he was very brave to stand up in front of everyone anyway."

"He was," I agreed, consistently amazed by Iris's compassion when the world had shown so little compassion to her.

Tilly bounded inside the moment Iris opened the door to her room, and I quickly formed a shadow cane for Iris before crossing the room to let Tilly out to the courtyard.

"Will you stay a little?" Iris asked, slipping off her shoes and making her way over to the bed, climbing up gingerly and sitting in the center with her legs crossed.

"Of course. What do you want to do? I had a very stressful evening, you know. I think licking your pussy until you've come so many times you can't walk would make me feel much better," I suggested solemnly.

Iris laughed, the sound brightening the entire room. "Tempting, but I have my period."

I groaned. Shade females had them too, but not nearly as often as human women got them from what I heard. I don't know how they coped—Ophelia complained fairly openly about it and it sounded unbearable.

"We can do other things, can't we? If you want to," I added. "Or I could send down to the kitchen for tea and cake, and read to you again."

Iris's scent sweetened delightfully. "You're so wonderful. Maybe... I could make you come? I really want to. It's not like I don't feel arousal when I have my period—sometimes it's worse than normal."

My cock stirred hopefully. "I can help with that."

"No, no, I wouldn't expect you," Iris said hurriedly, blushing scarlet.

"You do know I'm not scared of a little blood, right?" I asked, just to make sure. "It'd take a lot more than that to keep me off you if your cunt is aching for my attention, Iris."

I sucked in a breath, the scent of her arousal filling the room in an instant.

"Can we have sex?" Iris rasped. "Please, Damen. I just... I need you. And I probably won't get pregnant while I have my period. Maybe."

"Iris," I groaned, inching closer, wanting to inhale at the source of that sweet scent. "I can't be the responsible one and argue with you here. I'm very fond of the idea of getting you pregnant. If you let me, I'd give you as many children as you wanted."

She exhaled shakily. "Does this mean we're boyfriend and girlfriend?"

"Sure." That sounded a little flimsy for what Iris was in my head, and it was most certainly a human term—I was no *boy*—but I'd take what I could get.

"And you're going to have sex with me, right?" she pressed, her voice a little more stern this time.

"As often as I can."

"Okay, good."

"I probably shouldn't knot you though," I said regretfully. "Because pregnancy really is something we should talk about more seriously. I'll pull out. It'll be fine."

"Okay." She blinked up at me, her fingers flexing next to her on the blanket. "What are you waiting for then?"

I grinned at her eagerness, climbing up onto the bed and reaching for the bottom of her shirt so I could pull it over her head. "How rude of me to keep you waiting, princess. Will you let me make it up to you?"

"You'll have to work very hard," Iris sniffed haughtily, *almost* pulling off the petulant princess act, were it not for her needy expression and the pink flush that traveled all the way down her neck. It grew deeper for a moment before she spoke again. "Do you think you could put a towel down or something?"

I laughed, climbing off the bed. "The palace staff will be grateful for your thoughtfulness."

Whatever made it easier for Iris to get out of her head and let go, I would do it.

I fetched some towels from the washroom and laid them out while she finished undressing. I traced the curve of her jaw with my tongue then softly with the sharp points of my teeth, keeping my head up by hers and my gaze on her face because it was clear she was self-conscious.

That was okay. I'd have her relaxing soon enough.

"Can I kiss you?" Iris whispered, running her hands over my shoulders before trailing them into my hair and up to the base of my horns.

I hummed in agreement. "I've heard of this kissing thing. Be careful of my fangs, princess."

"You probably shouldn't call me that."

"I'm sure as fuck not calling anyone else that."

I pressed my lips against hers before she could argue with me, surprised at how pillowy soft hers were. Everything about Iris was soft and warm and inviting. I wanted to wrap myself in her embrace and stay there forever.

The urge to taste her sweet mouth was suddenly overwhelming. I'd never needed anything more in my life. I'd die if I didn't have it.

Iris gasped as my tongue swiped her lower lip, greedily opening her mouth for more.

"That's it," I encouraged, sliding my hand around the back of her head and gripping her hair just firmly enough to keep her in place. "Give me more. Give me everything, princess."

She whimpered, grabbing my horns tightly to pull me closer, brushing her tongue against mine, occasionally touching the tips of my teeth as she got bolder in her exploring.

Self-consciousness forgotten, Iris climbed onto my lap, grinding her pussy desperately on my aching cock. Her slick coated me, marking me with her scent in a way that made my territorial instincts bubble dangerously close to the surface.

Don't knot her.

Don't bite her.

Fuck, how was I meant to remember *two* things when I was holding onto my self-control by a thread?

"I want you *now*," Iris demanded, tipping her head back as I shifted my hands to her ass, giving her better leverage to grind on me. "Please, Damen."

Were we really doing this? I should have probably thought out the potential ramifications for our relationship going forward. But that was going to have to be a problem for Future Damen because my cock wasn't in the mood for thinking and it was making all the decisions right now.

I wrapped my fist around my shaft, squeezing the burgeoning swell of my knot.

Don't knot her.

"Is this pussy ready for me?" I asked, notching the tip of my cock at her entrance, suppressing a groan at how good just that felt.

Iris didn't even answer—not verbally. She grabbed my shoulders and slowly sank down, letting gravity do the work, at least at first. Eventually she gave my shoulders a squeeze of encouragement, and I held her hips, helping her take the rest of me.

"Fuck, Iris," I rasped, pushing in slowly, feeling her body stretch to accommodate me. "You feel *incredible*. Are you okay, my princess? How are you feeling?"

"Good," she replied. Each shaky breath made her breasts rise spectacularly.

The hollow pit that was my nearly empty power reserves filled at an almost overwhelming speed as I fed from Iris's lust. It was more pure, more satisfying, more *decadent* than any fear I'd ever fed on in the human realm.

I could very easily get addicted to this.

"What can I do to make it even better? Do you want to lie down?"

Iris smiled, leaning in to clumsily kiss the tip of my nose. "Yes, please."

"Hold on, princess." I banded one arm around her waist, keeping her securely in place—on my cock, which I felt very strongly was where she was meant to be—and carefully rolled us until she was lying on her back and my hands were braced on either side of her head.

"Come closer," Iris whispered, running her hands over my chest. "I want to hold you."

Fuck me. Maybe I should just bite her. She'd probably forgive me someday, right?

No. The idea of Iris being mad at me for even a second was agony. I wasn't about to be another suffocating presence in her life—she'd already had plenty of those.

I lowered my weight onto my forearms, bringing my chest close to hers, and Iris immediately buried her face in the crook of my neck, wrapping her arms around me as much as she could, nails scratching my back.

She held on to me like she'd die if she let go. I knew the feeling.

However close she was, I wanted more. I wanted to be connected to her in a way that couldn't be undone.

It wasn't just a want. It was a need. A craving like nothing I'd ever experienced before.

I turned my head to press my lips to her hair, sliding one hand beneath her neck to keep her face close to mine.

"Iris," I groaned, rocking my hips, grinding my pelvis against her clit with each movement. "Princess. I'm fucking obsessed with you, did you know that?"

She nodded fervently against my shoulder, teasing my skin with her own delicate teeth and tongue as though she wanted to mark me just as much as I wanted to mark her.

What *was* this sensation? I was almost feral with want.

"I need you to be obsessed with me too," I rasped, shifting my hand so I could gently tug her silky hair again, my claws faintly scratching her scalp.

"I am," Iris whined, planting her heels in the mattress so she could match my movements. We both sucked in a breath as I went deeper, her cunt clenching tightly around the base of my shaft.

"You better be. You're mine in all the ways that matter, Iris. I'm not letting you go."

Iris whimpered greedily as I used my hold on her hair to pull her head to the side, my tongue teasing a spot on her exposed throat.

Don't bite her.

But if I was going to bite her, that's exactly where I would put it. Nice and high up, front and center, so no one could miss it.

"Don't let me go," Iris whispered, digging her nails into my skin as best she could. "Please don't let me go."

"Never." Was she worried I would? I wasn't capable of leaving Iris alone.

And then there were no words, because nothing was sufficient and nothing was needed. The feel of her skin on mine, of her breath against my neck, her quiet, desperate moans in my ear... It was everything. She was everything.

Iris was embedded in my heart and soul, mating mark or not. She was lodged so deeply in there that there was no letting go.

"I want your knot," Iris whined, her pussy clenching tightly around me. "Please, Damen."

Shit. *Don't knot her.*

But she was *asking* to be knotted.

What was I supposed to do? Say no to her? The idea was offensive.

"You know you never have to beg me for anything. Are you sure?"

"Yes!" She wrapped her legs around my waist, digging her heels into my lower back like she was worried I was going to pull out. Probably because I'd said I was going to, though that seemed like a very long ago and idiotic statement now.

I pressed harder against her clit, wanting her to come before I did. I was so overflowing with power from feeding off her that it was nothing to form shadow limbs, sending them everywhere. They wrapped around her arms, her ankles, they swirled and teased her nipples, and formed a barely-there, elegant collar around her neck.

"I want one in my mouth," Iris whispered.

Fuck.

The moment I sent one thickening shadow through her open mouth and down her throat, I was done and so was she. Iris clenched around me so tightly that it almost hurt, and I rolled my hips forward to lodge my knot into place as it swelled, pumping her full of an obscene amount of cum. The shadow tentacles disappeared as my concentration shattered, both of us breathing hard and clinging to each other as pleasure swept us away.

This time I didn't cut off my purr as it rumbled to life, filling the room with the sound of my satisfaction.

There was no moving on. There was no letting go. Nothing about this was temporary.

Whatever I had to do to make this permanent, I would do it.

CHAPTER 25

I need to wash," I murmured sleepily, dozing with my head resting on Damen's shoulder. I was in a postsex haze that I had no desire to emerge from, and I knew that a bath would ruin it, but I was very conscious of how wet and sticky I was between my thighs.

"I'll carry you," Damen said easily, slipping away and climbing off the bed. He politely didn't say anything as I wrapped the towel I was lying on around my waist before he scooped me into his arms.

"Am I not too heavy for you?"

Damen scoffed. "No."

"You must be very strong. I struggle to lift some of the older children at the nursery."

"You probably haven't had much of an opportunity to strengthen your muscles, Iris," he pointed out gently.

Right. No, I hadn't. I'd never had to lift anything heavy when I was in the attic. Occasionally, Nana said we needed to exercise and we'd go for a short walk, but I knew I wasn't training the way people in movie montages did.

"Maybe I could start?" I wondered aloud. "I don't want to be too weak to lift the children."

Damen mumbled something that sounded suspiciously like *the children can walk* before clearing his throat. "Astrid and Soren are running training sessions for the ex-Hunters who want to learn to fight."

"I couldn't do that, Damen. I'd be a liability."

Damen's arms tightened around me. "You're never a liability. Soren and Astrid are great at what they do—they'll be able to tailor it to you, no problem. Would you want to learn to fight?"

I nodded, a sudden rush of emotion making it hard to speak. To learn to defend myself was an ability that I never thought I'd be capable of. I wanted it more than anything.

Nana wouldn't approve of course. Fighting wasn't kind. The only acceptable form of it was killing Shades, and I had no interest in that, of course.

I wanted to learn to fight for a purely selfish reason: to keep myself safe.

And maybe...

Maybe that was okay.

Maybe being selfish a little bit of the time didn't make me unkind or difficult or less worthy of love.

Maybe Nana had been wrong about that—and a few other things too. It was a liberating, terrifying thought.

"Oh, Iris," Damen murmured, squeezing me tightly as he climbed the stairs into the washroom. Instead of depositing me in the tub like I'd expected, he climbed in with me, so I was only touching his warm skin instead of the cold stone.

"Do I smell funny?" I asked, trying to lighten the mood. *Of all the times to get overwhelmed, Iris. How unsexy of you.*

"Just like you have a lot going on in that head of yours," Damen assured me, carefully unwrapping the towel and tossing it aside before turning on the water. Thankfully, it seemed like he was going to let it run for a bit so I could wash away the grossness rather than filling up the tub. "You're also coated in my scent, which I am very fond of and sad to be washing away."

I mustered up my limited courage. It was funny that it had been so easy to leave everything I knew behind and come here, and yet talking about my feelings seemed to be the scariest prospect I'd ever faced. "Well, you'll just have to cover me in it again."

Damen hummed, arranging me so I was leaning back against his chest and pressing his nose to my neck. "Would you like that? I am your boyfriend, after all."

"Are you teasing me?" I asked suspiciously, absently running my hands over his firm thighs.

"Only a little. It's been a long time since I was referred to as a *boy*."

"Shade-friend, then?"

Damen laughed, the sound echoing in the cavernous washroom. "You can call me whatever you want, Iris. What matters to me is that you're mine and I'm yours. I won't share you."

The words send a tremor of *something* down my spine. "You don't have to."

He made a rumbling sound of approval before encouraging me to lie back, gently pushing my knees apart and running a wet washcloth between them.

"You don't have to do that," I mumbled, trying to decide whether or not to be embarrassed. I knew the mechanics of sex, but I didn't know the norms around what happened afterward. And even if I did, the norms in the human realm might not apply here.

"I made a mess of you, it's only right that I clean you up. Are you sore?"

"A little tender," I admitted.

Damen gave me an apologetic squeeze. "I'll send for some healing tea." He hesitated for a moment. "You don't have any regrets, do you?"

"None," I replied firmly. "Do you?"

"Fuck no."

I exhaled a little. "Can we do it again?"

He shook with laughter. "Let's wait until you're not hurting, hm? For tonight, we're going to wash up, have tea, and rest. Sound good?"

"That sounds incredible."

I didn't have the courage to ask the question I wanted to ask. To find out if my rejection of Damen's proposal meant that marriage—and mating— was off the table for us forever.

I'd said that I needed to find a sense of purpose, and in hindsight—so had he. It was increasingly clear that Damen now wasn't the Damen who had proposed to me then.

He'd come into himself a lot more. He had a clearer sense of direction in life. He knew who he was and he wasn't afraid to speak up when the occasion called for it.

I'd always *liked* Damen. And since we'd started getting intimate, I'd definitely been attracted to him. But it felt like more than that now. When he wasn't around, I missed him. When he was near, everything felt easier. Better.

And the idea of him moving on, finding someone else, proposing to *them...* It was excruciating. It made my stomach lurch violently, like the time I'd had food poisoning.

I hadn't known what I'd been giving up when I gave him up, and now I was in love with him and I had no idea what to do about it.

Then again, maybe I didn't need to worry about it right this second. Things were going well. I could just... *go with the flow*, as they say. Focus on the present. Not worry about the future.

I could do that. I could be *chill*. I would be *so* chill.

"I need to go make arrangements for the first feeding trip back to the human realm," Damen whispered, gently rolling me off his chest and back to my side of the bed before tucking the blankets in tightly around me. "I'll open the outside door for Tilly. Keep sleeping, princess."

"Okay," I mumbled into the pillow, burrowing down further in the blankets to ward off the chill without Damen's body wrapped around me.

I gave up on sleeping not long after he left, climbing out of bed to get ready for the day. The process was much more seamless since he'd rearranged my room and had the drapes taken off the bed. There was a little flutter in my chest every time I reached out and found them gone, followed by a slightly panicky feeling because being in love was a lot more frightening than I predicted it would be.

Relax, I reminded myself. *You're going to relax. You're focusing on the present. You're enjoying this moment.*

"Knock, knock," Hela called, bustling in with my breakfast. "You've got visitors. I'll return downstairs for more tea and food."

"Oh, you don't have to do that," Cora said hurriedly. "We don't want to put you out. It's Cora, Iris. And Jade is here too. Have we caught you at a bad time? We can come back later—"

"Not at all. Please, sit. There are enough floor cushions for all of us, right?"

"There are," Hela agreed in a no-nonsense voice. "And I'll be back shortly with more breakfast."

I made my way over, hearing them sit down, and Cora immediately guided me to the free cushion. Tilly wriggled between me and her, resting her jaw on my leg, sniffing wildly in the direction of the breakfast tray.

"You've become very spoiled since we've moved here," I told her with mock sternness.

"There's a little bowl of plain meat over here," Jade said, tapping the side with her nail. "Is this for Tilly?"

"Probably," I admitted ruefully. "She's quite the pampered princess now. Would you mind setting it down on the floor for her?"

"No problem," Jade replied. Tilly's head vanished from my leg like it had never been there as she clumsily rushed behind me to get to her prize.

"What brings you to the palace so early this morning?" I asked as Hela quietly set down a second tray of items and excused herself.

"We came *because* it was early," Jade replied. "I'm trying to get out and explore more. Get used to the place, you know? But I find it easier to do when the corridors aren't crowded."

"Very understandable," I said sympathetically. For the most part, I preferred the hustle and bustle because it was so different from the silence of the attic. But I understood that we all handled change differently, and I could absolutely understand how it might be overwhelming.

"We were wondering whether or not to visit," Cora began, her voice deceptively light. "We suspected you might be awake since you already had a visitor this morning."

Jade laughed. "Don't be coy, Cora. Iris, we saw the prince leaving your room this morning. Or at least leaving the corridor, and apparently you're the only one staying down here."

My face felt unusually warm. "Yes. Damen stayed here last night."

"Get it, girl," Cora replied, impressed. "You're courting the prince?"

"Umm." My cheeks grew even hotter. Someone whistled, probably Jade. "He's my... boyfriend? I don't know if that means we're courting or not. He proposed quite early on when I moved here." I swallowed thickly. "I said no."

"Badass," Jade muttered.

"Why?" Cora asked curiously. "I mean, it seems like you like him at least a little bit if you're having sleepovers."

"I like him a lot. *A lot*. At the time, marriage felt like a bit too much of a leap to take—we'd just met."

"Yeah, rookie move proposing right away," Jade agreed, which did make me feel slightly better about saying no. I hadn't brought the topic up with the others because I was worried that I'd acted strangely with no frame of reference to go by, and they would think less of me for it.

"Romantic, though," Cora sighed.

Jade snorted. "Let's not normalize proposing to strangers."

"Agree to disagree," Cora laughed. "What would you say if he proposed now, Iris?"

"Yes, of course. In a heartbeat. But I don't expect that to happen—I imagine I hurt his feelings by rejecting him, and I understand why he wouldn't want to put himself through that again."

"Hurt his ego more like," Jade scoffed. "He's obviously still interested in you if he keeps coming back around. Have you asked him whether or not he's going to try again?"

I hesitated. "I think I might be a coward. If he says no, then everything will change. We won't be able to ignore the subject anymore. Maybe it's better to just keep as much of him as I can get, and be satisfied with that rather than risk losing him entirely. Live in the moment, you know?"

"That does seem cowardly," Jade agreed. There was a gentle thud, followed by a quiet curse word.

"That's a very understandable fear," Cora said softly. "But are you truly living in the moment and enjoying your time with him while this unresolved topic is hanging over your head? I get it—I don't like having difficult conversations either—but if you *love* him..."

She left the words hanging in the air, and I made a quiet sound of frustration. "I do love him."

"Yeah, you do!" Cora said enthusiastically, clinking her tea cup against mine on the table. "Then you've got to get your man. You can always propose to him, you know. That's always an option."

"Is it?" The idea had never occurred to me before. At least in the films that Nana had watched, that never seemed to come up as an option.

"Sure," Jade replied. "Was his proposal romantic? Would you need to go all out to match it?"

I gnawed on my lower lip. "He was very enthusiastic and eager to ask the question as quickly as possible."

"So, no then," she laughed. "Well, something to think about, right?"

It was all I thought about. We finished breakfast, and I made my way to the nursery with the intention of teaching the children some nursery rhymes from my own childhood, but my head wasn't in it.

I startled as Eadlin's little claws landed on my head, patting my skull as she sometimes did.

"Are you looking for horns? I don't have any, remember?"

She babbled something that sounded vaguely concerned, searching a little longer before playing with my hair instead.

"Oh!" I heard Yara exclaim, opening the door. "What's this?"

"An instrument. For Iris," someone grunted. I froze.

An instrument?

"Iris," Yara called tentatively. "There's a very large... thing here for you. It has strings."

"A harp?" I breathed. "How did that get here?"

"I suspect I know who might have arranged such a thing," she said, amused. "Shall we bring it over to you?"

"Okay." I shifted to the edge of the chair, and Eadlin climbed off my lap, slipping into the gap behind me on the seat to play with my hair. It was a little risky, given her claws. Even though she was the youngest, Eadlin was usually the most careful with her claws.

I exhaled shakily, helping whoever was delivering the harp to situate it in the right position, adjusting my posture to accommodate it. Tentatively, I reached out, sliding my hands up and down the smooth, glossy wooden frame before running my fingers along the strings, and finding the pedals with my feet.

"How does it work?" Jonan asked, startling me. "Can I touch it?"

"Absolutely not," Yara replied for me. "Only Iris can touch it."

"Shall I play something for you?" I asked Jonan.

"Yes." To my surprise—and probably everyone else's—it wasn't Jonan who replied, but Eadlin.

I twisted a little in my seat to smile at her. "Okay, then."

Nana's favorite piece of music had always been the *Waltz of the Flowers* from The Nutcracker, and after a few moments of orienting myself, I began to play. It wasn't my best performance—I was rusty, and this harp didn't feel quite the same as mine, but it was *so* nice to play again. To feel at ease and competent, and do something I was truly familiar with.

The nursery was eerily silent by the time I finished. Even Eadlin's hands had gone still in my hair.

"Iris," Yara breathed. "That was... I've never heard anything like that. This instrument can't stay in here—it has to go into the dining hall. You have to play for everyone. The court will adore you."

"Oh no," I said hastily, slightly horrified at the idea. "Maybe some day. But for now, this is the perfect audience for me."

"Another song!" Jonan demanded, grabbing my wrist and setting my hand back on the strings. "Play another one, Iris. Please," he added, somewhat reluctantly.

"Well, since you said please..." I laughed. "I'm a little out of practice, but let's try *Greensleeves*."

CHAPTER 26

Next week?" Allerick confirmed, his shadows shifting restlessly. "So soon?"

"The thinking is that it would be best to start with a small group and begin promptly, rather than let the pressure build," I explained, having hashed all of this out with Tallulah, Harlow, and Sebastian earlier this afternoon. "You can't go, of course. It's too risky. Us singletons are more dispensable," I joked.

"That's not true," Allerick replied sharply. "And you're hardly single—not really. No one has sat by your side at the high table before."

"Regardless. If I die, Iris won't be in the kind of pain she would suffer if a mate bond were to break, presumably." Allerick made a sound of disagreement. We didn't actually know what happened when one half of a mated pair died, and hopefully it would be many decades before we did. "We have it baked into the agreement that our own ex-Hunters will also come along to provide security, so at least one mated pair will be there. I doubt Astrid is going to let anyone go in her place."

"Likely not," Allerick agreed. "And Soren won't stay behind if she goes. Selene is pregnant, she'll need to stay behind and I suspect Austin wouldn't provide much in the way of security anyway."

I snorted. Austin hadn't even come up in conversation when Tallulah and I were discussing the most appropriate ex-Hunters to go along on the trip. Aside from the fact that he was too recognizable in the human realm, he was a lover, not a fighter.

"Andrus has already volunteered to come along—probably because he's desperate for a proper feed, but also undoubtedly hoping that being part of this small party will bring him glory. I think perhaps two or three more Shades—trained members of the Guard—would be the optimum amount to make up our numbers."

"Next week will mean that it is right before the Feast of the Modra."

I frowned. "So what? It's not like we celebrate it." I wasn't sure anyone did anymore—it was an ancient practice. From memory, it was a feast to celebrate all new life in the realm since the last Modra—to celebrate children and mothers, mostly. It certainly hadn't been acknowledged during our father's reign. He barely acknowledged his children, nor their mothers.

"Ophelia thought it would be nice to bring it back. She's liaising with Vespera and Cosima right now on the arrangements."

"Then the feast will be the perfect way to celebrate our success and the start of a new, healthy relationship between us and the Hunters. Or, at least, one small segment of their population. It's a celebration of newness, is it not?"

"*If* it goes well," Allerick pointed out, incapable of being positive about anything.

"Sure, sure. If. Anyway, do we have your approval? The others are taking a tea break but I'd like to go back and let them know if we can proceed on those terms or not."

Allerick leaned back in his seat, watching me from across the table where he'd been having his lunch before I'd interrupted. "Yes. You have my approval. You'd *like* to go back and talk to them? Voluntarily? I hardly recognize you these days, little brother."

"Is that a bad thing?"

"No. Not because you're finally being helpful and reliable, though I am glad for that fact. But because you're happier. Interested and engaged in the world around you. You *move* with purpose rather than aimlessly drifting from room to room, making jokes to hide your discomfort."

"I don't do that," I protested immediately. "I'm just very funny. You wouldn't understand because you are not."

Allerick snorted. "Of course. Go on then, go pass on my approval. A couple of the Elders want to meet with me shortly, they are still feeling slighted. I spend my days soothing bruised egos."

I shuddered at the thought. "I'm glad such a task falls to you rather than me. I'll see you at dinner."

In many ways, a weight had been lifted and my steps were lighter as I headed back to the meeting room to meet the others. There had been moments where any kind of truce between us had seemed like an impossible goal, so coming to an arrangement at all was an accomplishment.

On the other hand, it was impossible not to notice how subdued the mood was at court since Ruvyn's talk. His theories had forced all of us to reckon with some ideas that were long out-of-date. Ideas that *needed* to be reckoned with. It was an uncomfortable but necessary process.

What would the future of the shadow realm look like with potentially more Hunters in it? With the children of those Hunter-Shade unions running around? Were we capable of assessing value in any way other than the raw ability to channel shadows?

I slowed my steps at the sound of whispers up around the corner, wondering if I was about to encounter a satisfying piece of court gossip. Everyone had been dully well-behaved recently—a good scandal would be the perfect distraction from Ruvyn's talk.

"Don't do it," Meera whispered urgently, immediately making me lean in closer to eavesdrop. It was unlike Meera to give orders at all, let alone panicky-sounding ones. "Don't interfere. It's between them."

"Yeah, but they need our help," Jade complained. "Just need a little nudge in the right direction, that's all."

"It's romantic," Cora added. "We're just two little cupids, gently reminding the lovebirds that they belong together."

Who were they talking about? Was there another secret romance brewing at court? There was always something going on. I felt sorry for whoever they were, having these two meddle in their affairs.

"I'm pretty sure Cupid sent arrows, not gentle reminders," Meera countered.

"Love arrows," Cora replied smugly. "Now, shh. Tallulah said he would be coming back this way any minute."

Realization dawned slowly. Had they been talking about *me*? And Iris? There did seem to be a friendship brewing between them three of them, perhaps Iris had mentioned me in their conversations. I wasn't sure if I should be happy or nervous about that.

Then again, Cora had said something about lovebirds, hadn't she? That seemed positive.

And I was Iris's *boy*friend now, so I'd like to think she felt at least a little good about our relationship.

I made a show of noisily walking around the corner, too intrigued to wait a moment longer.

Meera gave me a slightly rueful look, and I wondered if she knew I'd been listening in. She was more observant than any of us had ever given her credit for.

"Sorry, I just remembered I have somewhere to be," she said, clearly wanting no part of this conversation.

"Where?" Jade challenged, planting her hands on her hips and giving Meera a defiant stare. I doubted she would have with anyone else, but Meera had something of a maternal role in Elverston House.

Meera's lips twitched as she backed away. "Somewhere."

Jade frowned before turning to face me. "Hello. Your Highness," she added after a moment's pause.

"Just Damen is fine," I assured her, crossing my arms and leaning my shoulder against the wall. *Don't laugh, you might offend them.*

The corridor was empty at present, and interestingly, there was nothing in their scent or body language that indicated they were uncomfortable being alone with me, which was nice. I'd sort of expected that from Cora, who'd been curious and enthusiastic about the shadow realm from the moment she arrived, but Jade had been extremely wary and hadn't even ventured inside the palace until recently. It was a great sign that she was more settled here already.

"Were you looking for me?" I asked innocently.

Jade gave Cora a look that clearly said *you tell him*, though I couldn't interpret the rest of the silent conversation they had with their eyes. I watched it with interest until they came to their resolution, though. Humans had such expressive faces.

"Okay," Cora began, blowing out a long breath and clasping her hands in front of her. "When are you going to propose to Iris again?"

I coughed. "She *told* you about that?"

I'd gotten the impression that she didn't want anyone to know, since neither Tallulah nor Meera had mentioned it, and they were growing increasingly comfortable reminding me to my face of all my flaws.

"Yes," Jade replied, finding her voice. "And she seems to think that it would be better to settle for this middle ground you're currently hovering in where you're sleeping together—"

"She told you *that*?"

"—but not talking about the future, just in case the answer is something she doesn't want to hear. And she obviously lo—I mean, *likes* you and hopes that it will turn into something more but she feels bad about rejecting you even though it's totally your own fault for proposing the minute you met her which almost anyone would find terrifying."

"I still think it's romantic," Cora mumbled.

"Anyway, things have changed now and you should propose again," Jade finished, crossing her arms and glaring at me as though she was daring me to disagree.

"This really feels like a conversation I should be having with Iris."

"But you're not," Jade pointed out. "And while we did remind her that she can propose to you and she seemed open to the idea, I kind of got the impression that she'd prefer if you did it. Maybe she was one of those little girls who always dreamed about weddings or whatever, I don't know." Her words had gotten quieter and more mumbled as she'd finished the sentence, and the flush on her face was getting increasingly more pronounced.

Perhaps Jade had been one of those little girls who dreamed about weddings. Perhaps she was more whimsical than she appeared, and a difficult life in the Hunters had made her feel the need to hide that.

"So?" Jade demanded, tipping her chin up and finding her confidence again.

While Theon's younger sister, Rainy, had been exiled at court, I'd spent some time with her to make sure she didn't make any more idiotic decisions. These two reminded me a little of her. Young. Headstrong. Absolutely convinced that they were right. Cora and Jade were probably more well-intentioned than Rainy, who would stage a coup and run a cult of worship in her own honor at the first opportunity.

"I appreciate you caring enough to say something," I said diplomatically. "Thank you."

They both stared at me for a moment before Jade threw her hands up in frustration. "What does that even mean? Are you going to propose or not?"

I grinned. "Iris will be the first to know if I do."

"That's the way it should be," Cora said quickly, cutting Jade off. "Thank you for hearing us out. We look forward to seeing you do the right thing. Come on, Jade."

I managed not to laugh until they'd disappeared around the corner. That was certainly a first. Usually, only Soren and my brothers told me off like that.

I doubled back as I passed one of the sitting rooms, recognizing the Shade sitting morosely within it.

"Ruvyn! What are you doing here?"

Why did I ask? I already knew.

He started guiltily, glancing around like the answer to my question might materialize in the walls. "I, um, wanted to stop by. And see you," he added unconvincingly.

"And see me? Really? You wanted to see me?"

He narrowed his eyes. "Obviously not, but you could have been polite and pretended."

"I could have," I agreed. "Come with me—I'm on my way to the meeting room now. Harlow is already there."

His shadows flickered. "She may have mentioned she was attending something today." Ruvyn hesitated. "I can't come with you. Those are for high-level diplomas and such, aren't they?"

"Technically, yes. Also the Crown Prince and whatever friends he invites along."

"This feels like I am inappropriately exploiting my connection to you."

I laughed. "What's the point in being friends with the prince otherwise? Really, you should make more demands. It's insulting how little everyone asks of me—you must all think I hold no sway at court."

"Unlikely. After your rousing speech at dinner the other night, I'm sure there's no doubt in anyone's mind that you are vastly influential at court. In the realm as a whole."

"That is very flattering to my ego. Thank you, Ruvyn," I told him sincerely.

He snorted, falling quiet as we approached the meeting room.

"There you are," Tallulah exhaled, twisting her fingers nervously in front of her baby bump while Evrin stood silently at her side when I finally made it to the meeting room. "I was worried you wouldn't come."

"Because you sicced Cora and Jade on me?" I laughed, remembering that Tallulah had been the one to tell them where to find me.

Evrin smirked while Tallulah's cheeks went pink. "I don't know why they wanted to talk to you, but they were adamant that it was important. I'm sorry—I hope I didn't make the wrong call."

"No, no. Not at all. Shall we head in?"

She clearly wanted to ask what they'd spoken to me about, but seemed to think better of it, biting her lip and nodding.

Harlow was in conversation with Sebastian and looked to be almost falling asleep. What had he said to woo Cosima? I'd yet to see any indication of wit or charm from him.

"I didn't realize you'd be joining us," Harlow said, her eyes brightening immediately when she spotted Ruvyn walking in behind me.

"Damen invited me," he grunted, almost apologetic as he took the seat next to me. Harlow's expression shuttered instantly, and I sent a small tendril of shadows to flick Ruvyn's leg under the table. Idiot. How hard would it have been to say something about wanting to see her?

I knew for a fact that Evrin didn't possess an ounce of charm either. I might be the only male in this room whose social skills weren't a total embarrassment. Fortunately, I was used to it, having spent most of my time with Allerick and Soren.

"So?" Harlow asked, looking at me and studiously pretending Ruvyn didn't exist. "What did the king say?"

"We have a deal." The room immediately smelled better as nervousness was replaced by relief. "Astrid will be acting as one of our guards for the first trip at least—I don't need to run that by her. She'd never agree to anything less." I paused, considering it. "She's also probably here right now, hiding in the rafters or something."

Sebastian startled, his gaze flicking upward. I hadn't meant it literally. She probably *was* hiding here somewhere, but the rafters were a little extreme.

"I don't know anyone who'd be willing to take on Astrid in combat. She's probably only gotten more formidable since she started training with your Guard," Sebastian observed.

"Probably," I agreed. And she'd been training the new ex-Hunters in Elverston House to be just as dangerous. It stood us in good stead. "Are you in a rush to leave? If not, I'll pour some wine. This is a success worth toasting to."

"I'm not in a rush," Sebastian said, offering me a tentative smile. It might have been a grimace, I wasn't good at reading expressions unless they were Iris's.

"I guess I could stay," Harlow added, cutting Ruvyn an unimpressed look out of the corner of her eye. I was giving him a golden opportunity to redeem himself, and I was going to be annoyed if he messed it up.

Fortunately, he was wise enough to immediately move around the table and engage her in conversation while I crossed the room to where the goblets and wine were set up. Evrin was already there, content to hover in the background rather than take any attention for himself.

"How have you been?" I asked him quietly. "You look well. Happy."

"Of course I'm happy. Have you seen my mate?" he asked, looking at me like I'd lost my senses. "She's a dream."

"I'm glad to hear it and not at all jealous of your happiness."

Evrin snorted. "You've got nothing to complain about. You're going to be mated soon enough."

"You sound more confident of that than I am."

"I hope you wouldn't be so stupid as to let Iris go. Part of my reasoning is selfish, of course."

I frowned. "What do you mean?"

"Some little courtly child came up to me in the corridor and told me that he wasn't afraid of my lack of horns anymore, even though his mother was, because Iris told him not to worry about it," Evrin replied, amused. "I'm not overly enamored with the idea of being approached and spoken to on a regular basis, but I suppose it's a nice change from everyone running away from me."

I almost swooned, like the lovesick swain I was. Where was Iris right now? It felt like we'd been apart for too long already, and I wanted to share the news about the human realm trip with her. I wanted to share everything with her.

I was barely allowing myself to think about it, but if what Cora and Jade said was true, if proposing to Iris was back on the table, if that was something she wanted...

Then I had some planning to do.

Ideally, I'd be married by the end of the month.

CHAPTER 27

Iris clung to my hand outside the portal in full sight of the entire court, her scent filled with nerves.

"It's going to be fine," I soothed, smoothing a hand down her hair and pulling her in for a hug. "I'll be back in under an hour."

"Don't take any unnecessary risks," she ordered raspily.

"I'll be on my best behavior."

"You'd better be," Astrid grumbled, stomping past to wait at the portal. I didn't take it personally—she'd outright refused to let any other ex-Hunters come with us, adamant that no one was adequately trained enough to help and insisting that they'd be more of a hindrance than anything. I understood the logic, though it meant that she was putting a lot of pressure on herself.

"I've arranged dinner for us afterward—just the two of us," I told Iris quietly. I couldn't let myself think about that now because all of my concentration *had* to be on the upcoming trip.

"Oh."

"*Oh*?" I pressed, alarmed by the faint concern in her voice.

"No, no. That's fine," she said hastily. "I'm sure it will be lovely."

"Are you really sure? Because you don't sound sure."

Iris smiled a little too brightly. "Very sure. It will be so lovely."

"Damen, hurry up," Astrid ordered, shifting her weight from one foot to the other. It may have been the most unsettled I'd ever seen her.

"Focus," Iris said sternly, grabbing my jaw with both hands and holding my head in place. "We can talk about dinner afterward, okay? Focus on the task at hand."

"Yes, princess." Her scent immediately sweetened, and I was incredibly smug about it. "I'll see you soon."

I pressed a kiss to the top of her head, wishing I could more blatantly tell everyone that Iris was mine in a way that wouldn't be off-putting to her, before joining the others and heading through the portal.

Our small party was comprised of Astrid, Soren, Andrus, Galen, and myself—and only Andrus and Galen would actually be feeding. The rest of us were there for protection, and to scope things out and make sure it was all above board.

"Everyone ready?" Soren asked, keeping a hand on Astrid's back as we headed toward the agreed-upon exit point near a park.

"Absolutely," Andrus replied, rolling back his shoulders. "I've been ready for this since the day feeding in the human realm was banned."

"Be smart about it," Soren warned irritably. He was too noble to say out loud that Andrus was one of his least favorite members of the Guard, but I was confident it was true.

Harlow was waiting for us when we emerged through the darkness of the trees, dressed head to toe in black with a look of grim determination on her face. In my incorporeal form, I couldn't communicate with her, but Astrid could translate. Her mating mark from Soren had given her the ability to hear us speaking to one another.

"How is everything looking?" Astrid asked, voice tight with tension.

"No concerns," Harlow replied, whipping out a device I'd come to learn was called a phone. "I've got a live feed going too," she said, showing Astrid the small, bright rectangle. "Um, do you guys need instructions or anything? You'll just do your thing right?" she asked, looking between our shadowy forms.

"They don't need instructions," Astrid replied, a faint smirk on her face as she glanced at us. "You've got two minutes. In and out this trip, remember?"

Off you go, Soren ordered.

As agreed, Andrus and Galen shot off in different directions. I trailed after Andrus since he was the more experienced of the two and better able to handle himself, while Soren went after Galen and Astrid waited by the entry point so we could leave quickly.

Andrus quickly zeroed in on his target—a woman tapping away on her phone, not paying attention to her surroundings as she walked through the dark, silent park. A chill ran down her spine as Andrus approached, and she shut off the bright light, tucking the device close to her chest and wrapping her arms around herself, looking around as though someone was going to snatch the phone away at any moment.

Andrus struck immediately, taking advantage of the opportunity the woman had unknowingly given him by turning her portable light off. He pressed his face close to hers, drinking down her fear like it was water, his form growing darker and more defined as he drew strength.

And then it was done. The woman's casual nighttime stroll turned into a jog to get back to the safety of the streetlights. Andrus was fed and pleased with himself.

It was dull and routine and predictable.

Exactly the way it should be.

This was the way it was always meant to be, and balance was finally returning. A little fear—the kind of fear that kept you cautious and alert—was part of the human experience.

But it was part of the Shade one too. The human realm was our equalizer, the one place where irrespective of power level, a Shade was vulnerable. Maybe some of the egos at court that had grown increasingly outsized over the past few weeks would shrink back down to normal when they experienced this level of risk once more.

Or maybe they wouldn't—only time would tell.

But for now, my priority was going home to my love. I had a question for her that I desperately needed an answer to.

"Why are you in such a rush?" Soren asked. "Where are you going?"

"I thought I might try proposing again."

Astrid coughed loudly, giving me a slightly disbelieving look. "Really?"

"Yes," I said decisively. "I can see now that I asked too early last time—a foolish error in hindsight. And then I labored under the ridiculous notion that I shouldn't propose again *at all*, which was obviously not the right call."

"And what is the right call?" Soren asked curiously.

"Keep asking until Iris says yes."

Astrid spluttered. "No, that definitely doesn't sound right. That sounds like the kind of thing that would get you a restraining order in the human realm."

"What an unromantic place," I observed seriously, wanting to see how red Astrid's face could go. Obviously, I fully intended to respect Iris's choices—that was never a question in my mind.

But if there were other requirements she wanted fulfilled prior to marriage, then I would work my way down the list until I'd met them all.

And I fully intended each proposal to be better than the last. Fortunately, that required very little work this time around since my first attempt had been so dire.

This time, I would give Iris the proposal that I should have given her the first time around.

Just in case she was ready to say yes.

Only my brother, Ophelia, and their small retinue were waiting for us outside the portal. Allerick quickly scanned each of us, checking that everyone who'd left had returned.

"Any problems?" he asked, scrutinizing Andrus and Galen particularly closely. They were both clearly content and well-fed, which I hoped would put his mind at ease.

"None," Soren replied, launching into a detailed description of everything that had happened. I walked right past them, heading for the palace steps. I guessed everyone had been sent inside—would Iris be in her room? I'd check there first.

"Where are you going?" Allerick called out.

"Soren will explain!" I yelled over my shoulder, picking up the pace.

Iris was in her room, sitting in the center of her bed and brushing her hair idly with her fingers.

"You're back," she said, exhaling with relief. "How was it?"

"Perfectly dull—the way it should be. Are you ready to go?" I asked, letting myself into her room.

Iris chewed on her lower lip, twisting her fingers nervously. I hadn't picked on it right away because the doors were open for Tilly, but her scent was definitely unsettled.

"Iris, what is it?"

"I want to ask you something," she said, her voice shaky. "But I'm scared."

I crossed the room, immediately grabbing her trembling hands and giving them a squeeze. "You can ask me anything, Iris."

"I already disappointed you once before," she whispered.

"You haven't disappointed me once since I met you."

She lightly squeezed my fingers back, sniffling lightly. "But I said no when you asked me to marry you. And I regret it *so* much. If I could go back—"

"You don't have to go back."

"Damen, I shouldn't have said no—"

"Can we go for a walk first? And then we'll talk more?"

"Oh. Um. Okay. If you'd prefer that," Iris replied uncertainly. "Should Tilly stay here?"

"If you're comfortable with that."

Iris nodded. "I'm comfortable with you. Stay, Tilly."

Fortunately, it was a short walk through the palace and a private drawing room to the small courtyard I'd set up for the occasion. Iris's nose twitched the moment we stepped outside.

"What is that smell?" Iris asked. "It's so nice."

"We're in one of the private courtyards. Some of the night-blooming flowers have been brought in—they're arranged in pots around the edge of the circular area we're standing in. There's a string of glowing orbs above us, though as few as I could manage—just enough to illuminate the space. There's also a fire in a stone pit here, would you like to move closer so you can feel the warmth?"

"Yes, please," Iris murmured, looking slightly baffled as I guided her closer. I'd wanted as many sensory experiences as possible, and there were platters of all of her favorite foods on the table too, but we could get to those later. "This is so nice, Damen. You did all this for me?"

I took a steadying breath, this time squeezing her hand to give myself comfort. "Yes. Because I wanted to give you the proposal you deserve. The one I should have given you the first time around."

Iris was silent for a moment before she laughed. "You're... proposing? You'd already planned this? But I'm proposing! That's what I was getting to."

"Cora and Jade hinted that you might—and I am more than fine with that, my princess—but I still wanted to give you the romantic experience you didn't get the first time around."

"Cora and Jade spoke to you?" she asked suspiciously.

I snorted. "Oh yes. And I'm glad they did—their intentions were pure, and I needed to hear that. My ego was a little bruised when you said no—but you absolutely made the right decision, it was foolish of me to have proposed then, even if I knew in my heart that you were the one. Even if I knew that I loved you then. I should have given you time to feel the same way about me. Maybe I was worried that you never would, and that securing your hand was the safest way of making sure I didn't lose you."

"You're the one for me too, Damen," Iris said gently, her scent sweet and perfect even as a rogue tear tracked down her cheek. "I'm sorry I didn't realize it when you did. I love you. I can say that now without a single trace of hesitation or doubt. It's you. It's always been you."

A piece of me that I didn't know I'd been missing settled into place.

"I'm not sorry," I assured her. "Your love was worth the wait, Iris."

It wasn't a Shade convention to get down on one knee, but Ophelia had mentioned that it was a human one and I didn't want to let Iris down by not meeting every single one of her expectations. I kneeled awkwardly, clasping her hand.

"Iris Nash, you are the other half of my soul. Would you do me the honor of becoming my wife?"

To my surprise, she kneeled down too, her fingers trembling slightly where she was clinging on to mine. "Of course. Would you do me the honor of becoming my husband?"

I let out a surprised laugh. "Are you proposing to me too?"

"I'd already hyped myself up to do it."

"Of course, princess. It would be the honor of my life." I stood up before lifting Iris into my arms, her legs wrapping around my hips immediately and her hands finding my horns. A shiver ran down my spine at her possessive grip. That wasn't what I'd intended for us to be doing out here, but I wouldn't say no…

"Wait, I have to give you the ring first," I mumbled, willing my cock to behave as I carried her over to the table.

"Kiss first," Iris demanded sweetly, maneuvering my head back with my horns and pressing her lips to mine.

It was sweet for a second, but only a second. Iris dragged her tongue across my lower lip, rolling her hips as I got us situated on a chair, grinding her pussy against my aching cock.

I explored her mouth with my tongue, enjoying the little whimpers she made as she struggled to accommodate it, her arousal perfuming the air more potently with each movement.

We broke apart panting, Iris's breasts heaving with each movement, practically begging for my attention. What would it be like between us a year from now? Five years? Ten?

I had the feeling that it would only be filthier as we grew more comfortable with one another and experienced more together. Iris was curious and unselfconscious, and I wanted to lick every part of her body I could get my tongue on.

She made a small whine of impatience as I reached behind her to grab the ring box on the table.

"Just a moment, princess," I teased, slipping the ring onto her finger and admiring the way it fit. It was a very Shade design, and I'd been worried it wouldn't suit her delicate human hands, but the contrast was very pleasing.

"Are they pearls?" Iris asked, rubbing her thumb over the row.

"Yes—or the Shade equivalent at least. They're black but shiny, and they sit on a silver band. I thought it might feel the nicest to play with," I added, slightly embarrassed. Perhaps she would have preferred something grander? But she was a very tactile person, and this would be the least obtrusive.

"It's perfect," Iris breathed. "Thank you. Is this place private?"

I laughed. "Did you have an activity in mind for us that requires privacy, princess?"

She smiled, sweet as always but with a slightly mischievous edge. "I need your knot, Damen."

I choked on nothing, not expecting quite that level of boldness. "Now? What about dinner?"

Iris pursed her lips thoughtfully. "We can eat while knotted, right?"

"Yes," I agreed immediately because why hadn't I thought about that? What a wonderful idea. "Iris, if we have sex right now, I might find it difficult not to put a mating mark on you. It's permanent. There's no turning back from that."

"Okay. Will you take my dress off?" she asked sweetly.

"Of course." She was wearing one of the flowy ones I'd requested Astrid get for her, in a deep purple color that I found very striking. With some maneuvering, we pulled the fabric out from under her legs and over her hips before I dragged it up her body, sucking in a breath. "You're not wearing anything under this."

Iris bit her lower lip, trying to hide a smile. "This was going to be my distraction plan if you said no to my proposal."

"Do you really think I can be distracted simply by the sight of your naked body, princess?"

Her cheeks flushed. "Honestly? Yes."

I pulled the dress over her head, tossing it onto the chair next to me and kissing the tip of her nose. "You're honestly right. I would probably agree to anything just at the mere sight of your breasts. And this sweet pussy?" A tendril of shadows snuck out to rub between her legs, making her jump. "It owns me."

"More, Damen," she rasped, spreading her knees as far as she could on the chair and gripping my shoulders tightly.

"So greedy," I teased, though my voice was too strained to sound like I was teasing. Iris *was* greedy for me, and I was just as fucking greedy for her.

I sent a thicker tentacle to play with her pussy, while increasing the pressure on the one that was grinding against her clit. Two more appeared to tease her nipples, and Iris opened her mouth and stuck out her tongue expectantly, so it would be rude *not* to send a shadow limb down her throat too.

"You look so beautiful right now," I told Iris, smoothing my hands over her ass as my shadows swirled around her. "So fucking beautiful."

Her scent sweetened again, the movement of her hips growing a little more urgent.

"That's not going to be enough, is it? You need my tongue."

Iris made a muffled, desperate noise of agreement. She cried out as all the shadows vanished at once, grasping at my chest and shoulders like she could pull the phantom limbs back out of my body.

"Stand for me," I commanded softly, cupping her ass and helping her to stand with her feet either side of my legs on the chair. "I won't let you fall."

"I know." The pure confidence in her voice was one of the best feelings in the world.

My claws lightly pricked her soft skin as I dragged her forward, sliding down a little in the chair so I could perfectly angle my mouth beneath her dripping cunt. "What a feast you're giving me, Iris," I murmured, swiping my tongue up her damp inner thighs, cleaning up the slick that was clinging to her skin.

"Can we maybe have less talking right now?" she suggested breathily. I laughed silently, nipping her leg with my teeth before getting to work. If my princess wanted me to be using my tongue for other things right now, then that was what she'd get.

I groaned as Iris lowered herself a little more, seeking out the pressure that she was craving. Even though the angle was slightly challenging, Iris was so primed that she was coming almost instantly, her legs wobbling alarmingly until I pulled her down onto my lap, rubbing my cock against her clit as she rode out her waves of pleasure.

"Damen," she gasped, reaching between us and wrapping her hand around my shaft. I almost came from the visual alone. The movements were clumsy and unpracticed as she lifted herself up on her knees and lined my cock up with her entrance.

"That's it," I encouraged as she sank down, taking me inch by inch.

"You're so beautiful, Iris. You're taking me so well. I fucking love the way you feel."

Her hands found my knees behind her, and I nearly swallowed my tongue at the view of her arching her body up, hair trailing down magnificently behind her. Most beautiful of all was the view it afforded me of her throat—smooth and unmarked, ready for my bite.

My ring looked nice on her finger, but not nearly as nice as my teeth marks would look on her neck.

Iris's movements were slow and intentional as she rolled her hips, using her arms and thighs to lift herself. She was clearly experimenting, figuring out what felt good, and I was more than happy for her to use me as she saw fit.

"Good?"

"So good," she breathed, pushing herself back up and wrapping her arms around my shoulders instead. I took over, bouncing her on my lap, the lewd, wet sounds we were making filling the courtyard.

"I'm going to knot you," I warned, acutely aware that the possibility I would get her pregnant was very much present.

"Good."

"And I'm going to bite you."

"Even better."

"And I'm going to love you for the rest of my life."

IRIS

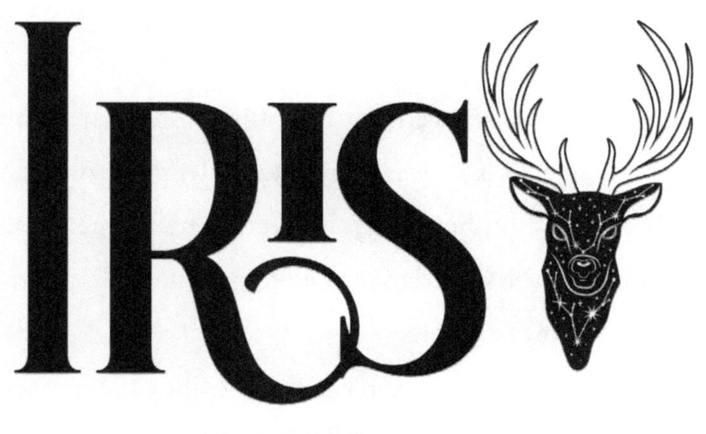

CHAPTER 28

I almost cried as I came. I might have actually cried. My skin was damp everywhere with a combination of sweat and slick, what was a few tears on top of that?

I was just so... relieved. *So* relieved. So grateful. So overjoyed. So overflowing with love—my love for him and his love for me—that I didn't quite know what to do with myself. Perhaps I'd been holding it back a little before now, not wanting to let myself get carried away in case things didn't work out. But the floodgates had truly opened and I had more emotions swirling around inside my head than I knew what to do with.

Damen murmured words of praise and encouragement to me as pleasure radiated out through my body, finding his own release as my walls clenched tightly around him. As the intensity subsided, I realized that I'd tipped my neck as far to the side as I physically could, silently begging for his bite.

I needed it. Something inside of me was missing, and I was convinced that Damen's mating mark was the only thing that could make it whole.

His knot expanded, briefly diverting my focus as I clung to him, breathing my way through the pleasurable stretch that walked right up to the edge of pain.

And *then*, he bit me.

Or, rather, sank his teeth into my throat and stayed there just long enough that I wondered if he was ever going to let go. It didn't hurt the way I expected it to, based on how sharp his teeth were. I barely even felt where the skin was broken. The sensation seemed to have immediately traveled much deeper, settling into my very core.

Damen withdrew slowly and carefully, tending the spot with his rough tongue. I shifted ever so slightly, setting off another relentless wave of orgasms where his knot was pressing on some highly sensitive nerves. By the time my soul had returned to my body, only the very faintest sting on my neck reminded me that he'd just had his teeth in my throat.

Something was taking root deeper, though. A connection between us that went beyond just the love we shared. That felt tangible somehow. I rested my cheek on Damen's shoulder, his arms banding around my back, holding me in place.

A purr rumbled out of his chest, and I immediately flattened my palms against it, wanting to feel the faint vibration of it through my hands.

"Talk to me, Iris. Are you okay? Are you hurting?"

"I'm good," I promised, surprised at how slurred my words were. "I'm very good. I'm happy."

"That's what I want to hear. I've never been happier. I'm going to move us closer to the table so I can pour you some water. You'll probably come a few times in the process," he added, not sounding altogether sorry about that prospect.

As he predicted, I was a writhing, panting mess while he shifted the chair closer to the table, adjusting our positions so that we could comfortably eat and drink while knotted together.

It was extremely... sensory. Decadent, even.

"Here, you need to hydrate," Damen murmured, pressing the rim of a cup to my lower lip. I took it out of his hand, quickly drinking the water that I hadn't realized I desperately needed, followed by a small sip of wine from the goblet he passed me next. "Can I feed you?"

I nodded sleepily, happily opening my mouth whenever Damen lightly touched a piece of food to my lips.

"Did you get all of my favorite things?" I asked.

"Of course. Like I said, I was trying to make this romantic."

"You definitely succeeded there. This was much more romantic than what I had planned for my proposal."

He laughed, kissing the top of my head. "What did you have planned, princess?"

"I was just going to ask you. Maybe cry a little," I admitted. "Not on purpose, but just because I was worried you'd say no."

Damen scoffed. "As if I could. Open, I've got some cakes here."

Eventually, his knot subsided, and we bathed in the bathroom of whatever guest room we were in before redressing and heading back to my room to sleep. Evidently, it was late enough that the rest of the palace was asleep, and it felt oddly rebellious to be walking around through the silent halls.

"This has been the best day of my life," I told Damen sleepily, my head resting on his chest in bed while Tilly stretched herself out over both of our feet.

"Likewise, princess. But I'm going to make sure we have some even better ones."

"Can you see my bite properly?" I asked Damen, smoothing down the front of the maxi dress I was wearing. It felt like it was made out of jersey cotton, and it was the most comfortable thing I'd ever put on. I really had to thank Astrid for all of the dresses she'd sourced, despite how busy she was furnishing Elverston House with human-realm comforts.

"Yes," Damen said smugly, pausing from playing on the floor with Tilly to reply. I'd even pulled my hair back into a ponytail to really show it off. The couple of days we'd taken to ourselves had been incredible, but we couldn't miss the Feast of the Modra. Ophelia had put so much work into organizing it, and the whole court was going to be there.

And while I was nervous about making our big debut as a mated couple, I was excited about it too. There was a possessiveness to it that I hadn't expected to feel.

Damen was mine and I was his. I wanted everyone to know that.

"Are you ready?" I asked. "Do you need to stop by your room first? Yours is probably much bigger than mine," I added, realizing that Damen was making sacrifices for me already.

"It is, but the courtyard with vegetation around the edges is far more comfortable for Tilly, and this room is easier for you to get to." He was quiet for a moment. "Though, perhaps we could renovate a couple of the rooms in this row. Join them together, and make more space for us that way. We probably need a formal sitting area for visitors at the very least. You were already popular, princess. It'll only get worse."

He sighed dramatically, like this was the worst thing he'd ever heard.

"Do you not like me having visitors?"

"I don't like sharing your attention, but have just enough self-awareness to know that this is selfish and unacceptable, and I'll have to learn to deal with it," Damen laughed.

"You'll have plenty of visitors too," I pointed out, moving toward him. Damen's hands landed on my hips the moment I got close, and he pulled me down into his lap on the floor. Tilly flopped her head on my stomach, and I gave her some enthusiastic ear scritchies. "What with all the projects you've gotten involved in recently."

"That's your fault too," he replied affectionately, kissing the top of my head before encouraging my head to the side, brushing kisses down my cheek and jaw until he got to the mating mark on my neck. "You were too wonderful. I had to learn to be less of a drain on society."

"You're ridiculous."

"Probably," Damen agreed. "Shall we go? The noise is dying down, likely most of the court is seated now."

I exhaled a little shakily. "Okay."

I'd sat at the high table before, but I'd never made the formal entrance with the king and queen down the center of the room with everyone watching. I had absolute faith in Damen and Tilly to keep me upright, but it was still a little intimidating.

We headed for the entryway, Ophelia's excited squeal letting me know we'd arrived.

"You look so beautiful, Iris!" Ophelia said the moment we arrived, grabbing my hand and giving it a squeeze. "Oh, that ring—Damen, you did so good."

"Would you expect any less of me?" he asked, standing a little taller next to me.

"No. When you apply yourself to something, you really go all in," Ophelia said confidently. The king hummed in agreement, but didn't offer any further remarks. I got the impression that from him, that was pretty high praise.

"What's that smell?" I asked, leaning forward to try and get a better whiff.

"Ooh, so there's an ancient tradition of decorating with garlands at Modra," Ophelia replied enthusiastically. "They're from a tree that grows all over the shadow realm and it smells so pretty, doesn't it?"

"We haven't bothered with it in recent years at the palace," Allerick added gruffly. "Neither my father nor I have much of an eye for decorations and such."

"I would have decorated every year if I'd been king," Damen announced.

"You would have forgotten about the Modra entirely," Allerick said dryly.

Damen laughed. "As you did last year, if I recall correctly."

"He'd have forgotten this year too, if it wasn't for me," Ophelia confided in me conspiratorially. "But Affra, my attendant, told me about it and I couldn't let it pass by unacknowledged. I know we all eat together every day, so that part isn't particularly special, but I miss the festiveness of a proper holiday season."

I nodded, though I'd never really experienced one. The holidays had been basically the same as any other day, except Nana and I had received leftovers from whatever meal the family had eaten downstairs.

In all honesty, the regular meals we shared that Nana cooked had been preferable to the stone-cold scraps we got on holidays as some misguided way of including us. And those days had always served as a reminder that I wasn't a part of my family and I never would be.

After all those years of diligently telling Nana that I was grateful for those experiences, I could admit now that I wasn't. I didn't like those holiday meals. I wasn't grateful for them. The life I had now was something I could be grateful for.

The noise in the dining hall briefly died down when the four of us entered, before building into a crescendo that had me clinging to Damen a little tighter in surprise. Were they stomping their feet? It was the cadence of applause, but a duller sound, and the ground vibrated beneath my feet.

"You all had such little faith in me," Damen called, laughing loudly. "I'm shocked that Iris agreed to be my mate too, believe me. The wedding will be held as soon as we can arrange it."

The stomping and whistles grew louder, and I felt myself relaxing into Damen's side, my face aching from smiling. The sounds were raucous, but they were warm and welcoming at the same time.

"If you recall, it's my job to make the introductions," Allerick pointed out wryly, though he didn't sound mad.

"Four stairs here," Damen told me, gripping my arm a little more securely before responding to his brother. "Why should you get to do all the fun jobs?"

"Historically, you've not had much interest in any jobs."

"I'm a new Shade now, clearly," Damen teased. "I have a mate to impress. I can't just lounge around all day."

"Very true," Ophelia agreed. "You don't want to give her the ick."

"The what?" Damen asked, though I had no idea either. That wasn't a term that had come up in the films Nana had put on.

"I'll explain later," Ophelia said as Damen helped me into my seat. "Everyone is staring, we should probably talk about something more cultured."

"Does anyone seem mad?" I whispered to Damen. "Aren't they worried about having more weak Hunter genetics in the royal family?"

"They better not be," he grumbled darkly, sounding surprisingly like Allerick for a moment. "But no, I don't think so. Everyone is riding the high of the successful feeding trips to the human realm, and the next trip is tomorrow. Their focus is there for now."

It wasn't a forever solution then, but at least a problem we didn't have to address right away. Besides, I had every intention of proving that I had value to add to the realm and to my new family, even if it wasn't in the form of physical strength. We all had something to offer.

"Harlow is here," Damen said cheerfully, narrating the surroundings for me. "Sitting with Ruvyn, looking very loved up—no mating mark. Or not that I can see, at least. All of the ex-Hunters in the realm are here with their partners—they've commandeered most of one long table. Sebastian is sitting with Cosima, that's a new development."

"I'm going to cry," Ophelia sniffed. "It really wasn't that long ago that I came here all by myself—wedding dress on, suitcase in hand, and now look at how many people are here! And they all look so happy. Isn't this amazing?"

"Sure," Damen agreed cautiously. "Are you feeling okay? You're weepier than normal."

She leaned in close, her hair brushing my shoulder to whisper to both of us. "I'm pregnant."

The relief and joy in her voice had tears pooling in my eyes as I discreetly squeezed her hand, congratulating her in hushed tones so we didn't draw any attention to ourselves. Based on her whispered announcement, I guessed she didn't want to announce it publicly yet.

"Are you crying now?" Damen asked, bemused, though he was rubbing soothing circles between my shoulder blades. "Is it catching?"

"Be nice," Allerick chided.

"This is me being nice!" Damen laughed. "We can talk more later when we don't have an audience, but I'm so happy for you both."

"And we're happy for you," Ophelia replied gently, nudging my engagement ring as she gave my hand another squeeze. "For us. And what the future will hold."

EPILOGUE

FIVE YEARS LATER

Roll over, princess," I told my wife, patting her affectionately on the ass.

"You're not supposed to call me that anymore," she replied ruefully, rolling onto her front and bracing herself on her knees and forearms, knowing exactly where I wanted her.

"I'd like to see anyone try and stop me," I replied easily, moving behind her on the bed and sitting up on my knees so I could admire the view Iris was giving me. "Your cunt is already dripping for me, *princess*."

"It usually is," Iris said mildly, undoing me with just three words. It was always like this with her. Whenever I got too cocky, she reminded me who really had all the power in this relationship.

Of the two of us, I may wield the shadows, but I'd lay down my life for Iris.

I sent tendrils of shadows up the back of her thighs, following the path with the tips of my claws before creating a crisscrossing pattern around her torso, snaking down her arms to connect her wrists together. Iris was practically panting as I repeated the process down her legs, a solid length of shadow connecting her ankles, keeping her perfectly in position.

It was only right that I take a moment to admire my work, so I climbed off the bed to walk around either side, taking her in from all angles. She was the prettiest canvas to paint my shadows onto.

"No gag today?" she asked, immediately opening her mouth and sticking out her tongue as I brushed a tendril over her lip.

"Not today. I want to hear you. Don't be shy now."

Iris whimpered impatiently as I climbed on the bed behind her, grabbing her ass a little more firmly this time and spreading her cheeks to admire the feast before me.

"Damen…" Iris warned, though her voice was too breathy to sound any kind of serious. "We don't have that long."

"We can arrive late."

"Absolutely not."

"Fine, fine, fine." I sighed, squeezing her ass affectionately. "The things I do for you. We could have made a whole evening out of this."

I adjusted my position before she could tell me off again, half hanging off the end of the bed so I could taste that sweet slick directly from the source, roughly massaging her clit with my tongue from behind, just the way she liked it.

Iris let out a breathy moan, instinctively rocking her hips back but my shadows were holding her in place. And while I accepted I couldn't take as long as I'd like when we were due to attend the Modra feast this evening, we still had a little time to ourselves and it was a rare afternoon off for both of us. I wanted to make the most of it.

I picked up my pace, feasting on my wife's cunt like it was the food of the very gods themselves. Iris was as desperate for me as I was for her. Within minutes, her legs were trembling, toes curled up as she came with a soft cry.

"You're impatient today," I teased.

Iris laughed huskily. "Less joking, more knotting, please."

I groaned. "You know I can't say no to you. I wanted to play with you a little more."

"Later," Iris promised. "You can tie me to the bed after the feast."

Well, in that case...

I used the shadows roped around her to roll her onto her back, grinning as she relaxed into the movement and let me position her body exactly where I wanted her. Without any prompting, she grabbed the back of her knees, pulling them up and opening herself to me.

Unable to resist, I settled my face between her legs again because Iris was the best mate and wife in the world, and she deserved more orgasms.

"Damennn," she rasped, throwing her head back. I glanced up the line of her body, admiring the prominent mating mark I'd put on her throat all those years ago. I never got tired of looking at it. I never got tired of the bond that connected us, that let me find her wherever she went.

I'd been lazy and often idiotic in my younger years, but I'd had the foresight to pursue Iris. At least I'd done that right.

My claws dug into the backs of her thighs just enough for Iris to feel the sting—exactly the way she liked it. The moment her legs started to shake, I moved over her, sliding my cock home as her orgasm hit, shuddering at the feel of her squeezing around me.

I lost control of my shadows completely at the sensation, and Iris took advantage of her free wrists by grabbing my horns and dragging my head down to rest in the crook of her neck.

"You feel incredible, princess," I breathed, pulling out so that just the tip remained before thrusting forward again, bumping her a little up the bed. "Fuck. Are you sure we have to go to this stupid feast?"

She used her grip on my horns to turn my head to the side, brushing her lips against the shell of my ear. "Very sure. But I'd like to go with your cum between my thighs, so get to work, husband."

"Anything you want, princess," I muttered, wholly focused on filling her with every drop of cum in my body.

It never took long when Iris begged, and it was even faster when she demanded. I had no willpower where she was concerned. I couldn't resist her.

"That's it," Iris murmured, teasing my ear lobe with her teeth, her heels digging into my back. "I love you, Damen."

Fuck.

She was playing me as adeptly as she played her harp—she knew I was helpless against those words.

I muffled my moan against her skin, pleasure ricocheting through my entire body as my knot swelled. The sensation tipped Iris over the edge, and I nearly came again as she tightened her grip on the sensitive base of my horns.

For a long moment, we stayed intertwined in silence, only the sounds of labored breathing filling the room.

"You did that on purpose," I accused affectionately.

"We can't be late!" Iris's hands absently drifted down my back. "You're just as excited about the feast as I am, don't lie to me."

"I'm more excited about getting you in bed."

Iris laughed, gently scratching my back. "Because it's such a rare occurrence? Don't you dare move, Damen. That knot needs to go down. I still need to get ready. Today is a big day."

Only somewhat resentfully, I left Iris cleaning up in the bath—so much for cum between her thighs at the feast—and headed for the nursery.

Yara smiled the moment I walked inside, but she didn't have a chance to speak before Adeon was climbing up my leg, clawless hands digging into my thigh.

"Must you?" I laughed, grabbing him under his armpits and swinging him into my arms. "That hurts, you know."

He may not have claws, but his strength was more Shade-like than human.

"Sorry," he said, not sounding sorry in the least. "Did you know Mama wasn't here today?"

"Yes, it was her day off. Remember? Yara and Alyndra looked after you." Usually, Adeon spent the day with us on Iris's day off, but all the children had been preparing garlands for the Modra feast today and he'd been desperate to attend.

"Is the feast now?"

"Soon," I assured him.

Adeon leaned his head on my shoulder, his pale blond hair stark against my skin. In so many ways, he was like his mother—both in looks and in temperament.

And then occasionally, usually with as many witnesses around as possible, he'd behave like a feral little beast. He got that from me.

"Let's go back and get Mama, hm? And then we'll go to the feast."

"Okay. Let's go."

"It smells so good," Iris murmured as we made our way into the garden.

There were too many attendees this year to fit everyone in the dining hall, so they'd moved the festivities outside instead.

"Calix and his crew are cooking the meat out here," I said. "One section of the garden has been taken over for food preparation."

Tilly sniffed hopefully in that direction, trotting along beside us. She was walking a little slower this year, and took a little longer to respond when we called her. Neither of us wanted to think too much about that, though.

"Can we eat now?" Adeon asked, patting Iris's arm.

"Not yet," she said firmly. "We need to wait until dinner time. Do you see your cousins?"

Adeon went up on his tiptoes, though it didn't help much considering how packed the place was. I scooped him up, carefully balancing him on one shoulder while he grabbed onto my horns and used them to wriggle until his legs were either side of my neck.

"They're sitting on the throne. How come they get to sit on the throne?"

"Because they're princesses," Iris laughed.

Adeon grumbled something under his breath that he *definitely* learned from a kid at the nursery. It was in a rural Shade language, and I was very glad his mother didn't understand it.

Allerick and Ophelia were on the temporary thrones that had been erected outside, surrounded by their gaggle of girls. All three had red hair, dark eyes, and a glare that could stop a Shade at fifty paces—even the baby. Everyone claimed that their perfect glare had come from their father, but I knew better.

The Glare was all Aunty Astrid.

Sophie was the eldest, and the crown princess for the time being. Her and Adeon weren't that far apart in age, and seemed to vacillate between being best friends and mortal enemies.

"There are so many of them," Adeon observed sagely. I snorted. There would probably be more, too.

As much as I loved Adeon, both Iris and I had decided that one was enough for us to handle.

"Is Mama going to play the harp?" Adeon asked, spotting it up next to the thrones.

"Later," Iris said. "And Austin will play his guitar—won't that be fun? Will you dance?"

"I will," Adeon replied solemnly.

Flynn—Evrin and Tallulah's son—waved as we walked past, sitting on the ground with his uncle as Austin taught him to drum on a stone paver with a couple of sticks. Austin and Selene's daughter, Thea, stood disapprovingly next to them, looking like an almost carbon copy of her mother though her eyes were human—with pupils and whites and everything. It had quickly become clear that the mother determined whether the child would be more Shade or human, which I was grateful for.

Iris was delicate. I didn't want anything with horns and claws growing in her fragile womb.

"Can I go see Thea?" Adeon asked, yanking roughly on my horn.

I lifted him down. "You can ask if she wants to play. You have to come back if she says no," I warned sternly as he darted off. All the children trailed after Thea—surely, she had to tire of it at some point.

"Are there many visitors from the human realm?" Iris asked, leaning in close to my side so she could hear me above the noise of the party.

"I would hazard to say there are hundreds." I brushed a kiss over the top of her head, pulling back so I could see her soft smile. "Families, too. Not all of the children you're hearing are from our realm."

"There are Hunter families? Here?" she asked in surprise.

"Yes. They've set up blankets on the ground all around the place, there are lots of clusters of them gathered. I assume different regions are sitting together."

Even Lucas was here—with his Hunter wife and their baby. I didn't tell Iris that yet though because I didn't want to say hi right away. I appreciated that he was the one who got Iris out, who brought her to the shadow realm and into my life, but I still thought he was a dick. Some things just couldn't be explained.

On the plus side, Verity still disliked him, and no one expressed haughty disdain quite like Verity and her mini-mes. They weren't here yet, though. They were probably still trying to convince Theon to get out the door.

"How incredible is this?" Iris whispered, quickly brushing away a tear, though her scent was pure happiness. That was my mate—always overflowing with sweetness and joy, even when life had thrown nothing but challenges her way.

The peace between the realms had held, though it wasn't perfect. But perhaps it never would be. Some regions of the human realm would never be safe for Shades to travel to. Some ex-Hunters who moved here weren't a good fit, and had been asked to leave. But Elverston House was never empty—Meera and Verner were constantly busy helping new arrivals get settled here. And ex-Hunters who'd gotten used to life here were now living all over the shadow realm. And some kept a foot in each realm—Harlow spent her days working with the Hunters, but her nights with her mate, living in the small home Ruvyn had found them near The Itrodaris.

It was a situation that would have seemed like an impossible dream when Ophelia first arrived here on her wedding day. A blending of worlds that had been at war for centuries, and peace that was rooted in the spirit of welcoming and togetherness.

It was an impossible dream that had come true.

THANK YOU

As always, I have to thank Steph at Rawls Reads and Marcelle at Books Checked. They've been rockstars not only for this book, but the rest of the series too. I'd also like to thank my PA, Nikki, my friends, my awesome Ream subscribers, and Dr T for being patient with any medical questions I have for my characters.

But my biggest thanks is to you, reader.

I had no idea when I started writing Luxuria in the midst of a cross-country move over two years ago that the Shades of Sin series would be what it is now. I'm so incredibly grateful to all of you for taking a chance on these books, and I've loved spending time with this interesting cast of characters. It's not goodbye forever—I'd love to write some bonus content and extended epilogues—but it is goodbye for now, and it's a bittersweet feeling <3

Until the next book,
Colette R. xx

P.S. To keep up with the latest news and releases, join my Facebook Reader Group or subscribe to my newsletter.

ABOUTTHE AUTHOR

Colette Rhodes is a paranormal romance author from New Zealand. She loves to write about love in all its forms, and adores imperfect heroes and heroines who find perfection in each other. You'll often find her trying to justify her degree by including ancient history and mythological influences in her work.

If she's not writing, then you're almost certain to find her reading—ideally with a cup of tea in hand and a scented candle burning to match the mood.

Keep up with Colette here:
coletterhodes.com
@coletterhodes_author

ALSO BY COLETTE

SHADES OF SIN:

Luxuria

Superbia

Gula

Avaritia

Invidia

Ira

Acedia

STATE OF GRACE:

Run Riot

Silver Bullet

Wild Game

Dare Not

Saving Grace

THREE BEARS DUET:

Gilded Mess

Golden Chaos

LITTLE RED DUET:

Scarlet Disaster

Seeing Red

ON THE SHELF:

Scheme

Excess

KNOTTY BY NATURE:

(omegaverse with T.S. Snow)

Allure Part 1

Allure Part 2

EMPATH FOUND:

The Terrible Gift

The Unwanted Challenge

The Reluctant Keeper

DEADLY DRAGONS:

The (Not) Cursed Dragon

The (Not) Satisfied Dragon

STANDALONE:

Dead of Spring (MF - Hades & Persephone retelling)